The Crooked Path

HARRIET GOODCHILD

HADLEY
RILLE
BOOKS

THE CROOKED PATH

Cover art © Yana Naumova
Cover design © Molly Suber Thorpe
Map of Ohmorah, the Later Lands and Lyikené © Douglas Reed
Typeset in GFS Didot

ISBN 978-0-9971188-1-0

Published simultaneously in the United Kingdom and the United States of America by:

Hadley Rille Books
Eric T. Reynolds, Publisher
PO Box 25466
Overland Park, KS 66225 USA

Edited by Terri-Lynne DeFino

www.hrbpress.com

For Maud & Hugo

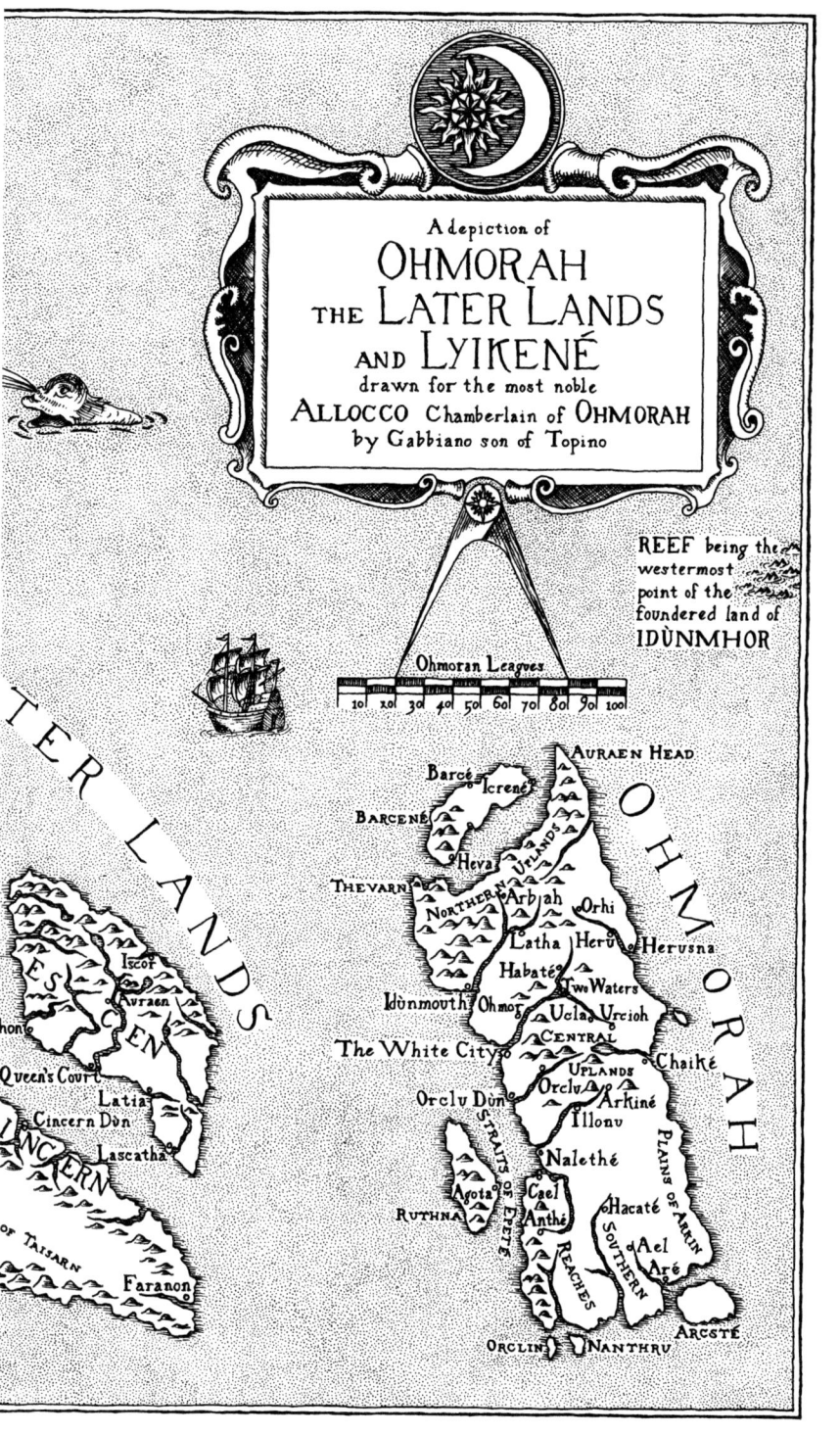

A depiction of
OHMORAH
THE LATER LANDS
AND LYIKENÉ
drawn for the most noble
ALLOCCO Chamberlain of OHMORAH
by Gabbiano son of Topino

REEF being the
westermost
point of the
foundered land of
IDÙNMHOR

Ohmoran Leagues
10 | 20 | 30 | 40 | 50 | 60 | 70 | 80 | 90 | 100

ATER LANDS

OHMORAH

AURAEN HEAD
Barcé
Icrené
BARCENÉ
THEVARN
Heva
NORTHERN UPLANDS
Arbiah
Orhi
Latha
Herù
Herusna
Habaté
Two Waters
Idùnmouth
Ohmor
Uclas
Urcioh
The White City
CENTRAL
UPLANDS
Chaiké
Orclu Dùn
Orclu
Arkiné
Illonv
Nalethé
STRAITS OF EFETÉ
Cael
Anthé
Agota
RUTHNA
Hacaté
Ael
Aré
REACHES
SOUTHERN
PLAINS OF ARRIN
ARCSTÉ
ORCLIN
NANTHRU

Iscor
Auraen
ES
CEN
hon
Queen's Court
Latia
Cincern Dùn
Lascatha
NCERN
OF TAISARN
Faranon

1: I offer you adventure

An outlandish knight came from the north lands
And he's courted a lady fair
He said he would take her to those northern lands
And there he would marry her.

The Outlandish Knight, Traditional

Beyond Ittachar lies the sea, and beyond the sea, Lyikené. And Lyikené is little more than a word these days, in Ittachar; it is a place of fear and fable, unknown, unvisited, save in tales told in winter by the fireside. On those nights stories begin, *At the back of the west wind, in Lyikené, there was once a man ... or a king ... or a tree.* But the man of this tale had his beginning in Ittachar, a western land but short of the utmost west.

He was a potter, turning clay upon a wheel, and a sculptor, changing the form of the cold stones of Ittachar. He was still a young man and lived alone in a cottage by the sea, keeping a few goats and a cabbage field, and a little rowing boat to fish from. All else he needed he bartered for his pots with the few traders who cared to venture along the coast, for there is little in Ittachar to tempt the mercatmen from Cincern Dùn or Escen. Yet all his pots were things of beauty, coloured with a glaze blue as the sky or grey-green as the deep of the sea, so it was a joy to hold one in your hands. Such was his life and, if he was not at all times content, he was at least no more unhappy than any man need be when he has enough and a little more than enough to live by.

But the day came when the potter found he had grown bored with the sea and the sky, of goats' cheese and cabbage soup, of mackerel and the talk of sheep. His boredom rose within him like a thundercloud and the glaze upon his pots became dull and lumpen. After a while his wheel fell silent, then his kiln grew cold, for he found that barleyspirit drove back his tedium and freed his dreams for a few hours, and by night his laughter could be heard within the cottage, mixing in the firelight with the songs of one woman or another. But such things could last for only a little while before his hearth grew cold again; the women returned to the village and the potter hid his face in his hands in shame at what he had become.

One morning, he tore at a lump of driftwood with his chisel. He worked all day and then by lamplight, calling the skill back to his hands. Late in the evening, as the moon rose over the hill behind him, he laid down his chisel and his plane and stared at the twisted thing he had made, half a fish and half a gull with an open beak and a thrashing tail and long, strong, feathered wings. It stood before him in the moonlight, a creature made of driftwood and dreaming that had no place within the waking world. The potter shrugged and left it where it was and went to bed, where he slept well and deeply for all he had strange dreams.

Next day the potter looked at his creation. The dew lay upon it and its eyes were silver bright and the wooden scales of its tail beaded with silver. "You are not yet whole," said the potter, and inlaid its eyes with mother-of-pearl from an oyster shell. With its eyes upon him, he painted its tail green and black and silvery blue, like the body of a mackerel as it is swung from the sea before it drowns and fades in air. He looked again, still not satisfied, then coloured the wooden bird-body white and grey after the manner of the herring gull, and the fierce, open beak he painted yellow lined with red.

"Now you are whole," said the potter.

That summer's day was long. His skill seemed spent on the carving, for the clay flopped on the wheel and, when he opened his kiln, another batch of pots had cracked in the firing. So much wasted time and clay sickened him. Late in the day he stood before his door and, as the waves beat their rhythm out against the shore, he saw his boredom reflected in the empty sea and the empty sky.

A noise came from the shadows, a rustle like silk, a thump like wet rope against the ground.

"If you are bored," said a strange, harsh voice, "I can carry you away."

The potter, believing he was drunk again or in a dream, took a step back and clutched at the door of his house.

Again the voice rattled out of the shadows. "I can take you 'cross the sea to the city of white towers and black streets, to the gardens where the willows dance, to the floating islands of the northern seas. I can show you queens and princelings, artists, musicians and mercatmen, sailors, liars, mystics and thieves."

Another thump, another rustle, and something moved into the evening sunlight beyond his open door. It stood upon the shingle and beat its grey gull's wings against the air, then folded them neatly across its back. Sidelong it looked at him, like any other bird, and its mother-of-pearl eyes were very bright. In wonder beyond fear, the potter stretched out his hand to touch its neck. Where before had been painted wood he felt now soft, white feathers. It thrashed its fish tail and the black stripes writhed upon it.

"You dreamed and looked beyond your life, you saw what other men did not, and so you set me free," it said. "I offer you adventure in return. Would you like to cross this sea that bounds your life? Climb on my back and I shall carry you. One mile or a thousand, all distances are alike to me."

"I've fished the edges of the sea these many years," said the potter. "Can you indeed carry me across it?"

"I can and I shall, if that is your desire," the creature answered, "but you must be quick deciding. The wide air and the stormy sea are my element; I cannot bide too long ashore but must away to the sea and the sky."

The potter fetched a bag and put in it his last good pot with a sea-green glaze, pulled on his sheepskin coat and locked his door behind him. Slinging the bag across his shoulder, he sat astride his creature's neck and buried his hands in its warm feathers. Again the creature beat its wings and this time it lifted itself high, high into the air. Twice it wheeled around the cottage in wide circles, rising on the wind so the cottage and the cabbage field stood clear and tiny beneath in the last light. Then it screamed in its gull's voice and flew out across the sea.

All that night, and the next day, and the night that followed, the creature carried him on relentless wings across an emptiness of sea and air. The potter had brought neither water nor food but found he wanted none and at night he slept, muffled in the warm feathers and his sheepskin coat.

At dawn upon the second day, the creature said, "The land yonder is not one of the Later Lands. It is Ohmorah."

The name meant nothing to him but the potter looked into the east towards a low land of meadows and trees. He saw a city built of white stone with four great towers and a black wall around it. The tops of the towers were gilded with the first light of morning.

"What can I do here?" he asked. "I know nothing but one coast and the fisherfolk along it."

"You freed me," was all the creature answered. It folded its wings and swooped downwards in a rush of wind, plunging from the sky like a gannet, but at the last it checked its speed and alit gently on the shore before the city.

On a spring evening, upon the day of the equinox, a stranger comes to the White City. He comes alone after the sunset in a fine ship, painted bright in green and red and gold, her prow carved into the head of a great grey gull. The sails are white in the darkening sky, whiter than any other sail in all the world. No man is aboard that ship save one, yet she flies neatly into harbour as a bird to her nest with only his word to steer her.

The people stare to see he does not fear Lyikené but dares to practise all the skills of wind and sea, which once were known across the world but now only in the west. There are many reasons why ships no longer sail boldly out from Ittachar or from Habhain or from Escen, and why the peoples of those Later Lands have put aside the art and knowledge of the open sea, but this is one of them. Much has been lost since fire and flood, since the lady came from the east.

The stranger says to the harbourmaster, "The Lord of Marac has come to Ohmorah and begs the lady's leave to stay awhile." The man lets him pass and so, by starlight and by lamplight, the Lord of Marac walks up the road from the harbour, a young and comely man to look upon. He comes up into the city but not to the great hall before all the court. The lady meets him in the garden of her house, and her daughter watches from behind her mother's chair.

The Lord of Marac says, "I have returned, Allodola, to the lands east of the sunset. Am I welcome here?"

The lady's daughter draws in her breath at his presumption: none in Ohmorah dares to call the lady by her name. The lady keeps her silence and makes no answer. Her eyes dwell long upon the stranger's face and she does not offer the guest cup her servant has made ready for them to drink a health together in friendship.

"What do you seek, Liùthion?" she asks at last.

"What I have always sought," the Lord of Marac answers. "To walk beneath the trees, as any man might do, and hear a blackbird singing in the twilight." His black eyes never waver beneath her steady gaze. "The gates of morning are long years closed and Averla is long years gone. Let us set the past aside," he says, holding out his hands, "and make a new beginning."

Perhaps the lady sees what she looks for in his face, for she says, smiling, "So did we come to this land, and peace we have found here, Liùthion. This city is our proof to all the world. Let you also find peace here."

She unfastens her silver brooch from her own gown and pins it on his coat. Then she embraces him as a dear friend and the old man beside her, her chamberlain, bows his head and speaks his greeting, though his face belies his fair words. He does not welcome this stranger truly; he is a man playing a part, and one he does not like.

Then the Lord of Marac smiles at the lady's dark-eyed daughter, as a man smiles at a pretty girl, and gives a gift to her, a white dove in a silver cage.

"Hang the cage in the window of your chamber," he says, "give her corn and water, speak kindly to her. After three days, open the door. She will fly free in the sunlight but always return to you when darkness comes."

So this she does, and it is as he said. On the third morning, and every morning after, the dove flies free into the linseed arc of the sky to wheel in the high sunlight around the towers of the White City. And each evening, as he promised, she returns and softly settles her white feathers and sleeps the night in her silver cage.

The potter climbed from his creature's back and stood at the highwatermark, looking up towards the city. Never had he seen so many buildings or such fine ones. It was very early in the day and the city gates were not yet open and so he waited, sitting on a rock upon the shore, his bag at his feet. When the sun had climbed two handspans in the sky, he heard a bell within the city calling out the sixth hour of the first and, as the last note died away, the great gate opened. A man came out of the city and the potter saw the guards standing at the gateway salute as he passed them by.

The man walked across the sand and shingle towards him. A young man, pale-faced, clean-shaven, his brown hair cropped to his chin; a man of his own age perhaps, or a little younger, but in no otherwise like to him; a nobleman with rings on his white fingers, his black cloak shot through with the shimmer of silk. This stranger spoke, but his language was not the one the potter knew. He shook his head and held out his own hands in friendship, to show they were empty and that he meant no harm.

"I am a man of Ittachar –" he began, but the other interrupted: "We are outside the city," he said, speaking now in the potter's own tongue, speaking slowly to make his meaning clear. "The lady's law does not run below the tideline."

He cast his cloak aside and the potter saw the knife in his left hand. Fear trickled in cold sweat down his back.

"If you would pass beyond the tideline to the lady," the stranger said, his lips twisting into a bitter smile, "you must first face my knife. Kill me if you can."

The morning wind blew cold from off the sea but that was not why the potter shivered. He tried to look the young man in the eye, and failed.

The stranger stood on the shore in his coat, poised like a dancer before the music begins, then sprang towards him and all the time there was shrank down into that moment.

The potter flung up his arms to shield his face and neck from the blow. The shore and the city faded away; he heard only the sound of his own heart; he saw only the bright blade of the knife aimed at his breast; he knew only he was like to die here and now, a stranger in a strange land where no one knew his name.

The moment ended with the knife's strike but all he felt was a thin line of pain no deeper than the tear of a briar or bramble. His foe had misjudged the blow for, instead of striking deep, the knifeblade had been caught and turned by the sheepskin of his coat.

With that thin pain, the potter's strength and will returned and, with them, the desire to have the mastery. He caught the stranger's wrist with one hand, twisting back his fingers with the other until he heard the knife drop onto the shingle. They grappled together on the shore. The man slipped and twisted in his grasp, hard to hold as water, and knocked his legs from under him, throwing him hard down onto the seaweed of the tideline. Breathless, the potter scrabbled to his feet. Mocking brown eyes met his, maddening him, and he smashed his fist hard into the stranger's face, bringing the red blood from his nose and dazing him; a second, lower blow brought him to his knees; a third laid him out upon the shingle. Then the potter knelt astride him and pummelled him in rage and fear.

It was not long before he knocked the stranger's breath and wits from him. Clay is heavy, and it takes strength to work it, and, before he learnt his craft, he had been brought up a farmer's son, used from boyhood to handling sheep and goats and ploughing the stony soil of Ittachar. He had never fought for his life before, and his victory sang sweetly in the blood pounding from his heart. He held the man beneath him by his throat and lifted a stone above his face so he might see it, and think what damage it could do to a man's bones. A stone is cruder than a knife but no less dangerous in the hands of a man who has forgotten himself.

He heard the creature screaming on the wind. There were no words in its scream. It was the raucous call of a gull, harsh and heavy on the air; it was the crash of wave on stone. Yet it was enough to make the potter remember what he was and call him back from the wild place inside his mind. A man lives for such a little time beneath the sun and so there is no act greater or more dreadful than to send another into the dark before his time has come.

He got back his breath and saw the question in the stranger's eyes, and, even now, a touch of bitter laughter. The challenge there he could not answer: he was a man again and had remembered what it was to kill. The potter put aside the hammerstone and showed his attacker his hands were empty, though he kept his knee pressed heavy on his chest.

"You should have killed me, stranger," the man spat out. His mouth was full of blood, his nose was bleeding.

"That's too great a thing for me," the potter answered mildly. "I'm only a potter and I've not the wisdom to know the time a man should die. I leave such matters to my betters. But I won't let you have my death. There's too much left I wish to do before I go into the dark."

"Then go home and do not enter the White City. All the roads from here are dark ones."

"Why should you want to kill me?" asked the potter. "We are strangers, you and I: you cannot hate me."

"I am Assiolo, Allocco's son." Even beaten and on his back, the man's tone said he should not have to explain himself. "My father died the night that creature was first seen in our city. That is why I met you with a knife."

"What's done is done. You must decide if your loyalty is with the living or the dead." The potter looked into Assiolo's face a long time, then having seen what he looked for, reached round and found the knife. He set it down by Assiolo and said, "Strike now if you will: a harder, straighter blow will kill me."

He turned his back, taking off his bloodstained coat. It was an ugly garment, the heavy hide and fleece of a hill sheep of Ittachar that still stank with the grease in the wool. Yet there was purpose in it: it had not been made for show but to keep out the rain and wind of a winter's night in Ittachar and today it had turned a knifeblade. He dropped the coat upon the shore and heard no stirring of movement behind him. It seemed he had judged rightly and Assiolo now had neither will nor strength to use the knife.

Blood was sticky on his hands; some was his own but most of it Assiolo's. The potter crossed the shore and knelt at the sea's edge, washing his hands in clear, cold saltwater. Behind him, he heard the rustle of the creature's wings and the rattle of its tail against the shingle. It said, in its harsh voice, "A man can fight and not be slain, and offer mercy to his enemy. A good beginning in this new world I offered you. Now I shall leave you to face the future you have made."

It turned its head, looking first at him from one eye and then at Assiolo from the other. "Do not fear: I keep my promises," it said, and he thought he saw a glint of laughter in its eye. "I was trapped, you freed me and I owe you a debt. So I shall come to you three times when you have need of me. That was the first. But remember, the third time the debt is paid and I shall come no more."

Assiolo picked up his cloak and walked back through the open gate into the city. When he had gone out of sight, the creature lifted itself into the bright air and circled the white towers screaming like a gull in the high sunlight. The potter watched until it grew small in the distance, then slung his bag on his back and, taking hope from the creature's promise, walked through the gateway into the White City.

Of course, he could not hope to go unnoticed, a stranger in a city of so many, and he was not left long alone. Armed men surrounded him as he passed the gate, making him halt. He held out his empty hands. No one touched him, nor threatened him with blade or word, nor would the armsmen let him go on. Soon the wide street was thronged with people. They gathered around, women and men, old and young, clad in all the colours of their trades and chattering amongst themselves, pointing down towards the shore and up towards the sky. The potter felt alone and afraid to be the sight in so many eyes; he tried to speak, but all spoke a different tongue to his and no one would look him in the face.

Then the clear high note of a horn sounded three times and the crowd fell silent. A man in a blue coat stepped through the crowd and spoke to the captain of the gate, who barked an order to his men. All but one stepped back. The man in blue beckoned to the potter to follow him. The potter did so, and the armsmen walked behind and so together they walked up the broad street into the city.

The sun is bright on the sea as Hadùhai the king leads the sailor to a green hill above a western shore towards the most precious thing in all Lyikené, the most precious thing in all the world. Many apple trees grow in many places but this is the only one of its kind. This tree does not grow in any wood nor within a garden wall. No man's hand planted it. It is gnarled and twisted by the wind from the sea, its roots go deep into the earth and it bears its fruit by day beneath one sky, by night beneath another, for here in the west the gates of evening are still open. A little spring rises at its foot and the waters run cold and clear down to the sea.

Hadùhai fills a cup for the sailor and he drinks a health in friendship; Hadùhai gives him an apple and he eats, the sun warm on his face.

Later, later, after the sunset, the sailor stands alone beside the tree beneath another sky and listens to the music of the borderlands, the song of sea and star echoing across the margins of the waking world. He hears the wind whispering his name through the leaves of the apple tree. In turn, he calls out, "If you are there, show yourselves!" and so they do, calling him to their dance upon the land and sea and empty air.

Time out of mind, he watches the liùthion weave their patterns across the land and the stars spin across the sky, until he sees there is another standing beside him beneath the tree, and all other sights are driven from his eyes and mind.

The king of the empty land holds out his hands. In his right hand he holds an apple, in his left a silver cup. "Eat, drink and be welcome."

The dancers of the borderlands are light and lovely as falling leaves, existing only at the edge of vision, in the world and out of it. But the king is the still centre, the fixed point, more solid than any flesh, more real than any dream. The wind from the sea blows his hair across a face that is a mirror to another face seen beneath the other sky, save for the eyes. This king's black eyes are beautiful and terrible as midwinter's night.

Time out of mind, the sailor considers his desires. To eat this apple is to forget his name, to drink from this cup is to forget the world and know only the dream that is the borderlands, the dance with no beginning and no end.

It is the hardest choice that he will ever make. This song was sung before his world began and will outlast it. But another song is singing in his heart, a song sung in a sunlit garden by a child beneath a rowan tree, and so he turns his back upon the borderlands. He does not eat. He does not drink. He takes up the golden apples Hadùhai gave him and sails back towards his city.

The street led up to the hill of the city, where it opened into a great courtyard. The man led the potter across the court into a hall of white stone and all the people waiting there turned their heads to look at him. The light within the hall was very clear and bright, yet it was no more than sunlight falling from high windows to lie in golden pools upon the marble floor. The far end wall was hung with a cloth of the richest blue and the device upon it was the moon and the sun. Beneath this, on a dais, was seated a woman whom he guessed to be the lady of the city. Beneath the dais was another, lesser throne that was empty and covered with a scarlet cloth. A man stood beside it and the potter knew him by his bruises, for all he had had time to wash the blood away and change his clothes.

This lady of the White City was not young, though her years did not yet sit heavy on her, and she was beautiful to look on, clad in a cloak of cloth of gold above a robe of silver, corn-gold her hair, sea-grey her eyes. The potter blushed to find himself so rough before such finery, in wool and leather where all the rest was silk and linen, but then some spark of pride flared in his breast and he raised his face and looked full at her.

There was silence for a few minutes. The lady raised her hand and a woman and a man came from behind the dais and walked side by side towards the potter. The woman held a silver cup and the man bore a platter covered with fine linen. The lady spoke but the words were strange, a language the potter could not understand. From his place beside the scarlet throne, Assiolo whispered softly to her, and the lady spoke again but now she used the language of the Later Lands and clear enough she spoke it, though accented strangely to the potter's ear.

"Eat, drink and be welcome, stranger from beyond the sea."

The man before him turned aside the cloth and there was fine white bread below it. He broke a piece and ate, and the potter did the same. The woman raised the cup to her lips and drank a little of the wine. Then she gave the cup to the potter and he drank also. The woman and the man stepped back as the lady spoke in the language of the city and all there spoke one word in answer. Then, in his speech, the lady said to the potter, before all the people in the hall, "You have eaten our bread and drunk our wine. You are a guest within the city according to our law. No hand shall be raised against you."

"Thank you, my lady."

The potter looked at Assiolo to see if the lady's words were meant for him. But Assiolo neither blushed nor blanched. He stood beside the empty throne and met his gaze, showing no shame as he looked into the eyes of the man he had, unprovoked, attacked.

The lady asked, "From where and how did you come to our city?"

"I am a man of Ittachar, far, far west of here," he answered, "and, if it please you, I cannot say how I came here but I think it was by magic."

"By magic," said Assiolo, with a slight and bitter smile. "And are you then a magician, to summon up a spirit of the air to carry you like a horse wherever you would go?"

For a moment the potter was about to say he was indeed a magician, for he felt very small before these great people, but he saw the lady's eyes upon him, not unkind but very shrewd, and he answered truly, "No magician, my lady, only a potter."

"A potter." Surely it was contempt in Assiolo's voice. "It is not fitting a potter should stand unwashed before the lady of Ohmorah." Again, the young man whispered something to the lady the potter could not understand.

"Hush, Assiolo," the lady said, gently. "Let the tale reveal the man." To the potter, she said, "But many saw the manner of your coming. Are such creatures then the steeds of potters in your land?"

Then the potter told the story of his boredom, the spoilt pots, and the making of the creature from the driftwood. He made a good tale of it and, whilst he spoke, all else were silent and, when he was done, the lady smiled.

"For what purpose did you come to our land?" she asked, and her voice was low and very clear.

The potter raised his face and met her eyes. "My life has been bounded by the mountains and the sea. Now I seek the adventure that creature promised me."

"Adventure?" asked the lady. "And fortune? And deathless fame?"

The courtiers around her laughed, and the potter flushed, thinking himself mocked. "My lady, I'm a craftsman not a nobleman," he stammered. "I need no fortune whilst my hands can make my pots. And I'm far from my home – few there have heard of this land so how would any deed of mine done here make me famous there? A tale to tell by the fireside when I'm an old man will be enough, so I know though I am but a potter that is not all I've ever been."

"That is the answer of a wise man and a modest one. How many of this land of Ohmorah would answer so, I wonder? Such a clear head ought to carry you safely through your adventure and beyond it." The lady smiled, her grey eyes soft as summer rain, and, as she smiled, her years seemed to drop from her.

The potter blushed and dropped his gaze in confusion. "My lady, I am your servant," he said, "and I would give you this." He stepped forward and placed the green pot before her, not daring to look in her face again.

"You are a courteous man as well as a fair-spoken one," said the lady, "and your gift is well given and does you honour. Go now and rest, and we shall speak upon the morrow."

The potter was led away from the white hall by the man who had brought him there. He was taken down long corridors, past gardens of bright flowers to a room that opened from an inner courtyard where a fountain played, surrounded by young rowan trees. Here he was invited to wash and to rest. When he woke, he found his own clothes gone and others in their place, much finer but strange to him. But his choice was wear them or go naked, so he dressed and flung open his window to look down towards the sea. The familiar smell of salt and the feel of the wind upon his face comforted him a little in this unknown place. Even his appearance in the mirror was strange, for he seemed no more the potter of Ittachar but a young lordling of a foreign land.

There were books within his room. Though he had learnt his letters as a boy, each he opened was written in a script that meant no more to him than seaworm casts upon a stone. But, having nothing else to do, he turned the pages and in one he found pictures of the city and its towers and – more strange – of a creature much like the one he had made. Two pictures of this beast were there; in one it was alone upon an empty sea but in the other it bore a woman on its back, her dark hair streaming in the wind. He mused upon these for a long while, wondering how his creature could have been here before him. Not knowing what was written he could know no more and at last he stretched himself, laid aside the book and went outside to sit upon the mossy stone in the afternoon sun.

The wind blows around her, the wind of the world and the wind not of the world. Hatred drove love out, and the little that was left behind lies dead beneath the apple tree. Now she is free to mourn for the life that was taken, for the hope that was stolen.

As midnight is called, she runs out of her mother's house into the night, screaming out her grief and loss. Though the guards at her mother's gate shout to her to stop, no man will lay his hand upon her now. No man dares to walk beneath the winter sky, though faces peer from windows at her wild running. No man knows what is best to do this dreadful night: the lady is absent; her daughter runs mad at midwinter; the chamberlain lies dying.

The streets of the city lie before her, stones she has known her whole life long, and, lying over them, the empty land that had been there before the light and will again be there when the light dies at the world's ending. She hears other voices in the wind, and wild, sweet music; she sees pale figures in the night. They dance around her in a great circle though she can see them only from the edges of her eyes. They have no flesh, no weight upon the world.

"Help me," she calls, but no answer comes there back. The liúthion are singing. It is a song with words she does not know, a dance she cannot join. They dance just beyond her reach; their cold fingers, hard to catch as water or starlight, slip through hers each time she jumps and snatches at them.

So she runs down the wide streets towards the city gate whilst the wind blows ever stronger and the kindred of the borderlands swirl round and around her, unseen by the guards upon the wall. She sobs in grief and fear and rage, pounding her fists upon wood and iron. It is of no matter: the great gate is locked against her and all her strength is not enough to open it. The storm beats down on it in one great rush of wind but it cannot undo the work of men.

One other has heard the music of the borderlands in the long night. The chamberlain's son comes from his father's deathbed, his cheeks still wet with tears. The captain sets his hand upon his shoulder, believing he weeps for his father as a son should do, but he will take no comfort. In a voice greater than the wind and storm, he cries out, "Open the gate. Let her pass."

When the gate is opened, she runs to the harbour where the sea crashes upon the sea wall. The little ship is bound still to the quay. Her sail hangs ragged from the mast. The dancers in the air crowd around her. They are light as feathers on the wind but at their touch the ship shudders into seafoam and driftwood floating on the waves. Between one heartbeat and the next they are gone, and only the world's wind, the west wind, is left behind; it blows, empty as a broken heart, across the sea to tangle itself into her hair.

The wind blows high, and the wind blows low, but the wind cannot blow her away. She cries out, fearing life far more than death, for death is only darkness and silence, "Since only death can make an ending, let it be mine!"

The chamberlain's son screams in anguish to see her cast herself into the water.

2: Green leaves and golden apples

And it's braw sailin' on the sea
When wind and weather's fair
It's better tae be in my love's arms
An' oh, gin that I were there.

Braw Sailin' on the Sea, Traditional

The afternoon had deepened into the first hour of the evening and none had come near the potter. As time passed by he grew fearful in the silence and so, as he sat in the late sunlight beside the fountain, he let his hand rest upon the trunk of one of the rowan trees, remembering his homeland where a rowan was planted close beside a house to offer protection from the night. He knew it no more than a childish charm but still the touch gave comfort in a place where all else was strange.

In a bowl on the table there are apples from her mother's garden. There are many apple trees in the White City but only one bears apples of this kind. They are golden-skinned and small; their flesh is hard but sweet to eat. They grew from a slip taken from the tree at the edge of the world. Her mother takes an apple, pares and peels it, and gives each piece to her. A hundred times in winter nights she has heard the singing in her mother's halls tell of the lady who, long ago when the world was young, when there was but a step between the lands of men and borderlands, when anyone could sail fearless beyond the sunset, came out of the east to Ohmorah. But the story her mother tells now is not the one sung in her halls.

"It is hard to give up life to return to darkness. In time, you will know how hard," her mother says when her tale is ended. "I was born into a land where women and men did not want death to be our end. I was not the first of them, but I was not the last. We saw one greater than ourselves, undying beneath this sky and the other. The greed of flesh for life took us, and, when he would not give us our desire, we looked instead to light everlasting the other side of the sunrise. We wanted to live forever and dance beneath a sun that never set. All things are possible if you are willing to pay the price; we knew the price was terrible and we did not grudge it."

She sees her mother is afraid to speak of these things. This frightens her, to see her mother flawed and fearful, for she has known her only as the lady of Ohmorah, great and glorious, and never before has she seen her afraid to speak the truth. She has never thought of darkness in her mother – always she has been light, warmth and brightness, the love at her root – but childhood is ending and the world grows larger. She is turned fifteen, standing on the threshold of her life. At her back are the safe certainties of the very young, ahead lie the crooked aims and blurred boundaries of adults.

At last his silent guide returned with food and wine upon a silver tray and, not long afterwards, the potter heard another step on stone and looked up from his meal to see Assiolo standing at the courtyard's gate, a bitter smile upon his face, poised as he had been whispering in the lady's ear beside the scarlet throne, calm as if half a day before he had not come with a knife to meet a stranger on the seashore. Rage rose in the potter's throat but he swallowed it down, remembering the lady's promise and that they were above the tideline.

"I have been instructed," Assiolo said as he stepped lightly in, "to answer your questions, and to ask any that seem good to me."

He wore his bruises like a badge of pride and all in his manner said that without such instruction he would not have looked again upon the potter, much less spoken to one so much beneath his degree.

"I'd have you tell me of your lady," said the potter, accepting his words and ignoring his manner.

Assiolo sat upon the stone lip of the fountain and dabbled his fingers in the water. "Allodola was not born to this country nor is she a woman of the common folk," he said. "She came out of the east and built this city."

The potter laughed at such a story. "This tale cannot be true. I'm no more a fool than I am a weakling, Assiolo. I saw the stones of your city are worn by rain and sun; I saw the blocks in the walls the masons have replaced. Such things don't happen in a score of years."

"What you saw is so, and what you say is true, but I'm no liar, clayman." It was Assiolo's turn to laugh, mocking the potter with his knowledge. "In your Later Lands, you have the Tions. Here in Ohmorah we have the lady Allodola. Did you think her merely a woman? She comes of the First People, the first to wake after the sunrise. In the utmost east they built their cities, laid down their laws and wrote their histories when all that dwelled in the Later Lands still lived in wattle huts within the forests. Even now, even here, even after she put her borrowed fire aside, she has a greater life than we do."

The potter shook his head, disbelieving such stories, but Assiolo sat quiet and collected in the western light falling across the garden.

"Look to the water, clayman; I shall show you what happened in that country."

Assiolo held out his hand to the fountain. In the spray of light and water dancing from his fingers, the potter saw a woman, not Allodola but another, a queen whose flesh was light and whose hair was fire. She was seated beneath a rowan tree with leaves of flame, and every berry of that tree was a coal burning red as the heart of a fire. A bright-haired child sat on her knee and a young man stood at her side. The man reached out, a word was spoken, and the sun stood still above a crimson sea. Between sea and sun, the sky was filled with fire above a ruined city and on three towers above the ruins swirled dancers made of flame. They burned and burned and were not consumed but stretched out their hands in exultation to the blood-red sun.

Then he saw a great wave come out of the sea and smash itself upon the ruins of the city, the waters poured over all, quenching the flames, drowning for ever even the highest towers and wiping that horror from the face of the world.

"Where was that?" he asked, though in his heart he knew.

"That was the day the rowan tree died in the east, the day the piper closed the gates of morning, the day the world was changed." Assiolo's answer came from far away, through the rush and tumble of the waves. "That day hangs heavy over all of us who were born later."

Now, in his fear, the potter clutched hard at the rowan tree beside the fountain. It gave no succour and no solace. It was a tree – only a tree. As in a dream, the potter felt the weight of water close above his head and blackness press upon his eyes.

"Enough," he gasped out, choking.

Assiolo pulled his hand back from the water. The fountain returned to its course, the nightmare drew back and the potter could breathe again.

Assiolo smiled. "Did you think all the world was quiet and small as little Ittachar, with no more to it than clay and sheep?"

"There are good livings to be made from clay and sheep," the potter answered, trying to speak easily for all his breath came fast. "It's not so bad a life, living where things are as they seem. We lack your art and knowledge but no man of Ittachar would greet a stranger as you greeted me this morning. We'd at least wait until he'd stolen a sheep or seduced a village girl before we struck at him."

As easily, but with a great deal more disdain, Assiolo met his gaze, and it was the potter who looked away. There was a depth of sadness or despair in those brown eyes that was too much for him to look upon. No young man's eyes should carry such misery within them.

"We live in the world they made, Averla and my father. Now our only hope lies in our own strength and will. Oh, clayman, clayman, I thought today you knew it." Assiolo pointed to the bruises on his face, and the potter looked and saw and did not understand.

Both sat silent for a while, each lost in his own thoughts, and the evening grew heavy around them. At last Assiolo said, "The sun rises, the sun sets, the days are counted out, and all who live must die. But my father would not have it so. He turned towards Averla, light undying before the waking world began; to live forever at her side, he stopped the sun at noontime. He stretched out his hands for what he wanted and did not count the cost. He made his people burn so bright with life and fire the darkness could not take them." Assiolo stood and faced the potter. His voice rang out into the twilight, hard and brittle as the snap of branches in the frost. "Always, clayman, always, the price of life is death. They would not die and so the rowan at the gates of morning died in their stead."

The potter touched the rowan's branch to drive away ill fortune. If Assiolo noticed, he did not heed it nor pause in his tale. "There was one had loved my father as his brother. But when he saw what had been done, when he saw the rowan tree aflame and the rowan berries tumbled into the sea, he opened his hands and let their friendship blow away on the wind. He said a word and sent a wave, Averla fled into the light, and so the long day ended."

The potter sat silent beneath the rowan tree. What could he say to match this tale, when he knew only Ittachar?

Softly, quite sadly, Assiolo told him, "Those who lived to that day's evening left the dead tree and their dying land and came out of the east. My father lived, and Allodola. They tamed the wild and built this city and put their past behind them. But what they did, we cannot undo: that tree is lost forever and with it all our hope of safety.

"Such was her past and my father's, long ago and far away, until a stranger came from the Later Lands, seven years since.

A stranger who was not a potter. He styled himself the Lord of Marac."

The potter started to hear the name of Marac. He knew it as a place with a black name to it, south from Ittachar, down the coast from Tarhn and beyond the great isle of Eilanmor. *A sorcerer's castle,* said some; *A haunt of ghosts,* said others; once, he had heard a tale that there the night grew thin and, when the time was right and the world was balanced, a man could step from Marac into another land.

Assiolo marked his start and asked, "What do you have to say to this, clayman?"

"I know as much of Marac as any in the Later Lands. But of a Lord of Marac no tale of Ittachar has ever told."

"He came here at the equinox with an empty heart, he left here at the equinox with an empty heart. He walked the streets after nightfall and left darkness behind him."

The memory of the knife below the shoreline was too strong in his mind. The potter asked, "What fate befell him here, Assiolo: did you try to kill him too?"

Assiolo smiled his bitter smile that never touched his eyes, and the potter glimpsed again the despair lying beneath his polished manner. Yet the young man said only, "Of his end, no man here can tell you. He was not a man of clay. I do not think he was a man at all." Assiolo bowed, his grace mocking the potter's awkwardness. "But now you've followed in his path, another stranger come to Ohmorah out of the west. What's in your heart, clayman, beyond a fool's dream of adventure?"

That was not a question the potter chose to answer. Instead, holding out the book, he asked, "What tale is here? The creature on the page is mine, I think, but tell me how you know of it."

Assiolo took the book and turned the painted pages until he found the picture of the strange beast of the sea and the air.

"This book tells of the lady's daughter, carried from this city the night my father died."

Assiolo's voice had softened. He looked at the picture, sitting surrounded by a little space of silence the potter could not cross, a shadow amidst the shadows in his black coat. Then Assiolo shut up the book and laid it aside, saying, "Liùtha's tale is not mine to tell. Allodola will tell you more, if it seems good to her to do so. I'll bid you good night, clayman, and leave you to your dreams."

But the potter did not seek his bed. Late into the night, he sat beside the fountain, looking up into the sky at stars whose names he did not know. His heart had been caught by these tales and, though he knew little of the world, he knew it was not by chance that the creature had brought him to the White City.

She has been a lonely child. Although she is the lady's daughter, she is of not much account in the White City. Her mother loves her dearly but she has had other children before her and has outlived them all. Her father sailed away long ago. He had loved the lady, and then his daughter, but over and above them both the sea had been his first love and always on the land he pined for her. But the sea is a cruel mistress and in the end, her mother says, she must have grown tired of sharing him, for surely he would have come back to them from any land of men.

Yet when she had been a little child, her father told her the tales he had brought back from the Later Lands. Of all the men of Ohmorah, only he has defied Lyikené and sailed across the open ocean to those lands. These stories are mostly of the Tions who do not wither and age. Yet because she is her mother's daughter, these tales fade from her mind; ageless beauty is no novelty to her, for though the lady and her chamberlain are not Tions their lives are very long.

But when first she sees the Lord of Marac she recalls one of her father's tales: once, long ago, a king of Eulana walked out of the waking world searching for his love. He found her dancing in an empty land and those with whom she danced had starlight in their hair. For, sometimes, when the evening shadows fall upon him, she sees a light like starlight at his brow.

Next day, the potter was brought word the lady wished to speak with him and would send for him in the afternoon. In the first hour of the third, his guide returned and led him through the city streets to a white stone house. The guard at the gate stood by to let him pass and he was ushered into a green garden where the lady was seated on a stone bench beside a pool. The potter stood awkwardly before her, feeling a fool in his fine borrowed clothes, but she smiled and signalled him to sit at her side. Somewhere in the garden a blackbird was singing of springtime and promises, and she put her finger to her lips that its song might not be disturbed by other voices. Within the pool he saw golden fish sculling slow and big beneath the lilies. The lady held bread into the water and the greatest fish came lazily out of the shadows to feed from her hand.

"So would my daughter feed him when she was a child, before the Lord of Marac came to this city," she said. "Soon, perhaps, we shall speak of her but first tell me of your own country."

So the potter told of Ittachar, that little land of fisherfok and farmers, a gentle land on the edge of the western sea where the sun does not burn in summer nor the cold bite hard in winter, where the people have enough and a little more than enough to live by. He spoke well, for he loved his home, the bracken on the hillside and the sunlight on the sea.

"But," the lady said, "it was not always so. I have heard it said Ittachar is not quite like other places in the Later Lands." She smiled at his surprise. "You see, even here, I have some knowledge of your histories. I know the Sea People came out of the west beneath bright sails and brought death upon a midsummer's morning."

"That was long ago," the potter answered after a little time. "Now that day is no more than a story to frighten children; now midsummer passes quietly in Ittachar and we no longer watch the west." Then, to turn the subject, he spoke of the picture in the book of the creature he himself had made from dreams and driftwood and yet was known to Assiolo.

All the time he spoke, the lady looked into the pool at the fish and the waterlilies. Her eyes were the silvery grey of clouds reflected in the water. "That is the past reaching out to touch the present," she said when he was done. "But what would you tell me of the future? What do you seek?"

" 'Twas I awoke that creature," he answered, his heart afire for glory. "Let me find out the truth of what happened to your daughter."

"Why would you go in search of a dream and a tale?"

"It is the adventure I was offered: to bring your daughter home."

She turned her head to look into his face. Her eyes were grey and wise; he had to steel himself to meet them and not to look away.

"That is not enough," said the lady gently. "That is a story told to amuse children with neither thought nor substance to it. I ask again, man of Ittachar, what do you seek from this adventure?"

He flushed beneath her steady gaze, and turned away to think awhile and gather his words. "It's as I said within your hall," he told her, "it's good to be a potter but it did not seem good to be only a potter. I wanted to find what I am, to test myself against the world. For Ittachar is a good place, but it is not the world." His face took on a look it had not had before, though he did not know it, but the lady, whose eyes never turned now from his face, marked the change. "I might be a hero or a coward, a wise man or a fool. There I'd never know. And, when I know, I shall go home and make my pots for the folk of Ittachar."

She smiled. "It was a fine pot you gave me. Your work shows you are a master of your craft. I shall take it as a token you are a man who can do what is required."

"What has my craft to do with this?" he asked, thinking she talked in riddles.

"Yours is a needful art," she answered. "I have watched potters here in the White City. They take raw clay and shape it to their will, using first water and then fire to change matter from one form to another without destroying it."

The potter said nothing. That was indeed his craft, though he would not have put it in such words. The blackbird filled his silence, singing loudly of its strength in challenge to the garden. Beyond the wall, the watch called out the hour and the shadows lengthened across the afternoon.

"I do not know if Liùtha wishes for her home," the lady said at last. "Perhaps, one day, she will return, but fetching her is not your task. If that were all that was needful, I, or Assiolo, or any of this city, could have done it in a month."

"What then can I do for her?" asked the potter.

"Lead her into the dark places where she is afraid to go. Bear her fear. Be her light. My daughter must go back to Marac but she cannot go alone. Another must go with her to do what she cannot." The lady's face was full of anguish and he saw she was afraid. She reached up to touch the branch of the rowan tree spreading its leaves across the pool.

"The world is not a safe place if you cannot trust your own heart," she said, and her voice was low and desolate. "She did not, she cannot; she is lost without trust or hope within the wilderness of her mind. Liùtha loved as much as ever woman loved, but love is not enough. There must be trust and hope and strength to give it substance. All she had was love, and so she was broken between two strong hearts and two strong wills that thought much of each other and little of her."

"Not all broken things can be mended," he replied. "A pot that cracks in the firing cannot be made whole by the most skilled of potters."

"A woman's heart is made of neither clay nor stone," the lady said. "Liùtha lives, she breathes, and so she can walk out of her sorrow back into her life, if only she can find the way.

That creature snatched her from the waves when in despair she sought her end. There are few men living can summon dreams out of air and longing. But here are you come from Ittachar – the west but not the utmost west – with skill and strength and dreams enough to free that creature and bend it to your will. I will take it as a sign you are the man can do this."

"Another called and trapped it. Did you send it to me?"

She shook her head. "That mystery is not of my making. Once, I could have done it. Once, I had the strength and will to call the elements to my bidding. No more: I put such things aside. Long before my daughter had her beginning, I let my borrowed fire burn out, content to live the days left to me as other women live. Because I chose not to be what I had been, Liùtha was born." Her face was sorrowful, her eyes were bright; sadly, softly, with her hand upon the rowan, she said, "Because I chose not to be what I had been, her father sailed a second time into the west and I could not keep her safe after the Lord of Marac came to Ohmorah."

Her grey eyes shone like light upon the water. She bent her head and, from courtesy, the potter looked away. "The past cannot be easily set aside," she said softly, "and the price of her happiness is very high. I cannot pay it, Assiolo could not. Yet I have already seen what you can do, and what you would not do."

Spring passes by, and the Lord of Marac comes often to her mother's house to spend evenings talking with the lady. By lamplight in the library, the captains of the White City spread out their charts before him. He shows them the sea lanes used by Lyikené when the Sea People come into the east and, more useful, those not used, and the routes of the grey whales. He marks the directions of the winds at each season of the year, and it is clear no man in Ohmorah knows the sea in all its moods and reaches as well as he. All this she watches, pretending to consult old books, whilst her eyes slip sidelong to his face so she might carry his image in her mind all the time he is not there.

One afternoon late in springtime, she lingers within the ante-chamber to her mother's hall, watching the rain fall down upon the garden and the people come and go about the lady's business. Dusk thickens grey light into black night and the lamps are lit. Then in comes the Lord of Marac shaking raindrops from his hair. Other men's footsteps echo on the stone floor but his feet make no sound.

*He has adopted the clothes of the White City in the month since his
appearance but still looks like a stranger.*

He smiles at her. "How does the dove?"

*"She does as you promised," she answers. "But she does not
care to fly in the rain and so today she sits sulking at my window."*

*"How did you find your name?" he asks. "I did not know your
mother's people had gone so far into the west."*

*"My father wished it," she replies. "It is all of his I have: From
a father nothing, if it is a daughter." The old and bitter proverb is
true enough: she has had nothing from him but her name and her
life. "Yet," she says, "it is your name too." For does not the lady
call him Liùthion?*

*"It is not my name. I have no name. Names are not the custom
of my people. Here I am the Lord of Marac, for I have made a
domain in Marac that lies beside the western sea." He forestalls her
next question. "My own land is far away. A man could walk all the
paths in all the world, sail his ship on every sea and never come to
that country. The world has grown old and the way out from those
lands is no longer the way back."*

*His voice is even and she cannot read his face to tell if this
thought saddens him. She is used to the tales of exiles. The lady
and her chamberlain speak sometimes, sadly and with longing, of
the wonders of the land they had left to die.*

The sunshine fell through the leaves into the pool and lit the
fish beneath the lilies in tones of red and gold and bronze.
The garden was a lovely place to sit in the sunny afternoon,
sheltered by stone walls that turned aside the wind. It was easy
to forget the world beyond the walls. The lady looked down
at the golden fish, she looked up at the green leaves and the
flickering light, but she did not look at the potter. She dabbled
her fingers in the pool and the great fish came to her hand to
take what he was offered. Shaking drops of water from her
hands, she turned back to the potter.

"There is one thing more you should know before you go
further. When I saw what creature carried you, I sent Assiolo
to meet you beneath the shoreline."

The potter stared. "Knowing he would kill me or else I
might kill him."

"He did not come to kill you. He came to make you believe
he would kill you."

His heart beat fast that she should treat life and death so
lightly. "And if I had killed him, being ignorant that here you
gamble with lives as your stakes?"

The lady did not flinch from his horror or his judgement. "Assiolo has cared little for his life these seven years," she said. "He would have gone gladly into the dark and your adventure would be over. But you did not kill him."

"Why would you do this?" the potter asked. He tried to look into her grey eyes but saw them dark as storm clouds above the sea, and, in a moment, he looked away, remembering what Assiolo had told him.

"When a smith beats out iron for a blade or a ploughshare it must be tempered and tested in fire and water," she told him. "So is it with a man. Only by your deeds can I know you. If I am to trust my daughter to you, I must know what manner of man you are."

The potter shook his head, thinking of a knife in Assiolo's hand and a stone in his own, of the spray of blood and a wild, fierce drumbeat. In Ittachar, he had known how to judge all he saw around him, for, in Ittachar, deeds were matched to words. In this place, a man came at him with a knife, and so he came to judgement; then words came after to twist that knife into another meaning.

The lady left him to his thoughts. He watched as she walked to and fro within her garden, casting a sharp, hard shadow across the stone. *Queens and princelings, artists, musicians and mercatmen, sailors, liars, mystics and thieves*, the creature had told him. He had not expected to find queens were treacherous, princelings were pawns. He crooked his fingers against ill luck and looked away, and saw green leaves reflected in the clear surface of the fish pool, green leaves and golden apples, another tree beneath another sky. Surprised, confused, he glanced upwards. The wind gusted around the garden, tossing up the branches of the rowan, shattering the image of the apple tree, scattering splinters of sunlight in a scintillation of light. For a few moments, the shadows and the sunlight danced together across the water before the wind dropped and all was still. Then, for a little while, the only sound within the garden was the blackbird singing in the rowan tree, a lovely, empty ripple, meaning everything and nothing.

When the bird fell silent the lady spoke again. "The Lord of Marac came out of the empty land to walk between the sunset and the morning. Iron burns him, fire drives him back, light diminishes him, but death is not his ending. Because of him, Liùtha knows too much of fear, of anger and of hatred. The old songs are true – listen."

She took the potter by the arm and drew him round to face her. Then she sang, and it was a little song of Ittachar sung by mothers to soothe their babes to sleep:

"Beyond the land where apples gold
Grow on the firstborn tree
There is the land where starlight cold
Shines on the empty sea.

"They dance upon the empty land
They dance upon the sea
And empty is each heart and hand
From life, love, death all free."

"What madness is in you?" the potter cried. "You talk nonsense, sing childish songs and play games with men's lives."

He struck her hand from his arm, startling the blackbird from its branch above their heads. It flew away across the garden, rattling its alarm call. Yet it did not fly far, only to an apple tree set apart from the other trees where it perched among the green apples swelling amidst the leaves.

She said, reasoning as with a child, "Assiolo consented to meet you and take whatever fate you gave him."

"I did not consent. You tried to make a murderer of me."

"I could not do that," the lady told him. Her eyes were clear as running water. He could not look into those eyes and see a monster, only a mother who had lost her child. "You have your own will to make your own choices. You chose to stay your hand and so your adventure is not over. But the world is bigger than you thought it, and far more dangerous. Take time and think what you will do, then think again before you act. You are a man of skill and strength and will. None of those is enough to keep you safe. Consider what it is that you desire. If it is the certainty you will live long and be the potter of Ittachar then forget all you have heard, turn away now and go home."

Her mother sighs and is a long time silent staring from the window towards the harbour. "Longtimes we have made this world our own, filling it with iron and light and fire. It was not always so. When I was young, we told legends of liùthion, the kindred that danced before the world began. Time out of mind, they danced in the wind and the starlight upon the sea and land, for all places were alike to them before the coming of men. But in the end the sun rose up out of the sea and the stars were dimmed. Then men came out of the forest and took the land for themselves, making the wild places tame when they worked the first iron and planted the first harvest. When these things happened, the liùthion were driven back to the wild sea and the open sky, to borderlands between dreams and waking. Yet sometimes they remember that once the land was theirs, that one day it shall be theirs again. Then they will take flesh and walk a little time beneath our stars, a man amongst men, a woman amongst women."

All he had heard and seen in the White City swirled in confusion through the potter's mind. The wind whispered in the rowan leaves and the blackbird sang its song of love and need from the apple tree. He sat on the bench beneath the rowan and thought, and thought again, yet his last thought was the same as his first. The vision Assiolo had shown him was long ago and far away, distant as a dream. A wider life was beginning here in this garden, where the blackbird sang in the tree and the fish swam in the water. He did not wish to turn back to Ittachar and be again only a potter. Adventure he had sought, adventure he had found and, with it, the discovery that not all ways run straight across the world.

"What I can, I'll do," he said. "I'll find your daughter and go with her to Marac. I shall mend what is broken."

The lady smiled, and her smile drove away all thoughts of darkness. "I think you can do this. To you then, I shall trust Liùtha, though I can only give you my hope in return for all you offer. But, sometimes, hope is enough."

The lady took his hand and they stood together under the apple tree. All in the garden was bright and lovely and the lady the fairest thing in it, fair as summertime itself. It was hard to remember winter follows summer and the time would come when the tree would lose its leaves and the garden lie empty, hard as iron, cold as stone. He knelt before her and the lady stooped to kiss his forehead, as if he had been a lord of the White City.

"She has suffered greatly," she whispered, as she raised him to his feet, her eyes as soft and sad as morning mist, "and been changed since last I saw her; if ever you think you have lost your way and all roads lead from falseness to destruction, remember this: A man can undo what a man has done."

The potter returned to his room where food and drink were set out and his bed made ready for the night. As he slept that second night in the White City, he found himself dreaming of rowan berries fallen onto moss, of yellow apples ripe upon a tree, of the fierce fall of a hawk out of the empty sky. In the night he woke with a mindful of bright images and a memory of singing. He was troubled because he could not remember the words of the song, for surely he had known it all his life?

He rose from his bed and looked out of his window. The many lights of the city drove back the dark but beyond the city lay the sea, calm in the starlit night. The sight eased him and his dreams were forgotten; he lay down and slept until the morning, and did not dream again.

The sailor walks the road towards the White City with the strange piper leading him. He passes through its gates to the sound of bells and trumpets. He is crowned with a garland of elderflower and honeysuckle, with the midsummer sunlight bright upon his hair. He holds the branch from the world's end high so all might see it and roses are cast upon him. He is the darling of the city; he has defied Lyikené and come safely to his home again. In truth, he has been further than any here know but that tale is not for telling.

In the evening, when the feasting is done and the speeches are all spoken, the sailor walks with the lady in her garden. Two children play beneath the trees, games of hop and skip and jump down the stone paths. The chamberlain rests on the bench beneath the rowan, an old man in evening light; he has been at the lady's side for longer than the White City has existed, her most faithful councillor, her dearest friend. Together they came out of the east. Together they built the city.

When the last shreds of sunset have faded from the west, when two nurses have coaxed away reluctant children, the girl to her bed, the boy to his home, when the only light is the midsummer moon reflected in the water, peace falls upon the garden. Beyond the city walls, the midsummer music plays; beyond the walls, the people dance but here all is calm and still. The sailor draws the lady down on the stone bench beside the chamberlain. The time has come for Hadúhai's gift: two golden apples wrapped in silk to protect them on their journey, and a slip from the tree that bore them.

The lady picks an apple from its swathings and breathes in the scent of it; she strokes its satin skin that is now a little withered, though the fruit within is sweet and sound. It is only an apple. It cannot undo what was done, it cannot remake what is broken, but the slip will grow into a tree, and there will be hope. No more than hope but, sometimes, in some places, hope is enough.

She gives the apple to the chamberlain. "Eat, Allocco," she bids him.

"What is this?" he asks, looking closely at the fruit. "There are apple trees a-plenty in the city."

"Hope, Chamberlain," the sailor answers. "A new beginning. The chance to be the man you were before the flood, before the fire."

The chamberlain drops his apple back into the lady's hand. "I ate my fill of apples long ago," he snaps. "I know the man I am. I learnt it in fire and storm. I was tested by the fire of the sun itself and it tempered me, made me hard and strong. I do not fear the darkness: fire drives back the dark."

"It is a shame," the sailor says, "to live so long in the world and never know how lovely it is to walk beneath the stars or see the starlight on the sea."

The chamberlain answers, "I am a man. I walk beneath the sun. I am too old to take another path now."

He kisses the lady courteously upon her cheek, bids her goodnight and leaves her with her sailor in her garden. She smiles and eats the apples he has brought. And he smiles too, as a man smiles on the woman he loves.

Later, later, she rises from their bed to look out from her window. That night, she looks beyond the lights of her city and sees the starlight on the sea, the wind upon the water, and it is indeed beautiful. That night, she remembers what she had forgotten, what the chamberlain long, long ago taught her to forget: that only half a life can be spent beneath the sun. And, in the time that follows, she walks by day and laughs by night with her bold sailor who has crossed the world, who has less life than she but no less understanding.

The potter breakfasted in the sunlight, sitting again beside the fountain. The man who had served him gave him a pack of food and a flask of wine to carry with him on his way. He also brought his sheepskin coat. It had been washed and mended but the potter could not bear to put it on and left it lying where the man had set it down. Bloodstains could be washed away but never anger or treachery. He walked the streets of the city until at last he found the gateway below the tower that opened onto the road to the seashore. The guard saluted him as he passed.

A man was waiting outside the gate, sitting on a stone beside the road. His finery and mocking smile were ill-matched to the bruises on his face.

"Are we to part as we began, Assiolo," the potter asked, and hoped all the scorn he felt was clear in his voice and face, "with lies and tricks and false pretences? If I had half your learning I'd not use it to deceive an honest man."

" 'Tis easy enough to fool a fool: a wise man can tell truth from seeming," Assiolo answered, with a bitter smile. "Nay, I did not come here to spar again, clayman. I thought to give you this before you go your way. It was Liùtha's long ago."

He tossed the potter a little bundle, something light and hard wrapped in grey velvet. "Give it to her as a token you are a friend."

The potter turned aside the cloth to find a little crown, a fine silver circle bearing one great stone glowing white and bright as the full moon itself, wondrous fine work it was, even to his craftsman's eyes. He ran his finger over filigree, delighting in its beauty. "I could buy half of Ittachar with such a thing."

"Does it tempt you?"

He flushed against Assiolo's mocking smile. Swallowing his anger, he wrapped the crown and pushed it into his pack.

"When I first saw you," Assiolo said, "I thought you were another, greater man. Now I see you are only a fool who has meddled with powers that are not his own."

"What I am, I am," the potter answered. "I told the truth to your lady and gave her my promise. I owe you nothing."

Assiolo shrugged and smiled. "It seems a fool can go where a man of the White City cannot. Do you even know what you must do?"

"Tell me," the potter said.

"You must bring death, clayman. Allodola knows many things. But I am my father's son and death is one thing I know even better than she does." There was a wild laughter in his voice, a laughter born of bleak despair. He had looked on the worst the world could offer, and mocked the potter for his hope. "You must decide a man must die, and find the strength to send him into the darkness and the silence. Only then can this be ended. Do you have that strength? Do you have that will?"

"I shall leave you to your city, Assiolo, to live in light or darkness as you choose," he said, though his skin shivered. "I go for Liùtha."

Assiolo's laughter died away. He held out his empty hands and the potter saw the line of an old scar running across his left palm. "She will burn you. She is fire and ice," he said, and his scorn was gone. The potter heard an honest warning and saw tears brightening his eyes. "I loved her once, but love is not enough. She will have your life, and you'll not dare to wrestle with her to win it back again." He took off his cloak and gave it to the potter. "I wrecked your coat. This may not stop a knife blade but it will keep out the cold. Go carefully, if you are to find your home again."

Then Assiolo turned back into his city and the potter went on towards the shore.

The chamberlain's son rambles in the places where the roses grow and marks the green tendrils of honeysuckle twining round the elder boughs.

At midsummer, he will walk beyond the city beneath the flowering trees; at midsummer, there will be light and fire, music and dancing. At midsummer, a girl bright as a candleflame will step beyond the walls of her mother's house and he will crown her with flowers.

All that will come in its own time. Now it wants a month of midsummer, the flowers have not yet opened, and she is safe within stone walls, sheltered by the rowan tree in her mother's garden.

At sunset, the wind blows from the sea. Shivering, he pulls his coat around him. "If you are there, show yourself," he calls, but the only answer is the rustle of the aspen leaves above his head, a thousand tongues whispering he is no more alone.

He walks out of the wood down the path towards the sea. The hawthorns in the hedges are laden with blossom soft and white as drifts of snow. There is no hurry in his step. He has all the time before the morning. The air around him drags thick as water and he walks across the shore as if wading through a dream.

At the first glance it could be a man standing at the water's edge, but no man could ever look so lovely in that cold, clear light. The Lord of Marac stands with one foot on sea and one on shore, weaving the threads of starlight into a silver crown. Whilst he works, he sings and his song has no place within the waking world.

The chamberlain's son says the words his father taught him and the song falls silent as the Lord of Marac turns around to face him. He hears him say, "On midsummer's night, I shall be waiting between the city and the shore."

"What care you for midsummer?" he cries out. "Your kindred do not dance beneath the flowering trees."

"Do you not think, Assiolo, it would be very sweet to meet the one you love beneath the trees at midsummer?"

Then their gazes meet, and each sees himself reflected in the other's eyes.

3: Frost upon a flower

He stepped away from me and he moved through the fair
And fondly I watched him move here and move there,
Then he turned his way homeward with one star awake
As the swan in the evening moves over the lake.

He Moved Through the Fair, Traditional

The potter stood at the sea's salt edge and called into the wind for his creature. To pass the time of waiting, he walked along the tideline, finding shells amidst the shingle, watching the flights of oystercatchers and turnstones as all the while the sea slipped gently down the shore and the sun climbed slowly up the sky.

At noontime he saw the creature flying low across the sea out of the east. It wheeled across the sweep of the bay, its white wings and the scales of its rainbow tail flashing in the sunlight and the sea spray, and dropped to earth beside him, ungainly on the land though in the sky it had been graceful and lovely.

"Will you carry me from this city?" he asked.

"Little time for freedom have you given me," it said in its voice of rattling stone, "but I shall keep my promise. You ask, and I am here to answer. Where would you have me take you now? Are you weary already of foreign lands and desire again your home?"

"Oh no, not yet, and my home can wait a while longer. In the city, they told me you rescued a girl from the sea seven years since and carried her away."

"That is the truth, after a fashion."

"What manner of creature are you?" asked the potter. "I made you myself out of driftwood and yet you were here before me."

"I had my beginning on the day when men first saw how great the distance was between what they were and what they wished to be. So it was a man with nothing left but his despair could trap me in the knot and fibre of wood and words."

The creature beat its wings against the air, it thrashed its tail against the stones and told him, "I am the desire to fly with the gulls in the high sunlight and the longing to swim with the fish in the deeps of the sea. So it was you could release me with your dreams of freedom."

It turned its head and gazed at him, first from one eye and then the other. The potter could not look into those eyes though he himself had made them. To look there made him giddy, as if he stood atop a tower and stared into the space below. There was nothing between himself and the void and surely he was falling, falling...

Frightened, he closed his eyes and felt the stones firm again beneath his feet. "Dreams fade with the morning," the creature said. "Can you go on when the wind blows hard against you, and the sun shines fierce and burns you, and you see the world for what it is?"

The potter had no answer. He did not know what he could do, only what he had promised. He settled Assiolo's cloak around his shoulders and felt its unaccustomed folds fall around him. "Will you help me?"

"Climb on my back and I shall carry you to where you need to be."

Fast and far they flew across the sea, a day and a night without a sight of land until, at the dawning, the potter saw a land of mountains and sea lochs with clusters of little houses and small fields set upon the hillsides. Again the creature came to rest at the boundary of land and sea, this time upon a sandy beach.

"I brought the girl to where she might find shelter amongst people," it said. "Here in Anach I set her down, and slipped sideways into seafoam and driftwood bobbing on the wave."

"Why did you bring her so far across the sea when you could have taken her safe to her mother?"

"That was not her wish. She did not want her mother, she did not want her city, she wanted a time out of the wind where she was safe." Its eye was bright and knowing but the potter could see nothing of its thoughts. "I knew her mind," it said, "and so I gave her what she wanted, just as when you freed me I knew your mind and offered you your dreams."

She asks the Lord of Marac in the library one evening, "Why did you come here?"

"To read your mother's books," he answers, laughing.

She tosses back her hair, disdainful he should tease her. "No! To the city."

"For the reason any man crosses the sea in search of strange lands, of course. For fame and fortune, to find out my fate. I came

to Ohmorah because I dreamed I would find here a jewel beyond price I could carry back to Marac."

She does not like it when he talks as if he thinks her no more than a child when in but a month, at midsummer, she will be a woman grown and surely he must see it.

"I know little of the world," she answers, very seriously, "but I know you have small need of fortune, and that you are no more a lord of the Later Lands than you are a man of the White City. I have heard it said you are come to court my mother."

There is still an edge of teasing in his smile. "I had not marked you as a gossip, child. Have you seen me court your mother? Is she then to be my jewel beyond price?"

"You wear her brooch." She points to the silver on his collar. It does not show her mother's own device, which is the sun and the moon, but is patterned with sea and stars. Between them a single figure dances forever on the waves, its head thrown back in ecstasy. "It was the loveliest of all her treasures from the land that was lost. My mother would not let me wear it, yet she gave it to you."

"But before Allodola had this brooch another wore it. He left the world long ago; she kept it so she did not forget why she came out of the east."

"Did you know that land?"

Again, she sees that laughter in his eyes, the laughter of an adult with a foolish child, not unkind but full of knowing patience.

"I am not one of those who came from Idùnmhor with your mother and Allocco. See — no mark of such age is upon me."

He holds out his hand before her face. It is smooth and pale in the lamplight, a young man's hand. Yet though, like his face, it bears no lines of age she cannot think he is young. His eyes are dark and deep, like a night without stars.

"Allocco is an old man," he says. "Even Allodola grows older, though the winds of time blow more gently on her than they will on you, for you were born in Ohmorah. Go and feed your fish, he must grudge the time you spend here."

She shakes her head and stands her ground. He sighs, and shuts up his book. "I see you are not done with questions. Ask on: I am at your mercy."

"You call my mother by her name. That is not the custom here."

"But I am a stranger in these lands, and if Allodola can overlook my discourtesy I am sure you can forgive me too."

"The chamberlain will not forgive it. You must beware the chamberlain."

Her voice shakes with her fear and he puts aside his teasing. His voice is gentle as he asks, "Little one, why do you fear Allocco? Far better pity him: he is only a man."

"You are greater than he, and that he will not suffer."

His eyes stare beyond her into the dark towards a man that is not there. At last he says, quietly, very sadly, "I know what Allocco was and what he is; he has no power to bind me. Love might be enough but he has only hatred left to him."

This answer does not calm her. There are words in her that must be spoken so she goes on, though she knows she sounds like a child gabbling stories. "He watches you, as once he watched my father. He would not eat the apples brought from Lyikené." She has not spoken of her father for many years, not since a day when she was nine years old and learned he would not return. "My mother ate," she says, "but he would not. So, long ago, my father sailed away. He left me behind with my mother and the chamberlain, and he will never come back to me."

She stares the Lord of Marac in the face; seeing anew the fall of his black hair and his black eyes, deep enough to drown in, she thinks she could not bear it, were he too to sail away and leave her.

He looks at her full tenderly, as if he heard the thought unspoken, and she finds she is weeping. She turns away to hide it, flushing to show so plain what should be hidden.

He takes her hand and holds her back. "I shall watch Allocco. And I promise you, I did not come to court your mother. It was to you I gave the dove."

He meets her eyes; in his face she sees all she could desire and, for a moment, there is silence between them. Her heart beats fast. Then the door opens and a servant comes in to trim the lamps and close the shutters against the night. The moment is broken; when next the Lord of Marac speaks, his teasing tone is back. "But now I think on it: Allodola is very beautiful. Perhaps I should think again."

She snatches back her hand and runs from him, from the smile in his eyes and the truth in her heart.

From the creature's naming of this place, the potter knew he was back among the Later Lands, though far from Ittachar. He went up around the fields of barley in search of people and news of the lady's daughter. In the village he had a hard time of it, for many people would not speak to him, mistrusting his fine clothes and his accent of Ittachar. But, at last, his patience was rewarded and he heard from an old man that in the next valley was the farm of Issa Gicocca, who had once found a strange girl, though that was long ago and he knew not if she was living there yet. The potter gave the man thanks for this news and wished he could give more, but his pockets were empty save for the silver crown. So he bade him farewell, and went his way back to the beach.

The creature was not there when he returned but the grooves worn in the sand by its dragging tail led down to the sea. Where it had gone he could not follow. He stood, alone and lonely, on the shore between the sea and the empty sky. Once more he might ask its aid, then the adventure must end and he return home and be again only a potter. But that day seemed far away and his home small and further still.

"I am not ready yet; the task I undertook is not half done and who knows when it shall be completed. My home will wait for me or else it is not my home. I am glad my path lay down such an unexpected road, for how many potters see the ends of the earth?" He spoke aloud to keep up his spirits, which had been quenched by solitude. "And I shall have such a tale to tell when I am old by the fireside, even if none believes it and think my wits wander further than I ever did."

He slept that night in a haystore wrapped in Assiolo's cloak against the draught leaking under the door. Before he slept, he heard the patter-pat of rain upon the roof and all the night the sound of water ran through his dreams. In the morning, he ate the last of his food and drank sweet water from the burn beside the village and went on to find the house he looked for. It was larger than the rest and set apart from the village, a white house soundly built of stone with a stout slate roof and surrounded by a garden within a stone wall. Hens pecked around the door, there were cows in the meadows and sheep on the hill pasture. An apple orchard was planted at its back, the trees protected from the wind from the sea by the high stone wall. Their boughs were set with half-grown apples; the crop promised to be a fine one when the autumn came. A rowan, an ancient twisted tree, grew each side of the gate, as at the gates of many houses all across the Later Lands.

The door was opened by a woman past middle age with a kind, worn face who curtsied to him in his fine city clothes, and looked askance when he spoke to her with the accent of Ittachar.

"Are you Issa Gicocca, mistress?" he asked.

"I am."

"I am a stranger here," said the potter.

"So your face tells me."

"I came yesterday across the sea from the east."

"We saw no boats from the east yesterday."

"I did not come by boat, mistress, but if I told you the manner of my coming I fear you'd not believe a word I said and think me a trickster or a rogue."

"Then tell me nothing of it and let me judge you by other means. If not how you came to this place, tell me why, and we might understand one another."

"Mistress, I seek one who was stolen away. A girl, a woman, brought from a distant land and abandoned on the sea shore. I seek her, to restore her to her friends or, if she be dead, news of how she came to her end."

"How can I know you are a friend to such a woman? There are many reasons why a girl might flee her home, never wishing to return, but a man lies at the root of most of them."

"My face is all the proof I can offer. I have other proofs for her, but none for you."

She looked hard at him, the look of a woman who has lived long enough to become wise to all the wiles of men, but he met her gaze steadily, having nothing he wished to hide. At last Issa Gicocca smiled, and stood aside so he might come in.

"Fairly said, stranger. It's taken longer than I thought but I always knew someone would come seeking her."

She brought him into her kitchen and sat him by the hearth to warm his feet, setting his damp cloak to dry. From courtesy, she did not ask his name, only his trade, for she knew enough to know the ways of names in Ittachar were not the same as in other places. He felt at home within her house, far more than he had in the glory of the White City. Here a farmer could talk to a potter as equals, their feet on the same ground. Indeed, it was very like the houses he knew in Ittachar with herbs drying in the rafters, plates on a wooden dresser and a tabby cat curled on the rug by the fireside. She sat down at her spinning wheel. The thrumming hum as the wheel turned, the purring cat and the sound of the rain against the window made the kitchen a very pleasant place to sit and tell stories.

"My man went down to the shore at twilight to call home a goat that had wandered to eat the seaweed cast upon the shore. The goat came home at its own will but in a hollow in the dunes he found a poor, drenched girl. He knew her for no poor man's daughter; though her clothes were ruined by the sea and rain, they'd been fine once, finer than any in this country for fifty miles around.

"He brought her home to me, so I might dry and feed her and coax out her tale, for he guessed she would be sought for and thought there might be a reward for keeping her safe until her folks came by. But she told me her name, and nothing more." Issa Gicocca stood up from her wheel and took bread from the crock. "So we warmed her and washed her and put her safe to bed. When the next moon's day came around, we told of her in the mercatplace in Anach, we asked of the ships come from foreign parts, and my man went over the hill to tell it in the town. Many came, to look and talk and wonder. But no one knew more than we did, which was nothing, and no rich lord ever came to seek her. So to us she came and with us she stayed. We could not turn her from the door, a girl alone and lonely, not after she'd eaten our bread and drunk with us."

The potter nodded. In his land, too, a stranger was no more a stranger once food and drink were offered and accepted: giver and taker were bound together by a bond that could not be broken. So, there and here, hospitality must be tempered with caution for it was no little thing to ask, no little thing to give.

"Who is she then?" She looked at him, curious to have the mystery she had lived with made plain. "Liùtha's none of Ittachar – I'll not believe it if you tell me that, potter."

"She is the daughter of the lady of Ohmorah," and he told of the city and the lady.

Issa Gicocca shook her head and looked at him, somewhat askance. "Well, that's as may be." Ohmorah meant nothing to her and the lady was as any wonder in a traveller's tale, good in the hearing but not to be believed. But since his tale was true he met her gaze. "Oh, let Liùtha be the judge of it," she said at last.

She set a plate before him with bread and cheese and onion and a beaker of new milk. He raised his cup to her, speaking her health, accepting what was offered. Issa Gicocca went on with her tale, munching her own meal as she did. "Liùtha's never spoken, from that day to this, of where she came from or why she left. Those early days, her misery was plain to see; I guessed it was the usual tale of man and maid and did not press her. The days turned into months and into years and I can tell you no more of her than that. She's a kind heart, mind you, under her silence and her sorrow. I tell you, when my man died, she was more comfort and support than any in the village with tongues in their heads but nothing of use to say with them."

"A sad, strange tale," said the potter, "and you know one end of it and I the other. If you'll trust me with her, mistress, I'll not rest until I can take her home again."

She shook her head. "That's not for me to say. I'm no kin to her and have no claim, fond of her though I am. You must ask her. But go gently," she warned. "Liùtha does not care to speak with men. She's burnt her hand at that fire, that's plain as wholecloth."

"Will she be home soon?"

"She went down into the village with the eggs to sell; like enough she'll be back before the evening. You can ask her will then, and be my guest tonight whatever her answer."

The potter bowed his head in thanks and left Issa Gicocca to her work. Outside, the rain had passed and pale sunlight sloped from beneath dark clouds. He walked on, not knowing where his path would lead but heading upwards. He found a rocky outcrop with birken trees above it and under it a patch of heather where there was some shelter from the wind and a view over the hillside to the sea. He threw himself down and stared through closed eyelids at the redness of the light and presently he slept a little, to dream of the great grey eyes of the lady of Ohmorah.

One evening, late in springtime, the white dove does not return at sunset to the silver cage. She calls from her window but still the bird does not come home. So she comes down from her chamber to search for her in the garden. She does not find her there and goes to the gate that opens onto the street. The guard salutes and stands aside, for she is no longer forbidden to go out alone into the White City. Yet she has never done so.

"But," she thinks, "I am no longer a child and may go where I please in my own city."

So she walks out into the street that runs down the hill from her mother's house to search for her white dove.

The sky is full of red and gold but in the city it is the time of the lighting of the lamps. They burn and burn and the shadows in the streets are driven back and broken by their brightness. She walks on into streets she does not know, that grow narrower and narrower, until at last she finds the dove that is become a tumble of white feathers, a pretty toy for a grey cat. She drives the cat away and picks up the bird. The dove does not flap or struggle but lies light as air across her hands, her heart fluttering against her fingers. One wing hangs down, a broken thing with no use left to it; her white breast is red with blood; her eyes are dull.

She does not know what to do and stands there, weeping, weeping, with the dove in her hands. A long time she stands there, while the shadows thicken round her. At last she feels a breath of wind against her neck and she is no longer alone. She looks up into the face of the Lord of Marac.

"What has happened, child," he asks. "Why do you weep?"

She holds out the dove to him. He takes the bird and strokes the bloody feathers gently back into their places. Then he bends his face to the dove and breathes upon her very softly. In a minute he opens his hands and holds them out. She sees the dove settled there as she might be upon her nest. Her eyes are bright and all the blood is gone.

"See, she is whole again," he says. He lifts his open hands and the white dove flies up into the sky, her feathers gilded by the sunset. He smiles, a smile she has not seen before. It seems as if a great wind had blown upon her, but the night is calm and still.

"She has gone to her home," he says. "It grows late for you to be alone in the city. Let me walk with you to your mother's house."

Quietly, she follows him, her head full of wonder at what she has seen. His feet make no sound as they walk down the paved streets.

The sun dropped down towards the sea and shadows lengthened across the hillside. The potter woke but did not yet return to the house behind the rowans. He sat with his knees drawn up to his chin and looked into the west, remembering the sunsets of his home and thinking of the women he had known there. As if thought created substance, he heard a rustle in the bracken and there she was indeed, a woman standing by a young birken tree, slender as the tree with her dark hair bound tight against the wind and the sunset catching at the silver brooch fastened on her coat.

Warily, she met his gaze, her face set still as if she wore a mask through which she could look out but none could see her as she was. Like her mother, she was lovely but, whereas the lady had been golden in the sunshine, her daughter was a flower nipped by frost that could not open to show its beauty to the day. A long time the potter looked at her until her disdain showed him he stared. Flushing at his discourtesy, he held out his hands in greeting. The woman did not move, and he remembered what Issa Gicocca had said and turned away. Presently he began to speak of what was in his heart so she might know and trust him.

"My home is on the shore of a land not so very unlike this. It is in Ittachar, to the north of here. This land is new to me but it is the same sun and the same light and the wind with its tang of salt reminds me of home. I am a potter, and I colour my pots with the patterns of the sea and the sky. It's a fine life to be a potter."

As he spoke, he mostly looked out across the hillside to the sea and the setting sun but now and then he dared to steal a sidelong glance at her, thinking it a shame she was so cold and hard when one so young and fair should be warm and sweet as a rose in summer.

He paused to see if she would answer but the woman kept her silence and after a moment he spoke on. "But it's not so fine a life to be only a potter and I was bored, despite my skill. It's a long time since I drew up the clay to shape a pot, making form where there was only raw matter, a long time since I fired my kiln, a long time since I saw what I made was good. I raged against the limits of my life; I wanted more than the wheel and the sounds of the sea, more people to talk with than my good neighbours, more ideas. To know I was not only a potter...

"That's why I gave my promise to your mother to go with you to Marac and meet the darkness there," he said. "I know I'm not a magician or a lord but I took this adventure freely and shall not turn back."

"A great man used all the power he had against me. You come to me with kind words and a brave heart, potter, but it will take more than those to stand against it." The woman had a hard, cold voice well matched to her face. "Strength and knowledge would arm you better. I am not your adventure. Go home to Ittachar and forget the White City."

He saw himself reflected in her eyes and what he saw made him afraid. She saw only a potter, a braggart from an unknown land; she had known men accounted powerful and wise in the White City and weighed him against them to find him wanting. Seeing her scorn, the potter doubted his words and purpose and thought himself a fool who had acted rashly.

There was a rush in the air, a sound of beating wings and a seagull's scream louder than the mew of any gull. Both started round, she with a loud cry. The creature circled in the air above them and the slanting light of sunset flashed on the feathers of its wings and the bright scales of its tail. It settled on the ground beside him and preened its feathers, as any bird would do, but all the while its fish tail thrashed against the grass.

It raised the potter's spirit to see the creature, and as much again to see that now the woman looked at him as if he were more than a foolish stranger bent on deeds of glory. He smiled and greeted it, rubbing its head as he would a dog's.

"So you have found already what you sought. I congratulate you," it said, "but adventures are not so easy as they first appear. Each tale leads on to another, and some are not yet told."

"Does he yet live?" the woman cried out to the creature, and the change in her voice told of some passion, but whether hope or hatred the potter could not tell. "You fly beneath both skies – tell me, does he yet live?"

"I cannot tell the tales of men," said the creature in its rasping voice of sea on stone. "Let the man tell you what he knows. But no man knows all there is to know."

"You see our fates are already linked, yours and mine," the potter told her. "This creature brought you out of Ohmorah – it carried me first to the city and then here in search of you. I do not know what you remember."

He saw a clenched look on her face that was meant to tell him nothing but said, clearly as the words unspoken, that she remembered everything. "I carved its likeness from driftwood. It came to life and it offered me adventure; it took me to your city and your mother. There I found its picture in a book I could not read and I knew you were my adventure." He fumbled in his bag and held out the moonstone crown to her. "I have this to give you as a token, and your mother's words. *A man can undo what a man has done,* she said."

She took it from him. The western light lit up her face and kindled a moment's warmth on her frosted beauty. "Then there is hope," she whispered to the wind, "and hope is the hardest thing of all to bear."

A cloud covered the sun, and the light faded. Her face was set and sad, as it had been when he first saw her. The sun set and the wind from the sea blew across the hill. The sky had darkened already in the east and the first stars pricked into light. The potter shivered; he had left Assiolo's cloak drying in the house and the evening wind was cold.

"Liùtha," he said, using her name for the first time. It was sweet as heather honey on his tongue. "Liùtha, you can't hide forever. You can be freed from your past."

"Did my mother tell you that, or Assiolo? Did they say also some costs are too great to bear?"

He turned back to his creature. "The world's truly a stranger place than I knew and I must ask your help again, though I don't know your nature. You're as hard to grasp as the wind and the sea themselves. But I've a question maybe you can answer. How I may fulfil my oath and bring Liùtha through the darkness of Marac?"

"I say again: you freed me. There is strength in you the equal of any man in this world. Trust your own heart – nothing else can keep you safe. Now I've said enough to help you on your way. You've one more call on me before I go free forever to the sea and the air, and you back to your home." Its voice was harsh, rasping like stone across stone, and gave little hope or comfort. It preened its wing a little time and spoke again. "I am not a man: I do not judge men or their actions. The world is as your kind has made it, and you must make your way as best you can."

The potter stood to face it, despair biting at his heart because he had not yet proved himself. He had found what he sought, knew where he must go, but was no nearer knowing what he must do there. Now he had seen Liùtha, fair and frozen, Assiolo's words were heavy in his memory. Yet what he had begun, he would finish.

The creature's voice cut into his grey thoughts. "Once more I shall come when I am needed. Choose that moment carefully, for the third time is always the most important."

It looked sidelong at him from its bright bird's eye and the potter saw a glint of laughter there that was not unkind but not like the laughter of men. It knew more of the world than he did, and had known it longer. He was only a man, far, far from his home where all things were known to him, and ordered.

The creature leapt into the darkening air and sped off into the evening. For a little while they could hear the sound of its wings beating into the distance, then it was gone. The sky was empty but for the rising, gibbous moon that dimmed the stars around it. The potter looked down at his hands. They were strong and shapely, hands of an artist, hands of a craftsman, but of a man of power? That he could not see.

"Maybe I cannot do what I set out to but I shall go as far as I am able," he said. His voice was faint, even in his own ears, and he did not look at Liùtha. "I shall not break my word."

It grew too cold to linger on the hillside. He felt Liùtha touch his arm and saw her face, pale in the moonlight, bleak and lovely as frost in springtime. She led him back to the house and, after supper, they sat by the fireside with Issa Gicocca, and drank hot milk sweetened with honey and talked together whilst she listened.

"Liùtha, will you come away with me?" the potter asked. "I think you're not made to hide yourself away, fearing life and all it can offer."

"I know the choice you offer, better than you do yourself," said Liùtha. "I can leave Anach to see if the Lord of Marac is yet in this land. Or I can remain here in exile and live alone forever." The look of sorrow on her face grew heavier and her voice dropped to a whisper. "I shall stay here. I have grown used to grief. To leave this place brings too much danger, to me and to any man who goes with me."

Issa Gicocca shook her head. "That's foolish talk, child, when he's been far across the sea and back for your sake." She put her hand onto Liùtha's, and the young woman grasped it tightly, accepting her comfort. "Best go with him, my dearie. There's nothing here for you. What the young men offered, you each time turned away. You've locked yourself away each year when the midsummer music calls the young folk to their dancing. That was not done by one who'd stay. This man offers hope, take it."

"Issa Gicocca speaks wisely. I can offer only hope, if you choose to leave Anach and come back into the world."

"I do not want to hope again. Hope has not served me well before."

The room was silent but for the crackle of the fire and the purring cat asleep on its mistress's lap. The house was warm and light and very safe, its stone walls keeping out the night. Liùtha stared ahead as if she looked beyond the fire into a great distance. At last she said to the potter, "It's a quiet place, Anach; a safe place of little farms. Its people have been good to me. Here is Issa Gicocca, who took me in out of the storm and was kind to me when all I knew was lost."

"Your mother trusted me. I brought the creature out of the sea and the sky. If you'll not come with me now, I'll wait, and wait, until you do," the potter answered, for he knew enough of women to be certain she wished to go to Marac but needed another's strength to bring her to the point. "I can manage a boat and can find work with one of the fishermen. It is hard for you to leave Issa Gicocca, perhaps, you've been here so long."

"The world is a dangerous place," replied Liùtha, turning her gaze from the deep of the fire to look him in the face, "and the worst lies in the hearts of men. If you take the path to Marac with me most like you will not come safely to your home again." Her eyes were opaque, reflecting the firelight rather than acting as a window on her thoughts.

"I'll take that risk," said the potter, more bravely than he felt.

"Though you are but a potter?"

"My kiln and clay are far away. In these lands I am not a potter."

"So I have seen, and for that reason I shall go with you," Liùtha said, and rose to go to her bed, lighting a candle at the lamp.

"I have one question in return: Tell me what the Lord of Marac was to you?"

"Enough tales have been told tonight. That one can lie quiet until it is needful to tell it."

The potter thought of ice upon the meadows, of frost upon a flower, of cold, dead, lovely things, and shivered in the firelight.

"It is long since I have eaten," says the Lord of Marac, as they stand before the gateway of the lady's house. "Will you let me eat and drink with you this night?"

She leaves him in the garden beneath the rowan tree and runs to find what food she can. She does not wait to ask for what the cook or kitcheners can offer but seizes the first she comes upon, a flask of wine and a basket of honey cakes. Then, suddenly, despite her haste, she is shy to be alone with him past nightfall, even within the boundary of her mother's house. She pauses beneath the apple tree to calm herself and still her breathing. The flowers have fallen, little buds of apples are setting on the tree, green and hard but within them lies the promise of sweetness. Somewhere in the garden a blackbird is singing of love in the springtime and, as she stands beside the apple tree, the same song fills her heart.

The Lord of Marac sits on the bench beneath the rowan. The tree is heavy with white blossom. He has broken off a great foamy spray to breathe in the faint perfume. A little while she watches as he sits in the shadow of the flowering tree where the lamplight does not reach and sees again, more certain this time, the touch of cold light at his brow. At last he raises his head from the flowers and stares into the dusk, a still, quiet figure in the twilight, and she does not know if the look upon his face is joy or sorrow. His eyes are great and black and neither the lamplight nor the starlight touches them. Then he turns his head towards her and she walks out of the shadow towards his smile.

She offers him wine and he drinks, and she drinks with him. She offers him food, and he eats; she eats with him, sitting at his side on the stone bench. All this is done in silence. Why this should be on his account she cannot guess but, for herself, she cannot think of anything to say. Though her mind is racing, her heart is too full to bring the words to her tongue. She wants to stretch out this moment so it will never end. She wants to seize the future and make it hers. She does not know if it is the world that is changing or she herself.

When all the wine is drunk and all the cakes are eaten, she watches the Lord of Marac go out through her mother's gate and hears him bid the guard, "Goodnight." She sits a long, long time on the bench beneath the rowan, thinking of him and of his silence. When, at last, she turns towards the house, she sees her mother with the light behind her, watching from the garden door.

4: A half-made man

And what were you all quarrelling about?
Son, come tell to me.
Oh it's all about a little holly bush
And it might have made a tree, a tree.
It might have made a tree.

Edward, Traditional

In the morning, after breakfast, the potter waited at the gate as Issa Gicocca held Liùtha tight a long while. At last, the old woman kissed her cheek, and pressed a purse into her hands. He took up Liùtha's bag with his own and, together, they passed between the rowans at the gate and left the old house behind them. Liùtha did not look back to Issa Gicocca, nor did she weep to leave her, but her eyes were very bright.

They walked along the coast road to the port of Anach. There, Liùtha sat on the harbour wall and flung bits of bread to the gulls screaming on the wind. The potter meanwhile asked around the ships' masters until he found one that would take them. This was not so easy as it might have been. There was silver and ivory enough in Liùtha's purse for him to have no need to trade his labour but the people of the port looked long and sideways at Liùtha, who herself looked only at the seabirds and the sea, and the potter knew tales were whispered, of her, of him, both strangers come by strange ways. Master after master sucked his teeth and shook his head, and so turned them away. But on one boat an old sailor was a man of Ittachar and he vouched for the potter as a countryman. After that, the master accepted the potter and his woman at the second glance, though he asked a high price for their passage. But when the master had spoken his consent and gone below again, the old sailor rebuked the potter, that he had not the heart to treat a woman better: "'Tis a shame to see so fine a lass with so sad a face."

This the potter swallowed, thinking it better all on the ship believed her to be his woman. What Liùtha thought of it he did not know: he could not ask, she did not tell.

Her mother says, "It is of the Lord of Marac I would speak."

On her mother's face is an expression she has not seen before. It is soft and sad, and she is afraid.

"He can do all the things a man can do. He can think all the thoughts a man can think. None of this makes him a man." Her mother reaches out to hold her tight against her breast and whispers, "I have seen you are lost in love for him, but does he love you?"

She keeps her silence, remembering his beneath the rowan tree.

Her mother strokes her hair. The blackbird sings in the apple tree, a ripple of swift notes meaning everything and nothing. Quietly, so as not to startle it, her mother says, "You have brown earth beneath your feet, blue sky above your head, white flowers to grow for you all the days of your life. There is nothing sweeter than a life well lived with the one you love beside you. But however sweet your love, however long your life, when it ends it is as if it had never begun. It is not so for him. He is not bound to the waking world as you are, as I am." Her mother stills her hand and asks again, "Does he love you?"

"He loves me," she says at last. Inside her mind, she sees him turn his head to smile at her, and knows her words are true.

"Then for your sake," her mother says, "I wish he had made a new beginning before ever he came to Ohmorah. I wish he walked beneath the sun. His heart has changed but not his substance. At his core there is a song of sea and stone, a dance upon the wind."

Her mother holds her close as she has not held her since she was a child, since the days before her father sailed away, and tears run down her cheeks.

"Go carefully," she says. "The wind blows straight across the sea but stone walls act as checks upon the wind and turn it from its path. The knowledge of what he is, and how to do him harm, is not lost. Outside stone walls the elements obey him, but he has eaten our food, he has drunk our wine, and, within the city, our laws bind him now. When you measure the men of the White City against him remember this: it is not a little thing to be a man."

They turned from the harbour to the town and market, buying blankets and food and a sheepskin coat for the potter. It was not so good as the one he had left in the White City but he was glad to trade the cloak for it, not liking to remember Assiolo. When all was done, he heard music. A beggar stood by the mercatstone, his hat laid out before him, and played upon a wooden pipe. The potter had heard a few wandering musicians in his time. Such folk were common enough upon the roads and came sometimes even to Ittachar to earn their bread, making music at a wedding or at a feast to mark the payment of childprice. This beggar himself was a dwarf, twisted and ragged, with his face made hideous by the birthmark across it.

Yet, for all that, he was a true master of his art and the potter stopped to hear the tune to its end.

He turned away when the pipe fell silent but felt Liùtha's hand upon his arm, bidding him pause a while. She dropped a bit of ivory into the beggar's hat. He looked up into her face and put aside his pipe to sing instead. Skilled and sweet as his piping had been, the beggar's voice was lovelier by far. A rare voice he had: sweet and welcome as the first drops of rain on a summer's evening; high and strong as a lark soaring in the blue dome of the sky. It was like no man's voice the potter had heard before but as if a spirit of the air itself sang, music fit for the courts of kings rather than a street in a fishing village. The beggar sang the song of the sea's daughter, and all the while his eyes were fixed upon Liùtha.

This is that tale: Once a young fisherman saw the sea's daughter dancing on the waves as he fished by night. He cast out his nets to catch her and brought her to the shore. She came into his house and ate and drank with him; for love of his handsome face, she put aside her nature, forgetting her life within the sea to give herself to him. But after seven years the fisherman grew tired of her and gave a golden ring to a farmer's daughter. Abandoned, the sea's daughter wandered weeping along the shore, having no place now on either land or water, until at last she faded into a brown bird, a curlew that flies low across the sea's edge and calls out the dying to their deaths.

The potter was glad enough to hear the song to its end, for it was a tale well known in Ittachar. When it was done, the beggar picked up his wooden pipe to play in echo of his song, music so sweet and sad it tore at the potter's soul. Liùtha stood silently beside him, her hand within his, and he saw with surprise something in the beggar's song had melted the frost in her heart, for her face was wet with tears. So they listened together until the tune was finished, then she turned away towards the harbour. The potter followed, leaving the dwarf to gather up his fee, put on his hat and limp away.

The piper says, "Let us walk awhile together, beyond the city, beneath the trees."

"And talk of the past?" the old man asks. "Your past and mine, piper. We have much in common, you and I. Both of us lost all we loved the day you closed the gates of morning."

"I would rather talk of the present and look to the future."

They walk together, beyond stone walls, across ploughed fields where the green corn stands. A lark is singing in the high air, and the song and the sunlight fall down upon them. They walk out of the meadows towards this song; they walk beyond the orchards to the places where apple trees give way to birch and ash and rowan and, as they walk, the day grows brighter and the birdsong sweeter yet, calling them out of their long past.

They walk together beneath the trees across mossy grass scattered with windflowers until they reach a place where they cannot see the city or the sea. Then the piper says softly, "All that was mine, I lost that day. You have all the choices I do not. You are a man who lives and breathes."

In his foul face his golden eyes are bright as a blackbird's in the morning. He is a broken, twisted thing but he has words in him that must be spoken, a truth deeper than the sea, clearer than the light. He holds out his empty hands to the trees and to the man beneath the trees: "All that was yours you can have again, if you will but live your life. You have blue sky above you, brown earth beneath you, a living son who would love you if you let him."

The old man does not look up to the sky. He does not look down to the earth. His voice is dry as the wind through summer grasses. "A son no son. A half-bred, mewling brat who listens to your music far more than to the things that I would teach him."

"Perhaps he finds in me what he does not find in you, a father kinder than his own."

"All that was washed from my heart long ago." The old man's face is still as a figure carved in ivory, a tired face, a strong face with its past of failure and of grief written into it. "You love him better than I can."

The piper sighs. He will not sicken or grow weak, his face has not a line upon it, but he is very old and the sorrow and pity in his face are enough to turn the hardest heart from its purpose, if the man had but the eyes to see it.

The old man stares down at him: he looks, he sees, and then he turns away. His own eyes, blue as the sky at midsummer, bright as the noonday sun, blaze with scorn for all the piper offers. He has no desire for pity, he cares not for compassion. He has lived long, and lost much, and rages against his fate. The light must fade, the day must end, but he will fight against the dark whilst he has life and breath left in him. Once he stopped the sun at noontime so he might dance forever beneath a sun that would not set with those he loved beside him. He stares into the distance and the past, remembering a boy who danced in fire as other children splash in the sea.

That boy is long years gone: the fire was quenched, the dance was ended, the sun set and death came in the evening. All that is long ago and far away but he has not forgotten the vow he made at that day's ending as a dead child lay in his arms and the starlight lay upon the sea.

He says to the piper, "The present is empty, the future has no meaning, the past alone has weight upon my heart. You are not a man: you know nothing of the hearts of men. All that was mine, the Liùthion took from me. I do not forget, I do not forgive and, when he returns, I shall not be kind. Only when I have kept my vow and had my vengeance shall I go easy into the dark."

The piper does not answer. There can be no answer. All his music cannot give peace to a man who does not seek it. The blue sky and the brown earth and the white flowers are as nothing against hatred in a man's heart.

That night was the first on board the ship. It would slip away on the morning tide and in ten days, or maybe a little longer, be in Marac Bec, putting in at ports along the way, a stout, small, trading ship carrying goods and travellers along the coast, never out of sight of land, never daring the open sea. Starting out from Tarhn, it put in first here at Anach, then next went on to Inchmar and from Inchmar on to Ountrie and so round the great isle of Eilanmor and the long, last stretch to Marac Bec. But on from Marac Bec, around the promontory of Marac itself, the master would not go. That coast had a name for storms. Those who had sailed it told strange tales of strange winds and jagged rocks that would tear the belly from a boat but could not be marked on any chart, for no two ships found them in the same waters. But sometimes, the sailors said, in the autumn and the springtime, on moonless nights round about the equinox, the sea round about the coast of Marac would lie quiet as a summer meadow, silvered beneath stars whose names no man knew.

In the morning, the potter woke to feel the ship moving beneath him, alive upon the sea. He climbed on deck to see the little port of Anach already far behind and the new day shining brightly on the sea. And, in the blue distance, he saw a shape, most like a gull, but no gull could be seen from so far.

Liùtha joined him at the rail, staring back at the land that had been seven years her home. She said, as she had said in the stone house on the hill, "It is a good place, Anach. There are no wonders there, no libraries or council chambers, no city walls, no gates or guards or gatehouses. A quiet place, a safe place, where all is as it seems."

"Ittachar's like that, a safe, slow place where a goat in the barleyfield can make a sennight's chatter." He looked at her, hunched and huddled in her coat against the wind, and the misery in her face called out his heart in pity. "What do you seek, Liùtha?"

"Hope," she answered, and did not look at him, only at the gulls soaring on the wind. "An end to hatred and grief."

All around their little ship, the morning sunlight danced upon the waves. Quick as the scintillations of sun on sea he found his answer: "That I can give you." But at his speaking, she turned her face to meet his eyes and the words died on his tongue.

Unsmiling, Liùtha said, "Perhaps in Anach things are as they seem. But we have left Anach behind us. Do not make promises you cannot keep."

Her voice was cold and hard as on the hillside the first time they had spoken. She had bound her hair beneath her hood but the sea winds pulled strands free about her face. Her dark hair blew about her and her dark eyes looked out wary on the world. She did not look at the potter but back to the hills of Anach. There, beneath the birken tree, the potter had seen she was lovely; there, by the fireside, he had seen she was sorrowful. Now, as he looked at her in the bright morning, he saw she was afraid, not of him but of the world. She stood close by his side but could not see what he saw, the light laughing in the wind as they swirled together across the waves. Seeing her fear, the potter made a new vow in his heart, swearing as men do in Ittachar by land and sea and by the empty air, he would take this task to its end, not for the lady, not for the world, nor even for himself, but only for Liùtha, so she might see the beauty in the world again and laugh in the sunlight in joy to be alive.

He reached out and took her hands. "I never made a promise yet I did not keep."

Liùtha let her eyes meet his. He smiled, and this time she did not turn away but let her cold hands lie between his until the hills of Anach disappeared behind them and her fingers had grown warm again.

The days that followed passed slowly, quietly, all the days peaceful and alike as the little ship made its way along the coast. The sunlight played across the water, dancing in the wind upon the waves. The potter's mind cleared of the past and of the future while he saw Liùtha sitting quietly with the ship's cat purring in her lap. He was content then to sit in the sun, watching the fishing lines trailing from the boat, taking his turn to swing a string of silver fishes to the deck to drown in air. Always, the first of the catch was thrown to the grey gulls, for all along that coast believed them the spirits of sailors lost at sea, their bodies never found. Without the embrace of the earth, they were doomed to fly forever on the wind, trailing the boats wherein their shipmates sailed, with wordless screams lamenting their lost souls. The potter knew as well as any sailor he must placate these spirits lest they grew angry, being envious of those that were yet men, and raised a storm to draw them to their fate.

The potter told Liùtha this tale one evening as they ate grilled mackerel. She offered no story in return but the next evening, and the next, she came to sit beside him and ask for the tales of Ittachar. So he told her of the seals that were women and might take a man and love him for a year and a night, then slip away into the sea never to be seen again; of the hunter who slew an osprey for love of its mate's beauty and became a bird to fly with her in the bright air, until his brother's arrow killed him and he fell back to earth a man; of the quiet king who danced in the long night of midwinter and left no footprints in the frost. She listened in silence and, all the time he told his stories, the potter looked sidelong at her face and thought that she was lovely and wished he could take away her fear.

Only the fourth night as they left Inchmar, as he sat with the sailors on the deck, passing round the bottles and telling tales of his homeland in trade for theirs, he looked up to see the moon, half past its fullness now. Then he saw Liùtha sitting apart, staring into the night with unseeing eyes, twisting over and over in her fingers the silver brooch she always wore. He said her name aloud and would have gone to her, but she was wrapped in her silence and did not turn to look at him, rejecting the light and the company of men. He remembered her mother, *She is gone into the dark*; he remembered Assiolo, *She will burn you*. Then the thought came to him, *It must be soon to find this place or it shall be too late. She has been too far, too long in loneliness and grief.*

A shifting of shingle, a rattle of stone against stone. He looks up and sees the chamberlain's son close beside him with wild flowers trailing from his fingers.

"So all my father says is true," the young man cries. "You are not a man: what have you to offer her?"

"All that I am, I will give to her. She shall have the stars to shine upon her, the night winds to caress her, the sea to sing to her."

He stoops and cups a hand full of saltwater. As the young man watches, he shapes it between his palms into a stone that glows round and pale as the moon itself. He fits it into the silver crown and asks, "What can you or any man offer that will equal this?"

In answer, the chamberlain's son stretches out his hand. A rose lies on its palm. In the sunlight it was red but all colours are quenched to black beneath the stars.

He takes the rose. Such a little thing, no weight at all upon the world. Laughing, he says, "Roses are sweet upon a summer's evening, but roses wither, they decay."

"Look at it, Liùthion: now it is a perfect rose. Its beauty is no less because it cannot last."

He bends his head towards the flower. It has a scent as sweet as love; it has a thorn sharp as the pangs of love; it has a petal soft as the touch of a lover's lips against his hand.

"The stars will shine forever," says the chamberlain's son, "but she is only a woman. Is this well done, Liùthion, to take your pleasure and to keep your freedom?"

"My love is no less than yours, though I am not a man."

"Fine words, fine words that have no meaning. When the sun rises, when she wakes to find herself alone with her fading dreams, where will you be?"

He bows his head, and does not answer. The chamberlain's son says, "Go, beg an apple from the king and dance her dance upon midsummer's night, a man as other men. Only then can you love her as she deserves."

For a long, long moment he looks down at the rose, tracing his fingers across the curve of a petal. When, at last, he speaks, his voice is balanced somewhere between tears and laughter: "Oh, Assiolo, Assiolo, even if I wished it, I could not do your will. Whenever were there apples ripe at midsummer, even in Lyikené?"

The next morning their boat put in at Ountrie, where they needs must stop a day whilst the master put off one cargo and took on another. Passengers being in the way at such a time, they left the little ship to see the port and buy more food to keep them until the isle of Eilanmor, where they would pass midsummer. As they waited at a baker's shop, they heard a sudden noise, a woman's cry of fright. Then another voice cried out in pain, and in the street men were shouting and boys yelling. Across the road a man had knocked another down and was kicking him upon the ground. The potter was amid the throng before he recognised the faded blue of the beggar's coat. He thrust the boys aside and pulled the man away, placing his body between the mob and the fallen dwarf.

"What is this?" he demanded. "What did he do that you must beat him so?"

"He looked at my wife, and spoke to her," the man of Ountrie muttered, and others offered their support. "She is with child," the man said, more loudly, "and I'll not have her bring forth such a freak as this."

The little crowd nodded, knowing full well the danger to the child unborn from such abominations. Harsh voices called to the potter to stand aside and let the monster get what he deserved.

The potter's temper rose. "That is lies and superstition. Shame on you, man, and pity on the child to come for having such a father."

The old sailor came shouldering his way through to stand beside him, rolling up his sleeves. Strengthened by the thought he was not alone, the potter said, loud enough for all to hear him, "I'll vouch for this man. I heard him sing in Anach and there's neither darkness here nor danger. Foul without and fair within – better than you, with your comely face and heavy boots. You'll not touch him again unless you've broken me to do it; aye, and my countryman here beside me. Shall you go to your wife's bed with our blood upon you?"

The mutterings from the crowd were more muted now. The potter looked the man of Ountrie full in the eye. "Let it go," he said to him. "You are not yet a murderer."

The woman pulled at her man's sleeve, shaking her head, and he fell back into the crowd, the boys at his heel. The mob dissolved into its parts, each melting away upon his own business now blood would not be shed. The sailor of Ittachar, seeing his part was played out, returned to the dice game he had left outside the alehouse.

"How badly are you hurt?" asked the potter, kneeling by the beggar and helping him sit up. His coat was more ragged than before and he was bruised, yet seemingly he had taken no great hurt of them.

"I'll live to see this day to its end," the dwarf answered, scrambling to his feet. "My thanks to you for facing down that rabble."

"A payment for your play in Anach."

Seen so close, the beggar seemed more ugly than in memory. The potter found his eyes flinching from the sight of him but, wishing to show the courtesy due to any man, he forced himself to look and saw that, whilst his face was foul indeed, his eyes were wide and golden. "We heard you play in Anach," he stammered, ashamed of staring and embarrassed to look away.

"Aye, lad, I also sailed from Anach," said the beggar, "but my ship was the faster. I was here yestreen and you came ashore but an hour ago. Long ago, I learned the dolphins like the sound of this pipe and sailors like the sight of dolphins. So, now I wanted to come again to Ountrie, all could be satisfied."

He took the potter's hand in his and turned it palm upwards. Many times the potter had seen fathers look at their sons' hands in this way to try and read there the map of a life that was not yet lived. So had his own father done when he was a boy, before he sent him off apprentice to a potter.

"You're a craftsman yourself?" the beggar asked.

"A potter."

"Like always knows like." The piper smiled, and his disfigured face seemed bright and clever. "It's by my design, not chance, we meet here, potter. You two I saw in Anach amongst the crowd, and I asked myself, *Why should there be a man of Ittachar here and with him a woman of the White City? There is no trade between those places nor travel neither.* So being curious, I asked, and was told strange tales for my trouble of foundlings from the sea and a stranger come from foreign parts yet no ship come to bring him."

The potter gasped and felt Liùtha's hand on his. "This is not Ittachar," she said, "and he's not what he seems."

"I see you know me now, Liùtha," the beggar said, drily. "I'd thought you might have done before."

She flushed red as any rose, and the beggar's lips curved in a smile. "Well, 'tis of little matter," he said. "You were a child when last we met, lass, and much has happened since that time. I owe you a favour, I think, for your father's sake. He made me welcome once. There are few enough who've done that 'neath this sky."

He offered her his hand. Liùtha did not take it and her face was set and blank. The beggar shrugged and looked to the potter, saying, "I asked in Anach, lad, where you two were bound and, when they told me, I remembered other times and places, older tales I'd heard years since of a spirit taking flesh and walking on the earth, a man amongst men. Then, being a wanderer by nature, I decided to wander in the same direction."

"You've wandered far indeed if you've seen both Ittachar and the White City," was all the potter could find to say in answer.

"Aye, wandered far and for longtimes," said the beggar, "but it was not the wish to see Ountrie again made me come this way. I've travelled this coast before and my face is not unmemorable. I've no cause to love this town; I learnt long ago it was a place of rogues and thieves, and that lad now has not changed my mind. I was come to seek you out, lad, and ask to travel with you awhile." He bowed to the potter with a grace and courtesy unexpected in a wandering beggar. "I am Kenu Vanithu, called monster, called musician."

As the dwarf's face turned to the light, the potter saw he was not an old man as he had first thought but, insofar as such a disfigured face could be read, one some years younger than himself, perhaps of an age with Liùtha.

"Don't goggle, lad, there's stranger things than me in this world, if few uglier."

The potter flushed to have been caught staring, and stammered, "Then you're also of the White City? One like the lady of Ohmorah?"

"Not of the city. Nor like the lass's kin. The First People are folk not unlike yourself: they too live out their lives, even if they are very long ones; this lass is proof of it. They meet in love and bear their children and in age they'll find their deaths." The beggar smiled, and it was like a grimace on his dreadful face. "Mine is a different fate."

As if she were explaining the world to a child, Liùtha said, "Not every son born in the Later Lands becomes a man, nor every girl a woman. Kenu Vanithu is a Tion."

"He could not know it, lass," Kenu Vanithu said. "There are no Tions born in Ittachar, not any more. And few enough elsewhere, since the world was changed. Tikai Incithu in Latia, Marwy Ninek in Felluria, Belata Vaa in Escen; in Vanin, One-Eyed Ku... Far and few we are, and mostly forgotten. Even those who remember do not think to see a Tion with my face. Tions are beautiful, old stories say, never to sicken, never to grow old; they look at me and see only a half-made man."

That was true enough. The beggar was twisted as an old man, his left leg shorter than the right, but far worse than this was his face. This was hideous, piebald pink and black, the face not of a man but of a monster.

"We heard you sing in Anach of the sea's daughter," said Liùtha. "Is it a true tale?"

"All the tales I tell are true, after a fashion," said the beggar, looking straight up into her face. "Do you know that tale in the White City?"

That there was some depth of meaning beneath the question was clear but what it was the potter could not tell. It seemed, however, Liùtha had the key to his meaning for she dropped her eyes and answered shortly, "We've other tales, like and unlike to that one, but no singers so fine as you to tell them, not even in my mother's hall."

"A good place, Ohmorah, and your mother is the best of it. There were few who came through Averla's fire and the Liùthion's flood to walk gently beneath the sun and stars."

The beggar turned to the potter, as if he had had what he needed from Liùtha, and asked him, "May I then walk beside you for a while?"

"Kenu Vanithu," said the potter, bewildered still but making the best of it, "you're welcome to come with us although your music is worthy of better ears than ours."

"My friend has a kind heart but better you find yourself a warmer hearth," Liùtha said, cold and quiet. "It's a dark place we go to, and we expect no welcome."

"I'll take his *Yes* over your *No*, lass." The beggar laughed, a short and hard laugh with no humour to it. "Don't fret yourself on my account. I'm no stranger to dark places and my face has taught me to expect no welcomes."

She sits on the bench beneath the rowan tree in her mother's garden. In the pool are golden fish swimming ever round and round. Her favourite is a giant of his kind, a fish longer than her arm who had been king of the pool for many years before her birth. As a child, one of her great joys had been to dabble in the water and have the old fish take bread from her hand. Even now she is grown she has not lost her pleasure in this play. She leans, as in those earlier days, over the stone lip of the pool to feed the fish whilst her mother and the chamberlain walk together in the garden.

When the lady returns to her house, the chamberlain pauses underneath her apple tree. The sun has not long set, the western sky is still bright with dying fire as he says softly to the summer twilight, "If you are there, show yourself."

For a moment she wonders if he speaks to her but then the Lord of Marac steps out of the long shadows cast by the apple tree.

"I am here. What would you say to me, Allocco?"

"*Let us put aside our pretences and politenesses,*" *says the chamberlain. He is like a hooded crow with grey hair above his black coat, the first man of Ohmorah, even without the scarlet of his office.* "*You know me as well as I know you, Liùthion, though I have aged and you have died since we last met.*"

"*What little faith you had in me at the end. My flesh might have died by the rope's drop, or with a knife between my ribs, or old in my bed with the years of my life upon me, but never by drowning. I did not die, old friend. I fled, as you did.*" *The Lord of Marac holds out his right hand to the chamberlain. There is hope in his voice, not fear or anger.* "*There is so little left of that time. The dead are gone into the dark. We were friends, Allocco, you, I and Allodola, before you grew envious, before the sunlight called you to folly and the white wave called me to doom. You made me your equal then: I will not be so again. Let you make your peace with the past, as Allodola has done.*"

The chamberlain strikes down his hand. "*I will not turn to you because you walk again amongst us, fair of face and tongue. I am not Allodola.*"

"*That is true,*" *the Lord of Marac says.* "*Her years have not been empty ones. She has found her balance. I have seen the White City she has built, safe and strong with a loving, peaceful people.*"

"*Because of you, all that I loved is lost. Because of you, I must die. I must leave the sunlight and go into the dark.*"

"*I never was your enemy, Allocco. I did only what was needful. I did not come to fight you then, nor was it for that that I returned.*"

He glances around the garden, turns back to the chamberlain, holding out his hands again, pleading with him. "*Before you were anything else, before you turned from me towards Averla, you were my friend, Allocco.*"

The chamberlain's voice is quiet and calm and full of hate. "*You are neither my equal nor my friend. The dead are long years gone, I am become an old man withering towards my grave but I have not forgotten the oath I swore at that day's ending. You had not the courage to share the fate you made for us. Only then shall you be free of me.*"

He also glances over the garden, looks long where the Lord of Marac did not. She sees him looking across the fish pool to where she sits beneath the rowan tree and meets his steady gaze, for all it makes her heart beat fast.

The chamberlain turns back towards the apple tree, stretching out to cup one of the half-grown apples and feel its sun-warmed weight against his palm. It is not ripe yet; when it grows sweet in the autumn its skin will flush to gold.

*"You have given me the means for my revenge before I die,
Liùthion; you are in my hand. A life is due to me. Before the apples
are ripe, I shall destroy you."*

*The Lord of Marac shakes his head. "I shall trust love over
hatred, Allocco."*

*The chamberlain laughs. The wind blows, the shadows shift, and
he is alone, an old man standing in the dark beneath the apple tree.*

So when the ship sailed from Ountrie on the evening tide
a third traveller sailed with it. Kenu Vanithu stood at the
ship's prow to play his pipe in the moonlight and, as he had
promised, the dolphins came to dance in the bow wave. Their
coming eased the sailors' distrust of the ragged beggar for
dolphins had ever been friends to sailors, being heralds of calm
seas and favourable winds. But, when the moon set beneath
the sea, leaving only the ship's lights and the stars to shine
upon the water, Kenu Vanithu turned to Liùtha.

"Liùtha, lass, I knew your father once. Would you have me
speak of him a little?"

Liùtha nodded. In the lamplight the shadows leapt across
her face and her eyes were black and big.

"He was a sailor, a bold sailor with the swiftest ship ever
built in Ohmorah. Even now, he's the only man of Ohmorah
to make the westward run to the last land, to Lyikené, the
westermost land before the sunset and the endless sea. He
came across the sound beyond the five islands where the sea
boils amidst sand banks and reefs and the bones of many men
tumble in the tides. The Sea People are the children of the sea
and the storm bird," the dwarf said, and the potter shivered
and pulled his coat around him. "They sleep upon the deep as
easy as you or I might beneath a flowering tree at noon time.
They do not welcome another's mastery of the open sea. Yet
their king gave him his own son's name, calling him *Liùthai*,
after the evening star that is the first to shine out after the
sunset, and he carried the name home with him."

Liùtha looked into the west, at the stars above the sea and
said nothing. Then Kenu Vanithu also looked for a time at the
starlight on the sea until a sailor, sitting nearby upon a coil of
rope, called out, "There must be more than this."

The piper shook off his thoughts and took up his story. "I
saw Liùthai when he returned in triumph. The towers of the
White City were hung with pennants, green and red, blue and
gold and all the people were waiting for their bold sailor on
the walls or all along the road from the harbour. The sunlight

burnished his hair as he came ashore and flashed on the silver at his throat. He raised his hand so all might see the golden apples set upon the branch of the tree from the land at the world's end. And at that sight, the crowd roared out in hope and wonder.

"I was alone then, a stranger in a foreign land. Then, as now, I'd only my pipe and my voice to keep me fed and whole. I heard the cheer for Liùthai but more than that I heard the rush of my blood in my ears as I was pressed among the bodies of the crowd, for all looked up at him and none down to me. I thought I'd be crushed and forced my way forward with all my strength until suddenly the crowd fell back and I was alone on the road before Liùthai. I heard hissing, for who was I, a beggar and a stranger, to force myself to notice at such a time? But Liùthai himself held up his hand for silence.

"*Who are you?* he asked.

"*I am the piper from the gates of morning.*

"*Then, piper, play for me for I am come back into my city.*

"And so I played my wooden pipe and we walked together up the road from the sea to the white gate, and the roses that were flung to him fell as soft and sweet on me. He was a gentle man, your father, as well as a bold one."

And the dwarf raised his pipe to his lips and played the song of homecoming he had made for Liùthai the sailor, years ago in the White City of Ohmorah.

"You fear Allocco," the piper says as evening falls on the White City, "but when he was young, he was not so very unlike you. He also decided he would follow the call of his own strength and will; he also would not be bound by laws and rules made by lesser men. He also had his time of glory before his people."

The sailor remembers the day he came back into his city upon midsummer morning: the shouts of triumph and the scent of roses, the sound of bells and trumpets upon the city wall, the sunlight warm on his back. Above all else, he remembers his fierce pride in having outdone other men. Of all the men, in all the world, only he has defied Lyikené, and lived.

The piper, who speaks only the truth and does not judge, sees the pride on the man's face and smiles. His smile is twisted and broken in the gloaming. He says, "I had lived a long time in the world before the rowan tree died in the east. The hearts of women and of men were much then as they are now, desire for glory mixed with simple needs, joy and woe mingled close to make a life. Then, as now, we died and went into the dark. But, then, we were protected against fear and hate and vain hope; then, we had our times of dancing in the empty air. Then, there was a song ringing out from star and sea and stone across the daylight world for all to hear."

"At some times, in some places that song may still be heard," the sailor says. *"I have seen the tree that grows yet at the gates of evening."*

"But how the world is changed. Now you dance to make the land safe. Now you fear the dark. Now the west is guarded by bronze spears and the eagle's strike from the empty air. Now we must trust our hearts, for nothing else can keep us safe."

The sailor holds his daughter in his arms; the child has fallen asleep and on this last evening he cannot bear to take her to her bed. He bends his head to kiss her hair and hears the piper tell him, softly, very sadly, *"You have done as much as any man may, my friend. Given love to your lady, life to your child."*

He opens his mouth to answer but a blackbird sings in the apple tree and the piper puts up his hand for silence. Music is strong in him, strong enough for his song to make men forget his face awhile, but he keeps silent whilst the blackbird fills the evening with a song born of need not art, a call of life to life. His own music is art alone, his life can call no other to him and his heart has long been desolate.

When the bird is quiet and night is deep upon the city, the piper tells the sailor what he has not heard before: *"There were many deaths the day I closed the gates of morning but only one that matters to Allocco. All you feel for your child, he felt for his. His heart sank with his son into the depths of the sea. Some things that are broken can never be mended. He will not forgive, no more than you would forgive, and so he seeks a reckoning."*

The sailor shakes his head. *"Hadùhai offered hope and a new beginning, but Allocco turned away. Now you have also failed to turn him from his path. If he cannot be swayed, the other must: I shall seek the Liùthion in the empty land."*

"What of the oath you swore? Think you, because Hadùhai had mercy, the world is again as it was? If you sail again into the west you will die before you set a foot upon that country. That is as certain as the sunrise."

So has his love said to him, and more. She lay at his side this morning, knowing his heart and all his plans, and together they watched the dawn slide across the sky. *"You have sailed the western sea,"* she said, *"and seen the land beyond the sunset. You have met two kings beneath the firstborn tree and brought the gift that freed me from my past. Let this be enough for you; my love, let us live out our lives together and watch our daughter grow."*

She turned his face to hers so he must look at her. She has lived longer than he has and knows when hope is false. "Because you dared to do what others dare not," *she says,* "because you have gone where others have not, does not make you more than a man. Not even you can turn the wind from its course, nor look for mercy from the open sea."

Now that day is come to its evening and he sits within her garden beneath the flowering trees. The shadow of his apple tree reaches out to him. The little tree grows straight and strong in the brown earth of Ohmorah, sheltered by the stone walls that turn aside the salt wind from the sea. There are three things in this city he loves more than his own life: his daughter and her mother, and this tree. Tomorrow he will leave them all behind him to take his chances on the open sea.

"Did you read that in my hand or in the stars?" *he asks the piper, quietly.*

"I had no need of either. Te-Meriku keeps each oath he swears, and expects no less of other men."

"Where there is necessity, there is no choice."

"This is folly, not necessity, my friend. Hadùhai is dead. Te-Meriku had a cold cradling in Kistoru's hall and is yet young enough to cleave to justice, not to mercy. He will see only what you do and care not for why you do it."

"The Liùthion lives, he breathes as if he were a man. The call of life for life will draw him back into our waking world, where Allocco waits, more dangerous than any other man." *The sailor speaks softly, so as not to wake the sleeping child.* "You know this as well as I: why else did you come to the White City? You fear his return, as Allodola does, as I do. Only Allocco yearns for it, so he might match himself a second time against his enemy and this time have the mastery."

"I know full well I shall die but I shall speak before I die and that, perhaps, will be enough to turn one future to another. Before the fire, before the flood, he had a gentle heart."

He looks the piper in the eye and sees the sorrow in that golden gaze.

5: The dance beneath the flowering trees

Oh and she rose up and she let him in
She kissed her true love cheek and chin
She took him between the sheets so thin
And she opened and she let him in-oh.

Cold, Hailey, Rainy Night, Traditional

On the day before midsummer, their ship rounded the Isle of Eilanmor. No craft of the Later Lands would put to sea upon the morrow nor any man choose to stay on a ship rocking on the water on midsummer's night, if he could instead dance the short night through or leap laughing through the fires beneath the flowering trees. About the middle of the afternoon, they put in at a tiny harbour by a village of white painted houses and all came ashore, save the old sailor who was a man of Ittachar. He cared no more for midsummer than any other of his countrymen and would act as watch upon the boat.

The master had bespoken lodgings for himself within the village, and the sailors would camp up on the hill to be near the midsummer fires when the dancing began, so, with Liùtha and the beggar, the potter walked up the only road out of the village to find where they could stay. At a little farm above the harbour they found a farmer who would give a place to them until the ship sailed. He showed them to a dry stone bothy, caulked within to keep out the wind, with a wooden door that had no lock. There were many such bothies upon the hills and glens of Eilanmor where travellers might find a night's shelter. This one was small and clean, a single room without windows but with two bunks built into one wall, and a great hearth and chimney built into another. It was set in a pleasant place looking downwards past the village with rowan trees growing all around and a silver burn running close by towards the sea.

In the late afternoon the potter made up a fire in the hearth and, as they ate, he told the beggar of the creature he had made of driftwood and of how it had carried him to the White City. Liùtha sat outside the open door and watched the light upon the sea. In the last days out of Ountrie she had no longer come to his side and asked him for his stories, and the potter had regretted her quiet company. Instead, often and often, he had seen her watching the dwarf and heard her catch her breath each time he spoke as if she feared what he might say. But never after that first night had Kenu Vanithu said anything beyond the commonplace; he had stitched at sails and tidied ropes and played his pipe upon the deck whenever a sailor called out to him to give a tune as the price of passage. Only now, upon the hillside, had he asked the potter for his tale and so the potter gave it, well aware of Liùtha listening beyond the door. In her hands she held her moonstone crown, her restless fingers tracing the curving silver about and about.

"You've a tale worthy of the telling and your words reveal the man. Yet all tales change with their teller. I know it well: songs and stories earn me my bread and keep," said Kenu Vanithu, "so I'd ask Liùtha to tell her own tale, so you know what she has become, as you have become more than a potter."

Again the potter heard that little catch in Liùtha's breathing and saw the faint flush upon her cheek as she glanced sideways to the beggar. Kenu Vanithu met her eyes, and she looked away.

"I've lived a long time in the world, lass," he said. "You wear your pain and sorrow clear for all the world to see but there is more than that, hidden away behind your suffering. Do not forget, this man has sworn an oath to help you. If he is to bring you to your heart's desire, he must know what you are and what you wish from him."

"He is a man who chose to go to Marac of his own free will," Liùtha answered, cold and clear. "The rest is no concern of yours, Kenu Vanithu, for all you knew my father and my city."

"I've lived in the world a long time," he said again, "and in that time I've seen many sights and heard many stories, and some of those are of great concern to me."

"Did you come here to judge me?"

"Nay, lass, it's not my part to pass judgement on another. What was done cannot be undone. It's what you choose to do that is the more important now. You've all your life before you, and so does he. Consider what it is you that you desire."

Liùtha gave her answer in her mother's tongue and the potter knew she did so to be certain he would not understand. Her words had no meaning in his ears but he needed no words to hear the pleading in her tone or to see the fear in her face. Kenu Vanithu said nothing in reply. He turned his gaze towards the potter, waiting for him to speak.

The potter looked from Liùtha to the dwarf and back again; one was fair, the other foul, and both were strange to him. Liùtha too was silent. She looked at him with great dark eyes, and he remembered how he had held her hands as the boat sailed from Anach: she had trusted him then, he would trust her now. So he said, speaking into the silence Kenu Vanithu had made, "It's as Liùtha tells it. I made my choice and gave my promise freely. When the time's right, all things will be known. They need not be now since she does not wish it."

"Fair enough, lad." Kenu Vanithu held out his hand to Liùtha. "Let us be friends again."

She touched his fingertips but briefly, looking at the potter. "Thank you," she said. "I'll tell you all my tale in Marac and there you'll know me as I am, and why I need you."

"When you speak, I will listen. And when you need me, I shall be ready."

As he spoke, he saw something in Liùtha's face he had not seen before, a startled look in her dark eyes as if at last she saw him not as a potter, nor as a fool, nor as a stranger set on his adventure, but only as a man. She stood up, staring at him blindly, and asked in a ragged whisper, "Why are you not afraid?"

In answer he reached out but her face set back into its look of wary sorrow and she stepped away, only a step but the space between them was suddenly too wide for him to cross.

Kenu Vanithu took up his pipe. Sitting cross-legged outside the door, he played late into the evening, the notes flickering fast as the bats across the summer's twilight. All the time he played, his strange, golden eyes watched the potter and never turned aside towards Liùtha, who sat beyond the lamplight lost in her thoughts and silence. When the night had thickened around them and the stars pricked into life he put down his pipe and said, "One thing I do not know, my friend the potter, is your name. Tell me, if you will."

"Where I come from we don't count names very high. We're known by our skills and trades," the potter answered. "Our names are for whispering in the dark and only when we step alone into the dark are they written on the stones above our heads, for dead men have no skills. I am a potter, though skilled enough in my craft that if one man in Ittachar spoke of *the* potter, another knew he spoke of me."

"High praise indeed," said Kenu Vanithu. "One day I shall claim a pot in payment for my many songs. But we are not in Ittachar, we are far from clay and you've not practised your art for many days. Whisper your name in the dark to me and to Liùtha."

"I am Almecu mor Thorrian," said the potter, softly, and a little breeze rattled the open door as he spoke, "but keep my name far from your tongue, each of you, for it is not the custom in Ittachar to speak a name aloud in company."

"Many customs have been changed in Ittachar. All across the world people will dance tomorrow night to press down the earth and make it safe. It is otherwise in Lyikené in the utmost west, and in your home of Ittachar, the west but not the utmost west," said Kenu Vanithu, and the potter found he could not now meet those golden eyes that saw many things men did not. "You do not dance at midsummer, for the land did not keep the dancers of Ittachar safe against the waves and sea, the day the Sea People came."

The potter knew his own story. He crooked his fingers to banish misfortune and looked to the sea, for all there were no square sails in the twilight.

The piper whispered to the wind and stars and to Liùtha, "The Sea People are no kin of the Later Lands. They do not dance upon the land, not at midsummer nor on any other day. They use no iron and live in Lyikené beyond the sea at the furthest edge of the world, and they are the stuff of nightmares, the monsters in tales told to frighten children into being good."

The potter had heard those tales when he was in his cradle: *Now hush your noise or the sea eagle will snatch you away.* When he was grown he had heard all the other stories, the ones not told to children, the ones that told why, even after so many, many years, white bones washed up onto the stony shores of Ittachar when storm winds blew hard out of the west. There is a price for all things and the price of a broken oath is very high, when that oath has been given to the king of the Sea People.

Kenu Vanithu said, "Once the sailors of Ittachar grew bold in their craft," and surely Liùtha was listening, in her place beyond the lamplight. "They too sought the mastery of the open sea, forgetting all the pledges that bound the peoples of the Later Lands. From Ittachar went out ships that followed the paths of the great whales, that fished the shallow northern banks where codfish spawn, that sailed into the west and made landfall on Lyikené. Because they did these things, the Sea People came raiding on midsummer's morning with swords and spears and arrows all of polished bronze.

"In the red light of morning the Sea People came out of the west. By the red light of sunset the farmers lay dead in the field margins, the ships burned in the sound and the fishermen floated as flotsam to the tideline."

The potter was angry he should speak so. That this tale was true did not make it needful to tell it aloud. Perhaps Kenu Vanithu saw his anger, for all the time he spoke, his golden eyes looked neither up towards the stars nor down towards the sea but only at the potter, yet, if he did, it was of no matter to him. He continued with his tale, though every word fell heavy into the potter's ears. "When it was known abroad what had befallen Ittachar, the little left behind when the tide of Lyikené went out, the women wailing for dead children with their bellies full of halfbreeds, all others in the Later Lands took the warning. None, since that day, has dared break the covenant made after fire and after flood or challenged that king's mastery."

Hunched in his wrath, the potter said to the piper, "That day has passed into memory and tales, and Ittachar is again a peaceful land of fisherfolk and farmers. We live quiet lives and harm no one."

"Have you not asked yourself what lies in the west that the Sea People guard so fiercely?"

He flinched from the question but the piper paid no heed and asked, "Are whale ivory and codfish so precious they need declare war on all the world to keep them to themselves? Amber and bronze are fine things but, even in Lyikené, the land could be ploughed. But they will use no iron and live hand to mouth through the winter on dried meat and salted fish and face the winter sickness. Is this not strange?"

"I have not considered the ways of the Sea People. All I need know of them is that they sent every man of Ittachar from the boy of ten into the dark before his time."

Hard and quick came back the piper's answer, and every word of it was true: "Though you choose to forget it, half your blood is theirs and more than half your stories. It is their songs your mothers sing you in your cradles, their tales you tell beside your fires in winter. You know what is in the west, Almecu mor Thorrian, you have always known it."

Liùtha stepped out of the darkness. Passing the potter as she went inside the bothy, she glanced down, a puzzled look in her eyes as if he were a man she did not know. The piper sang softly in the darkness and the firelight, beating out his time upon the stone wall:

"Beware, beware you sailors bold
That sail the western sea
And go in search of apples gold
Upon the firstborn tree.

"For death dwells in the western land,
Death sails the western sea,
Death holds a bronze sword in his hand
And guards the firstborn tree."

"They are barbarians!" the potter cried, silencing the song.

"Did you judge the lady so in Ohmorah? How do her deeds differ from those of the Sea People?" asked Kenu Vanithu, mildly enough. "Allodola has not always lived quiet and safe within her garden walls. It was her kind who broke the world. All you see are the reflections in a broken mirror and yet you seek always the straight road, the simple answer."

"And you see clearly?"

"I am a Tion. I told you, I have lived a long time in the world. I do not love, I do not judge and so I do see clearly. The pattern of the seasons is real enough. Life and death balanced across the year: seedtime, harvest, fallow." He took the potter's hand, saying, "It is not so in Lyikené, they have other ways and jealously they guard the west. And you – you are a man of Ittachar: do you think it is by chance you made that creature from driftwood found on your shore?"

He could not answer, for he did not know. He was only a man; he had neither the wit nor the knowledge to see the patterns in the world. He turned away and lay down on his bunk to sleep and all the night he had bad dreams.

The ships come with the sunrise out of the edge of the sea. Ships winged and toothed like dragons, their bellies full of death, their square sails all the colours of the sea and sky. The greatest has not a dragonhead but an eagle at its prow and its white sail is blazoned with the banner of Lyikené: three blood-red eagles, their talons outstretched to rend the world asunder.

The Sea People surround the little ship as a pod of piebald whales surrounds its prey, harrying it across the morning into exhaustion and submission. There is no escape here upon the open sea, no shadow beneath the sun in which the ship can hide. This is the domain of the Sea People.

When they board they kill the sailors, cleanly, quickly. The Sea People have no quarrel with the crew and give their bodies to the sea with as much honour as to their own kind. But not their captain. Him they bind, making him kneel beneath the noonday sun upon his deck to await the sentence of Te-Meriku the king.

For, far away in the west, Te-Meriku had met this man upon the shore before the king's hall in Lyikené and given then fair warning. "I am not yet king," said Te-Meriku, "and so I shall abide by the will of Hadùhai. Let the little tree grow and bear its fruit in the east, as Hadùhai wishes; let it be an echo, a reminder of what is guarded in the west. But," – and he took his oath by land and sea and by the empty air – "when I am king, I will brook no challenge to the mastery of the Sea People. Let the peoples of Ohmorah and of the Later Lands keep to their own," said Te-Meriku, "there is space enough upon the brown earth there for dancing. The open ocean and the older lands beyond the sea are for the Sea People and the great grey whales alone. All others who venture there shall die. Long ago," he said, "the world was changed, long ago the rowan died, long ago the piper closed the gates of morning, but, in the west, the Sea People, who guard the firstborn tree and keep the balance made that day, remember: death is the price of life."

And the man of Ohmorah swore by his life to abide by this, for he had what he came for and did not want to go untimely into the dark.

Yet here and now he is foresworn; here and now on the open sea death comes to oathbreakers, certain as day follows night.

The morning dawned in a red sunrise and it was midsummer, much light and little darkness; that night, fires would burn all across the hillside and men and women dance beneath the trees. Kenu Vanithu set aside his pipe and would neither play nor sing. Liùtha too was ill at ease and restless all the day. She had put away the moonstone crown but oftentimes her hand went to the place where it lay safe in its velvet wrapping. Always she left it there and set to pacing the bothy again, five steps from wall to wall and back again, like a wild creature in a cage.

Of the three, only the potter sat easy with his back against the stone wall in the shade beneath the trees. His dreams slipped away in the sunlight as he watched the day go by and all the while swifts screamed of summer in the tall air. This night's dancing was not the way of his own country and today the mystery was not his. But on this isle of Eilanmor, and many other places within the Later Lands, lived peoples who had come out of the east long, long ago, tracing the path of the sun across the world. They danced each year to make the brown earth kind so there might be a harvest and life after midwinter.

A little plant grew along the bottom of the wall, a plain thing with four-petalled white flowers and seedpods growing where the flowers had fallen. The potter saw the piper stare at it awhile, as if it were a rare and lovely thing and not a common weed.

"What is it?"

"Valley cress, they called it in Escen. It grows along the roadside."

"What use has it, what purpose?" Liùtha paused her pacing for a moment to look with scorn upon the beggar and the flower.

"No use I know," said Kenu Vanithu. "Its purpose? Same as yours or his or any living thing's upon the face of the earth. It grows strong in the sunlight and sets its seed and withers, dying from the world as if it had never been."

"Not you."

"Not I," agreed Kenu Vanithu.

There were no Tions in Ittachar and maybe the potter's question had shown itself upon his face, for the piper asked, "Did you think I was like you because I know your stories? Look beneath the rags and tatters, the show put on to fool a crowd. Look beyond my ugly face. I'll tell you what I am, Almecu mor Thorrian." He picked up a little stone from the ground beside the plant and held it out upon his hand. "The sun will shine, the wind will blow and the rain will fall upon the plant and the pebble. Then what will happen?"

Feeling himself a fool, the piper answered, "The plant will grow towards the light, spreading leaves and flowers, setting its seed, and it will perish. But the stone has no life to it and will sit unchanged by sun and wind and rain."

"Even so, lad, even so." He picked a stem and gave it to the potter. "If this is you, then this is I." He tossed the little stone into his lap. "When this plant's seed has blown away across the world, when your great-grandchildren have aged and died, I shall still tread these roads. As I am now, so shall I be then: never sickening, never quickening, never growing old."

Liùtha turned away to walk alone upon the hill but the potter looked at the plant a little longer. A tiny life upon the wide world and yet more akin to him than the piper was.

"I am a cold, hard thing upon the earth," said Kenu Vanithu. "I was born of a woman's pain and so I must die, but not peaceful in my bed with my age upon me. I know I must end in violence. It is a dark thought in the night, my death. I cannot choose to be a man."

"If you were born of woman, you were not born a stone."

A bitter smile, a brittle laugh. "Oh, I was young once, as you are young, as Liùtha is young. You are all so young that walk beneath the sun and moon. When I was young, I had my loves, my hopes. Love died in a woman's laughter at midsummer. Later, much later, hope died beneath strange stars in a strange land. Yet I live on and, because I am a stone, I see the world clearly and all the people in it."

"What was your home?" asked the potter. "You are a Tion, where is your domain?"

"I have no home. Not now. I was born in Escen and left my home as you left yours to see what the world would offer. If it was not cruel in those days, neither was it gentle. Once I found sanctuary beneath a rowan tree, once I was the piper at the gates of morning." In a voice harsh as stone grinding against stone, Kenu Vanithu told the potter, "That tree died in the fire, I closed those gates against the flood. The world was come to ruin and it fell to me to make a new balance this side of the sunrise. When I found my way back into the Later Lands, my domain of Escen had forgotten me and another had been born to take my place, a Tion fair of face with no music in him. I was left to wander all my days and call no place my home, a half-made man with no shelter from the wind." He checked himself and said, more softly, "Nay, that is too harsh and not quite true. A child in Ohmorah once loved me for myself, though I was not his father. I can never be any child's father. Mine is a lonely life, and a long one, and my years weigh heavy on me."

"How old are you?"

"Very old. You cannot think how old." He stared into the afternoon, keeping his silence, hiding his thoughts, and the potter watched Liùtha who had walked up the hill a little way, following the path beside the burn. When the piper spoke again it was to ask quietly, "Do you know what you're doing, lad? It's a dark road to Marac."

"I have that creature's word I will come safe home again," the potter told him, but his mind showed him Assiolo in his fear and misery. What had he begun?

"Do you trust it?"

"It carried me safe the first time and followed my bidding when I called it back. It plucked Liùtha from the sea when she was drowning."

"A fair answer, lad, had I not heard you crying out against your dreams last night. Liùtha's not the only one with secrets. What else did you hear in the White City, beyond what you've told me?"

The potter looked down at the plant crushed in his hand. "That I must bring death to a man."

"That's about the truth of it, in the end," the piper muttered, "though tales change with their tellers."

"I will not do such a thing," the potter cried. "I am not a murderer."

"Where there is necessity, there is no choice," said Kenu Vanithu. His eyes and voice were steady and, as he spoke, the potter saw clearly he was not a man, that he had known times and places no man would see.

"Even so, there are some things I will not do," the potter said, remembering with disgust the stickiness of Assiolo's blood upon his hands.

Now the noonday sun falls upon Te-Meriku the king. It lights the red leather of his jerkin and his flaming hair; it kindles a fire in the great ruby brooch binding his cloak. Te-Meriku looks down at the captain and at the little piper who stands beside him. Te-Meriku knows who the piper is; Te-Meriku knows what he is, though none of his kind is born among the Sea People. The piper is not a man and so he stands outside the laws of men. Te-Meriku will raise no hand against him.

The piper watches all the Sea People do that day. He does not flinch; he does not hide his eyes. All this he has seen before; all this he will see again in many times and places before his death. He does not weep, he does not judge, though every death is branded in his memory. He is a witness to these deaths, as he has been to so many deaths since first he walked upon the land.

He must make his music in the west, in the king's hall in Lyikené, Te-Meriku says as the light grows red. He bids his helmsman take him to the ship of the sea eagle. The piper follows without a word but first he stoops to kiss the captain gently in farewell, one kiss upon his brow as token of their friendship. When the Sea People carry him away, he stands with the wind at his back beneath the square sail that is as red as blood, as white as snow, and sings the lament he has made for the sailors of Ohmorah who will never now return to the White City. The Sea People are silent while his song drifts out across the sea, as high and pure as if it were the stars that sang or else the wind upon the water.

The potter and the piper sat together all the afternoon in uneasy silence. The potter's peace was broken though the day was yet as fair. Liùtha did not come down the hill until the evening. Her hands were filled with wildflowers and she sat beside the bothy door twisting them into a crown.

Slowly, the sun sank to its rest and the light lengthened across the hill; all across the bay, the sea was a shimmer of gold as the long day lingered and the evening rose up to meet it. At last the sun set and the day ended; then came the dancing and the firelight. They saw the fires lighted on the hillside. They heard the heartbeat rhythm of the drum, the calling of the pipes and the many voices lifted in song at midsummer. The old moon rose like a splinter of bone above the rowan trees and the wind tossed up their branches so the rowans too were dancing on midsummer's night.

Liùtha's face was tense and troubled beneath her crown of flowers. The midsummer fires had melted her frost but brought no joy. She stood before the door, looking down beyond the harbour to the starlight on the sea. In the bay, the sea was patterned with silver ripples as the wind blew over it, dancing on the starlit waves. The music of pipe and drum called across the night and suddenly she crouched beside the open door, rocking to and fro with her hands over her ears to deaden the midsummer music.

"I am afraid." Her whisper was no louder than the wind rustling the rowan leaves.

Without thinking, the potter answered, "I am here."

She turned her head and met his eyes.

He had not been afraid before, yet now his heart beat out his fear in time to the drumbeats of midsummer. In all the days since first they met he had scarce been more than a dozen paces from her side; he had eaten with her and drunk with her and, all the while, had thought he felt no more for her than pity and believed his only desire was for adventure, that, when he had kept his promise, he would go home to Ittachar. Now he saw her glance at him with firelight reflected in her dark eyes and, with that look, his world was changed: he knew the truth in his heart and that she could read it in his face, if she had but the eyes to see it. She was near enough for him to smell the honeysuckle tangled on her brow and he flushed in the darkness, knowing how midsummer was kept in this country.

But Liùtha did not look at him again. She said, very wildly, and maybe she spoke to him, maybe to the piper, or maybe only to herself, "This is what I was told long ago: in the days before the sun rose, the wind blew across the land and sea. When the last of us has gone into the dark, the wind will blow unchecked across the land and the sea. But, in the time between, this land is ours, and that is why we dance on midsummer's night."

Then she ran out onto the hillside, towards the fires. The potter called her name but she did not answer or turn back.

Kenu Vanithu's face was troubled. "It's best you follow her," he said. "Go carefully – midsummer is not like other nights. The pull of life for life is strong and sweet... There should be no shame to it, but she's so far into the dark that here and now the light of this land cannot redeem her."

"Will you go?" He was afraid to leave the shelter of stone walls. The fires burned too bright and dazzled him; the song was too sweet and tempted him; the drums were the heartbeat of another life calling him to a dance that was not his.

"Not I, lad, there's too much light tonight and the world is out of balance," said Kenu Vanithu, sourly. The potter saw some ill memory came upon him so his face was dark as well as ugly. "This is not a night for either beggars or Tions, and I am both. I have not enough weight upon the world to bring a hope of harvest. Tonight is for your kind. Go now: she is in your care."

The potter caught up with Liùtha at the edge of the dancing grove. Very lovely she looked in the firelight, but not happy. She did not smile to see him; there was in her face none of the joy that should come with the midsummer fires. The light of the great fires flickered across her face as she watched the dancers of Eilanmor weaving their lines around the trees. She had a hungry, eager look, craving the light and the company of dancers. When he came to her side, she said, "I have been seven years alone and have had enough of solitude."

He could not think of an answer. Nor did she did not wait for one but ran from him into the shadow of the trees. The wind blew around her, tossing up branches of birch and rowan and elder. He saw her stop, saw her look from the firelight and dancing to a place beneath the trees where the light could not reach and the shadows were deepest. She held out her hands to the darkness but the light from the fires shone all about her, outlining her in brightness. He heard her call, "If you are there, show yourself!"

On the edge of vision, like a distant star seen sidelong from the corner of his eyes, the potter saw a man standing among the ghostly trunks of birken trees, a pale-faced man whose dark hair was bound back with the brightness of starlight; he heard him whisper on the edge of hearing, "You must come to me."

The drumbeats grew louder, and the singing. The fires burned brightly fierce and sparks flew up, far brighter than the stars. The wind blew, the trees shuddered and shook their branches, and when the potter looked again the place beneath the trees was empty. The only voice was the wind whispering through the leaves. Liùtha cast herself upon the ground and sobbed aloud. But she did not mourn for long. In a few minutes she put aside her grief and came to him from the darkness.

"It is nothing," she said. She swept her tears from her cheek and her eyes glittered hard in the firelight. "A ghost, a fragment of a dream, crossing into the waking world. Tonight I shall put aside my past."

The days roll on and the year turns until it is midsummer. Her birthday falls upon midsummer's day, but she has never been allowed to join the music and the dancing on midsummer's night, and this year her mother says again she is too young. They had not kept midsummer in the country where her mother was born and it never beats in her heart as it does in her own, for the blood of Ohmorah flows through her veins. But this day she has turned sixteen and she vows no power in the world, not even her mother, can keep her from midsummer. The lady speaks against it, but she rages at her mother because she is no more a child and at last, for sake of peace between them, they agree a truce: she may join the dancing on midsummer's night whilst it is still her birthday. Yet when her birthday ends so too must her dancing, when midnight is called she must be back within her chamber.

She puts on her finest dress and brushes out her hair until it is smooth and bright as silk for she wants all to see that the lady of Ohmorah's daughter is grown up out of childhood and come into the city.

As the sun slides down towards the sea the sky grows bright with evening. Down in the dancing fields beyond the walls, the pipes are singing, the drums are throbbing, the trees are hung with a thousand silver lights like stars come down to earth. She kisses her dove in the silver cage and takes her place among the dancers. She dances through the evening with many young men, even with the chamberlain's son though he stares so at her face he treads hard upon her foot. It pleases her that the young men like her beauty but, in truth, the only man she wants to see her is not there.

At last the midsummer sun sets and she grows tired of dancing. She thinks she wasted her time in raging; she would have lost nothing by pleasing her mother and spending the night quietly within her house. So she draws apart from the lights and the dancing and the heartbeat rhythm of the drums to walk alone beneath the summer trees. She walks between hawthorn hedges that are a tumble of roses; elderflower and honeysuckle scent the night as she passes by; great moths in search of the moon drift by her head on feathery wings.

And there upon the hillside she meets the Lord of Marac looking down towards the sea. His face is pale, his eyes are black and there is starlight at his brow. He holds a silver cup and, as she comes to him, he offers it, and she drinks deep. It is not the wine she drank with the young men but water, very cold and clear. When she sets down the cup, he smiles, and it is the smile she has come to crave from him.

"I have heard it is your birthday," he says. "I have a gift for you."

He holds out his hand and in it is a silver circlet bearing one great moonstone that glows pale and cold in the starlight. He places it on her head. "Now you are the queen of the night." He raises her fingers to his lips and kisses them.

"All across the world people are dancing tonight," she says. Thinking to draw him into the circle of dancers, into the company of men, she asks, "Will you dance the midsummer dance with me upon my birthday?"

He shakes his head. "I do not dance this dance. Other beats than the seedtime and the hope of harvest rise in my blood. I do not draw my strength from the earth but from the sea and the stars." He smiles, but it is his common smile, the one that turns her back into a child. "Return now to the dancing and make the boys of the White City vie for your smiles tonight."

Almost, she does his bidding but then she stops. "You treat me as a child," she says, "but I am not a child."

"It is safe to be a child. The world is a dangerous place and the hearts of men more dangerous yet. That is why the men and women of the White City dance upon midsummer's night. They dance to tame the wild, to make safe a world that is not safe. Go now and dance your dance with folk who love you, who will keep you safe until you know how to make your own way in the world."

"I know what I want," she cries. "I want you. I want you to talk plainly to me. The dove was dying and you made her whole. The ship has no crew but you sail her with a word. The wind does your bidding. Speak of these things to me."

"As well try to capture the sea with a book as speak of these things. They are not stories to be told in words. One day I might show you."

His face holds more life in it than any man's. Her heart beats faster: whether she stays with him or no, her life will never be the same again. This moment of midsummer is the pivot on which it turns.

"Listen," he says, "what I am, I am. Your mother comes from a people lost beneath the sea before your father's great-great-grandsire was born. She is a woman, but more than a woman of Ohmorah. So here am I a man. I walk the streets and gardens of this city as any man might do, yet I am not always a man."

"And what am I?"

"You are a child," he answers, and he does not smile. "It is late. Go in. Go back to your mother's house before she misses you."

She remembers the look she saw an hour ago when she found him beneath the trees; she feels his gift upon her brow. "You do not think I am a child," she says. "You choose to treat me as a child because you are afraid."

"If I am afraid it is because I know the world better than you do. I have seen in other times and places that love is not enough."

"But I love you and I am not afraid." She puts her arms about his neck and kisses him full on the mouth. In daylight she would not have thought of doing such a thing, another night she would not have dared, but it is midsummer and the beat of the dance and the wine flows through her blood. As she kisses him, she knows her words are true: she is no more a child and can never be treated as one again.

His kiss is soft as summer breezes, sweet as honey, strong as wine. She forgets the world, forgets everything but the touch of his lips on hers, his hands upon her, her hands upon him.

Too soon, he pulls away. "Come," he says, "let us walk awhile together to talk of the present and decide the future."

The night is thin, the stars are bright, and lamplight shines around them. As they walk together beneath the trees in sight of the sea she hears the watch call out the midnight hour from the city wall. It has no meaning in her mind. Her promise to come home is part of another life and can no longer bind her. She has chosen another path than to be her mother's daughter, safe within the stone walls of her mother's house.

"You claim my love," the Lord of Marac says, "and I shall give it to you for all the time we both have flesh for loving. But think before you answer, consider what it is that you desire. Love is not a

*game played on midsummer's night and cast aside in the morning.
I am not a man of Ohmorah."*

*She sees the starlight on the sea. She sees his pale hand on her
arm, the darkness of his eyes. Seeing all this, she does not think
beyond the night. She tells him, "I will love you with all my heart
and soul and mind, forever."*

*"You do not have forever. Your fate is not my fate, howeverso
much I love you. But I shall love you until the ending of your
life, until the stars no longer shine upon your face, until the sea no
longer sounds in your ears."*

*"I knew you from the first. I knew you were mine," she says.
"I love you and I am ready."*

"Three times you have sworn it. Let it be so."

*He catches her up into his arms and a great wind blows around
them.*

The song of midsummer beat through the night with a pulse of
green and gold. Liùtha took the potter by the hand and pulled
him into the dance, joining a chain of dancers circling the fires.
They made their ways down the line of the dance, twisting and
turning in the patterns of midsummer. Sometimes the chain
would break and a pair of dancers leap high across the flames.
Always, the potter watched Liùtha, fearing he would lose her
as she swung through the dance with the men of Eilanmor.
Here, at midsummer, she was transformed from one creature
to another, her element no longer frost but fire. The sorrow
in her face had been driven back by exultation born of wild
despair and she danced as if upon the edge of doom, her hair
blowing on the wind like the smoke rising from the fires, and
all the while a light like firelight burned in her eyes.

At last the pattern of the dance brought them back together.
Liùtha held out her hands. "Dance with me, Almecu mor
Thorrian. We are both strangers here. Let us keep midsummer
together."

She had used his name and so the potter crooked his fingers
to ward off the ill luck that must surely follow. They were far
from Ittachar and her customs were not his. He remembered
the calm eyes of her mother: *She will lead you into the dark places.*
He remembered Assiolo: *She will burn you.*

Liùtha laughed, a mocking laughter with no joy or kindness
in it. "If you'll not dance with me, others will," she said. "It is
not good to be alone at midsummer."

Uneasy, troubled, he took her hands. She led him round
and through the fires and sparks flew out beneath her feet.

At last the potter could dance no more and made her pause beneath the flowering trees. The scent of elderflowers tumbled all around them, honey heavy at midsummer. He looked down at her, seeing her flushed and panting from her dancing, very lovely, more desirable than any woman he had known but for the wildness in her eyes. He reached out his hand to steady himself against a birken tree.

Again Liùtha laughed, seeing his desire in his face. "I've been seven years alone," she said. She put her arms around his neck, pulling his face down to hers, and kissed him, hard and greedy, amidst the firelight and the drumbeat of midsummer's night.

The potter closed his eyes and kissed her mouth, his hands tangled in her hair, forgetting the past and the future for a while, knowing only he was a man and she a woman and it was midsummer. Very sweet it was to feel her body pressed against his, the taste of her mouth on his lips, but then he opened his eyes and saw her face. What he saw there made him hold her from him. This was not his dance, this was not his song and, though he longed for her, this was not his love.

"I was never with a woman yet who did not care who she kissed," he told her. "I'll not be used to still your ghosts. Tonight any man would do for you. When you want me for myself, I'll kiss you."

He felt her shake within his arms. "You should have taken what I offered, potter. I'll swear it is enough for any man."

Her anger flared, then her face closed and her mask of frost was back. The creature he had glimpsed of rage and fire was gone. He preferred it so. Fire and frost both burned, but one was fast and one was slow.

"Enough of this foolery," the potter said. "It is time to go back."

"Did the wind blow?" Kenu Vanithu asked as they came in.

"Look you at the trees in the night," Liùtha answered. "The wind is blowing all across the hill."

"It wasn't the world's wind I asked of," said the piper, "but a wind that blew in Ohmorah seven years since."

"That wind is stilled."

He looked at her. She tried to meet his eyes but he outstared her. "It is not stilled," he said. "It blows yet from Marac. Why do you doubt what you saw?"

"I saw nothing," Liùtha said, and both knew she was lying.

"Which do you fear more?" Kenu Vanithu asked. "To find out he is in the world or fled from it?"

Liùtha filled a cup with water and drank it, her eyes opaque within her face, seeing all, saying nothing.

"The Lord of Marac waits in flesh and blood, and keeps his gate against your coming. He has waited for you these seven years. Do you think you can make your peace with him?"

The piper's words passed through her armour like a dart. She swayed and sank onto her bunk, covering her face with her hands. "How do you know?" she gasped. "How can you know?"

"I have lived in the world a long time. I felt its balance change when the Lord of Marac came into it. I would have felt it change again if he had gone out of it."

Liùtha stayed still a long while with her face turned to the wall and silent tears rolling down her cheeks. She made no move to wipe them away. Outside on the hill the music of midsummer sang wild all through the night but within the bothy all was quiet.

Maybe Kenu Vanithu slept through the remnants of the night, wrapped in a blanket with his coat for a pillow on the earth floor beside the hearth, but the potter lay awake, listening to the wind blow across the hill and the drums that would not stop until dawn was bright across the eastern sky. He thought over and again of how Liùtha had kissed him, and of the kiss he had given in return. Whatever had been in her heart, his kiss had been honest. He had learned that night he had come to love her, despite her silence and her secrets, and wondered if she had guessed, or cared. Or had she only been using him for her own ends? It was a bitter thought, and yet every drumbeat beyond the door drove home it had been so.

He lies beside her, naked in the starlight, and she reaches out to his cool flesh that she now knows better than her own. "Truly," he says in wonder, "it is not a little thing to be a man."

"I had thought you knew all things," she answers, so seriously that he must laugh. Still laughing, he takes her in his arms again, teasing and caressing her until first she laughs with him and then cries out with joy.

"I knew the song of star and stone," he tells her, later, tracing the patterns of his love upon her breasts and belly. "I knew the path of the wind across the water, but this I did not know. In the borderlands there is no time for love, no joy. All the old tales are true."

It wants perhaps three hours of dawn and the room is soft with shadows. Beyond her window, the stars are very bright and very many, each point of light reflected in the stillness of the water. The city of her life is gone; her only view the starlight and the sea, lonely and very lovely.

"This is Marac, my domain in the waking world," he says, softly. "You will pass back into Ohmorah at sunrise. I shall come to you at nightfall – do not bar the way."

"Why did you come to the White City?"

"Where else would I have gone? Allodola was there, and Allocco. The world had changed so much since last I walked it and they were all that was left to me. Then I saw you, standing behind your mother's chair."

His eyes are soft and black as he gazes at her, the smile she loves upon his face. Very gently she kisses him, a feather touch to make him shiver with delight. He turns her face towards his own and tells her, "When you looked at me I wanted to be only the man I saw reflected in your eyes; he was a far better creature than the one I had become, after the fire, after the flood. Your mother had begun the world anew, and, when you smiled at me, so too did I."

"You gave me the white dove."

"I gave you my heart, love, and waited for you to come to me. Life calls to life, love calls to love. I knew you would come to me and so you did, tonight."

"But what are you?"

"Until the sunrise I am the man who loves you."

"And after the sunrise?"

"Then I am what I have always been, the star that fades in the morning, the song you cannot sing, the wind upon the water."

She presses herself against him, desolate at the thought of parting. He wraps her in his arms to comfort her. "Each of us is what the other is not: for us, love must be enough. But I swear to you, by land and sea and by the empty air, I shall come to you at sunset and be again the man who loves you."

The white dove sleeps quiet in her cage, her feathers silvered by starlight. Soon she too sleeps, in his arms, on his breast, but when she wakes the sun has risen above the towers of the city, the dove has flown, and he is gone.

6: What I am to you, I do not know

If my love were an earthly knight.
As he's an elfin grey
I wad na gie my ain true-love
For nae lord that ye hae.

Tam Lin. Traditional

Late in the afternoon, four days later, their ship docked in the larger of the harbours of Marac Bec, that great seaport where ships came from all lands, where all languages were spoken and all ways known, a noisy bustle of a place, smelling of spices and fish. The potter stared to see the mercatmen with their hennaed beards counting up their beads and tally-sticks in the great warehouses along the docks and the hawkers on the quayside calling out their wares in voices louder and harsher than seagulls.

In the time since they had left Eilanmor, Liùtha had spoken little, and the potter little more, and mostly to Kenu Vanithu. All had been changed between them at midsummer. Despite this, as she stepped onto the quay, Liùtha shrank towards him, her face bleached by the onset of so much new. The potter felt his heart beat fast at the sight of so many strangers. Still he went on, bidding farewell to his countryman and giving many thanks to the master, who slapped his shoulder, wished him luck and thought no more about him.

The three went on together, the potter finding he must push his way against the crowds, Liùtha clinging to his arm lest they be parted by the press. The potter remembered his creature's promise: *Artists, musicians and mercatmen, sailors, liars, mystics and thieves.* Surely all were here, he thought, as he looked around in wonder, surely all the people of the world were here.

It was too late to set out that evening and, besides, the town gates would soon be locked for the night. They had been told of an inn near the port kept by a sailor's sister. In exchange for four of ivory, she agreed to give Liùtha a room for the night and to let the potter and the piper bed down in blankets by the fireside after the inn closed, a favour usually granted only to her brother's shipmates ashore for a night's drinking. The

price was steep for such a place but none thought it wise to
try to camp by the roadside outside the town wall. Marac Bec
was a rough, hard town and the innkeeper reputed honest, if
not generous, and her inn was at least clean.

But, come the evening, it did not seem so wise a choice, for
sailors new ashore are as wont to let a woman be as wasps
are to resist spilt honey. First one and then another set himself
down beside Liùtha, as she sat in a corner eating fried fish and
barley bread and over-boiled turnip, to offer ale and drunken
company, to chuck her 'neath the chin and try to kiss her
when she looked up, affronted. Though each time she told
them "No!" men's eyes kept sliding sideways over her, and
men's hands likewise. All this, the potter watched, grimly
amused and minded not to interfere unless real trouble came
of it. At last Liùtha could take no more. Against loud regrets
and whistles, she rose up to seek her chamber and leave them
to their drinking, sweeping a black look behind her to the
potter, who in answer raised his cup in mocking salute to her
beauty.

Then someone started a chorus of a shanty and Kenu
Vanithu took up the tune on his wooden pipe. But one sailor,
more drunk than all the rest, snatched it from his fingers to
play on it in parody. The piper waited until the man drew
breath and held out his hand to have his own again. The sailor
laughed and held up the pipe just a finger's breadth too high
for him to take it. Another called out, "Jump for it, manikin!"
Many laughed at such a joke, a ragged dwarf straining upwards
for what was ever out of reach. A slow chorus of calls and
handclaps began, "Jump, jump."

This the potter could not bear. He stepped forwards, to
spoil the game and take the pipe. Seeing the man's eyes, he
thought a fight would come of it, and that the other likely had
a knife, but the innkeeper jumped onto a keg and shouted
loudly, "There'll be no more ale if blood is spilt!" and so it
came to nothing.

"Go, keep Liùtha company," the potter said to Kenu Vanithu,
who nodded and slipped away to sit the night through by
the cold hearth in her bedchamber. But the potter stayed
downstairs to drink beer brewed at the inn and swallow the
sailors' jibes and jests as best he might. Often and over, as
the night grew old and heads grew thick, they named him a
fool, and worse than a fool, to have his chances and not take
them. And on what would surely happen when a beggar found
himself alone with such a woman they had much to say. He

shook his head, and kept his temper, and supped his drink in silence, watching the stair in case some drunken fellow got it in his head to climb it.

She stretches out upon the bench beside the pool, languid and lazy as a cat beneath the summer sun. She does not see the sunlight, she does not see the garden. Behind her closed eyes she sees only the starlight and the sea. These sunny days are but a dream, the night alone is real. Her life begins each evening when the dove settles to sleep in her silver cage. Then she hears the wind at her window and the beating of the sea; then, the daytime world fades away. She opens her chamber door to walk through the short summer nights into the halls of another place, an empty keep built of black stone beside another sea, and there he meets her with loving words upon his lips and starlight in his hair. Before the morning, worn out by love, she falls to sleep in his arms, soothed by his beating heart, and wakes alone within her chamber as the white dove rouses herself to fly free into the sunlit sky.

Bees hum within the lavender, butterflies dance above the mallow. She drowses through the afternoon until she hears footsteps on the stone and at last opens her eyes. It is only the chamberlain walking to and fro within the garden, an old man in a scarlet coat amidst the summer flowers. He plucks a sprig of rosemary and pins it at his collar and says, "Tell me, what happened at midsummer?"

"The fires burned, the music played," she says, facing him and trying to speak boldly though her face flushes. She knows he knows everything that happens in the White City. "The people danced beneath the trees. It is always so at midsummer."

He laughs at such an answer. "You are a candle to your mother's fire; you are a pretty toy, an oathbreaker's daughter."

She bites her lip upon her first retort. It is true enough: her father broke his oath and died for it.

"Midsummer is past," says the chamberlain. "After summertime, comes harvest. The wheat grows gold and is cut down; the apples grow sweet and are devoured. You know this as well as I – all born beneath our sky know it." He asks her, sharp and smiling, "What thinks the Lord of Marac of harvest time?"

She stands, turning away, thinking to leave the garden and go into the inner part of her mother's house where he cannot follow.

"He is not a man," he says. "He is starlight on the sea, wind upon the water. His boat is ever ready at the quay to be away on the evening tide."

She whips around to face him, the old crow who dares to cast a blight upon her happiness. "That is not true. He loves me! He swore it at midsummer."

"What does he care for midsummer – did he dance with you beneath the trees? You are a green girl – what do you know of him? In the borderlands there is no time for love, no joy. All the old tales are true."

She dabbles her hand in the water whilst she searches for an answer. The great fish rises cold and shining out of the dark beneath the waterlilies. The chamberlain says, "You must live all your days without him, knowing in the end he will not follow you into the dark."

All he says is true, and she can find no better answer than, "He loves me."

The old man nods his farewell and leaves her to sit beneath the tree and think of the borderlands. They lie far away, in the past and in the future, anywhere but in the waking world. They are remembered in tales told to children and old folk glimpse them on the edge of dreaming. Beyond life they lie, beyond time, and she can never come to them. Time blows on her like the wind. She cannot escape its dominion. It measures out the hours, the days of her life, counting them off with the rising and the setting sun.

But her lover is not a part of this: he danced with wind and starlight before her world began; he will dance, between the sea and the empty air, when it is ended.

The potter had asked the master of the way they must follow before they came ashore. Three days journey down the coast from the harbour and the town, the man had answered, was the fortress of Marac, its walls black against the bright sky. It had an evil name, the master said, and was a home of ghosts and spirits; ships put to sea to keep out of its shadow, and he knew of no man yet who had willingly gone towards it.

In the morning they set out along the road. Three days, they had been told. The first two passed easily enough, for the road lay through farmland and hamlets and the going was gentle. Though neither Liùtha nor the potter had much to say, one to the other, there was Kenu Vanithu's pipe to cheer their hearts. The third day was very hard. Their pace was slower now for the path through the heathland was rough and Kenu Vanithu could go but slowly on his twisted leg. The towers of Marac had seemed near when they woke but they found the seeming was deceptive for, though they walked all day, by evening they had not reached their goal.

Two hours before sunset they rested in a scrub of little trees, scanty and scarcely a windbreak. It was chilly for all it was so soon after midsummer, so the potter and Liùtha gathered fallen wood and Kenu Vanithu kindled a fire with flint and iron and tinder. It burned up bright beneath his hands but they had not fuel enough for useful warmth. At dusk, the rain began, a fine, cold rain that made the dreich night sourer still as darkness rose around them without stars or moon to lighten it.

When their food was eaten it was too damp for easy sleep, so all huddled close as could be to the fire and told stories to drive back the fear of the dark that pressed so heavy. Kenu Vanithu told of times and places he had seen, long ago and far away; Liùtha spoke of how her mother's people had been driven from their first home by fire and wave, sailing for years upon the sea before they came to Ohmorah and settled there, mixing their blood with the people of that land and building the White City; and, last and late, the potter told the tale of Tamarhak of Tarhn and the woman of the Sea People, who left her kith and kin behind for love of him, who bore a son to him, yet killed him when he broke the oath he gave her.

"A dark tale, that one," he said, after it was ended. "No other woman has set so high a price upon her love."

"No price at all, if he loves her," said Kenu Vanithu.

"Have you loved so?" asked Liùtha, from the shadows.

The piper was quiet for a long time, turning his pipe over in his hand. Though his eyes were bright, his face was grotesque in the leaping firelight. His lips moved silently, shaping a word unsaid, a name not spoken, *Averla*. And that was most strange, the potter thought, remembering Assiolo's tale of his father. But, he thought, most like he was mistaken; the piper had not named that golden witch and, when at last he answered, it was not of her he spoke.

"Once," he said, "when the world and I were young, there was a woman in the queen's court in Escen to whom I'd have made that vow, had she wished for it. She could sing like a blackbird in springtime and it was joy to me to hear her. I would play and she would sing; with her I could be happy. She was dark, and merry, and full of laughter.

"But when, still laughing, I told her of my love, her laughter stopped and her face changed. Only for a moment, but it was a look I've seen upon a thousand strangers' faces when first they see me. And, after that moment, she was kind." His face clenched with anger. "I could not bear her kindness; I wanted love returned or nothing, so I left her, left that place never to return, and, since that day, I've met no one I cared to speak of love with. Now she is long dead, her ashes blow on the wind and I have not yet forgiven her her kindness."

Then he put his pipe to his lips and played. The potter knew well the words of that song, an ancient lament made by a woman waiting for her sailor lover to return from across the sea. But the man does not return, only a grey gull forever screaming for its lost soul in the boundary between land and water.

All the time the piper played, the potter watched Liùtha, bright-eyed in the firelight. She pulled her hood close across her face but not before he had seen her tears. Then he put aside his wrath and pitied her; her sorrow was real and whatever she had done at midsummer it had been because her hope was gone.

At that thought his own hope returned, a quick, sharp pain stabbing his heart. He told himself, "Don't be a fool. It was midsummer, no more than that." He jumped to his feet and muttered a tale about finding more wood before they slept and so found excuse to walk alone in the dark a while, brushing tears from his eyes as he told himself, again and yet again, Liùtha did not love him. But he could not drive his love away, for all he willed himself to do so.

When night comes, and her love is with her, she speaks of what her mother has told her of the borderlands. She knows there is another tale she should tell, but that way leads into the dark. It is easier to ask him of borderlands that are far away and long ago. If she does not speak of it, if her lover does not know her thought, she can pretend a while longer to herself her fear does not exist.

She laughs to keep back tears. "The sea and storm obey you," she says. "Surely I am safe with you."

"Here, you are safe. The White City is far away. But you must return at dawn to the waking world."

She says, as they look out together upon the other sea lying beneath the other stars, "Let us stay together past the sunrise."

He takes her face between his hands, surprised. "Little love, is not the night enough?"

"Please," she begs him, "as you love me. I must live by day, as by night. Only half a life can be spent beneath the stars."

"What I am, I am," he says. "You have all that I can give. It must be enough." His arm around her, he gazes out into the night.

"Is any sight more lovely than the starlight on the sea, the patterns of the wind upon the water?"

The night is lovely, dark and deep, the stars as diamonds set in ebony, the sea as molten silver. He too is lovely, shining with starlight, more beautiful to look upon than any man. To love him is to know the caress of a summer breeze, the rising of the sea against the shore, the velvety oblivion of midnight. But, sometimes, in her mother's house in the hot days of late summer, by night time in his quiet keep beside the other sea, she thinks of life to come, and wishes he could come to her by sunlight as by starlight, a man as other men.

Liùtha was asleep when the potter returned to the fireside, wrapped tight in her coat and her blanket with her hands around her face. He spread his own blanket over her, wishing he could do more to shelter her from the rain. Kenu Vanithu was still playing his pipe, a haunting ripple of sweet, sad melodies, poignant as memory. The potter built up the fire and lay beneath his sheepskin coat listening to the music, much of his mind still measuring the distance between a potter and a lady of the White City.

"What happened to her father?" he asked, when the dwarf at last put his pipe aside and held out his hands to the fire.

"He died, lad," Kenu Vanithu answered, "upon the open sea."

"And why should he leave his lady and his daughter to sail across the sea?"

"Because he feared what would happen should the Lord of Marac come to Ohmorah."

"He went to fight him? Is that why he died?"

"Liùthai died, lad, because he gave an oath and broke it, thinking he would be pardoned because all he did he did for love."

This was not what the potter had expected. He kept silent, waiting for the rest.

Kenu Vanithu poked at the fire with a stick. "Only the very brave, or the very foolish, dare to defy Lyikené. You know that better than the rest," he muttered, "you men of Ittachar." Aloud, he said, "When Liùtha was a child her father crossed the world to beg a king be kind. Haduhai was an old man; he'd seen too much of death and so, against the custom of his people, he let him live and gave him what he wanted. It was no more than hope, but, sometimes, hope is enough." The piper jabbed at the fire again, sending sparks dancing out of its red heart to die in the dark. Harsh and hard, he told the potter, "Sometimes, lad, not often. And when it was not enough, Liùthai sailed again into the west. Perhaps he was a brave man, perhaps he was a fool. Either way, the ending is the same."

The potter started from his thoughts. "What is it to me what Liùthai was?" he demanded, and pulled his pack closer to use it for a pillow.

All through the night Kenu Vanithu sang quietly in the damp darkness, watching over the sleepers by the fireside and his song mingled itself into the potter's dreams; his tune was a cradlesong sung years ago in Ittachar to sooth a child to sleep but his words were all his own:

> "There was a sailor brave and bold:
> So bright and brave was he
> He passed the land where apples gold
> Grow on the firstborn tree.

> "The north star held at his right hand,
> Beyond the west sailed he.
> He sailed to find the empty land
> Of starlight on the sea."

He paused his singing when the potter stirred in his sleep. "Who in these days can tell a brave man from a fool?" he asked the dying fire, his face twisted with remembered pain. Though his eyes were dry, tears would have added nothing to the sadness in his face. After a little while he took up his song again, more softly than before:

> "But death came from the western land,
> Death sailed across the sea,
> Death held an apple in his hand
> Grown on the firstborn tree.

> "The blood runs from the sailor bold,
> Runs red into the sea.
> He lies beneath the starlight cold
> Beyond the western sea."

The first time this man sailed from Ohmorah into the west the king of the Sea People was an old man who loved a young man's daring enough to forgive his folly. For, in the stranger from the White City, Hadùhai the king had seen what his own son might have been, had he lived past the year the winter sickness fell heavy on Lyikené.

That king has gone into the dark. All men must die, even the kings of the Sea People. When Hadùhai died, Te-Meriku sent him into the sunset in his burning ship with his sword in one hand and an apple in the other, the bones of his son and his son's son at his feet. Now all of that line of kings that came in long descent from Imacah mor Tamarhak are dead. Te-Meriku the sea eagle is king now in Lyikené.

Whilst he kneels upon his deck, waiting for death with the sun scorching his bare back, the captain of Ohmorah remembers Te-Meriku, standing at the tideline 'twixt land and sea. That image is seared into his mind: Te-Meriku gilded by the evening sunlight, a red-haired man of Lyikené with eyes wild and fierce as an eagle that, alone of all creatures, can outstare the sun. Te-Meriku is not like the men of Ohmorah. They live quiet and safe within their walls and laws, within the peace the lady has made. Te-Meriku is not like Hadùhai the old king, who lived long and lost much and learnt mercy from his loss. Te-Meriku is brightness and terror, his place and purpose in the world as simple as those of the sea eagle that stoops from the high sunlight to its kill, beyond good and evil because it is unthinkable it should do otherwise.

For reasons of his own, the man of Ohmorah has broken his oath and sailed again into the west, beyond Lyikené. And, as he promised, Te-Meriku the sea eagle has hunted his prey across the open sea, and he has caught what he hunted.

As the sun sets, Te-Meriku leaves the captain alone in his own ship. It has been left without sail or rudder and drifts westwards across the face of the sea, following the paths of wind and current beneath the stars by night, the sun by day. His blood runs slowly out upon the deck. The man will die – Te-Meriku has made this certain – but he will have no easy passage into the dark.

In the morning the fire had fallen to ashes and the light was grey with raindrops that misted grass and blankets and all with silver. No one spoke, aching and cold as they were. Liùtha filled their flasks at a stream and divided bread and cheese between them. *Today we must reach Marac,* the potter thought as he rebound his pack. *Today I shall find out if I can fulfil my oath.* His heart was heavy as lead.

As they walked, Liùtha pulled him by his sleeve so they with longer strides left the piper a little behind on the track. "I saw you looking at me last night when Kenu Vanithu spoke of love. I was half-mad on Eilanmor. You must not love me. Can you forget midsummer?"

The potter flushed, for often and often he remembered it; each time he looked at her, he remembered, and was angry again that still she must treat him as a fool.

"Don't be afraid, Liùtha. I see nothing done at midsummer in these lands can be binding. I'll not force my love upon you or expect you to give yourself to me as a prize for valour, like a princess in a story told to children. When I've kept my promise I'll make my farewell and then you can forget me."

"I did not mean to slight you. If we're friends, forgive me." She looked up into his face. "It was midsummer and I was driven from despair into folly. My mother told me once love is not enough. Lovers are too easily hurt," she said, her hand upon his arm. "I fear for you if you love me. You are not safe. You deserve a kinder fate."

He stared at her for a long moment. "Liùtha, none of us is safe from the moment of our birth. I didn't choose to love you to bring brightness to my life, as I'd choose a glaze to put upon a pot." He fell silent, taking a little time to find the words, for midsummer's night still stood between them, the distance between his heart and hers. "I've seen wonders since I set out on this journey. I didn't know such things were in the world. But when last night Kenu Vanithu said no price was too high for a true lover I knew full well his meaning, as I'd not have if I hadn't met you."

Liùtha did not answer but turned away, white-faced and miserable.

Autumn comes again to the White City and the trees burn with red and gold. She sits an afternoon beneath the rowan in the garden. Its berries have grown ripe and red and some have fallen to lie like beads of blood upon the bench. Soon the first frosts will come but for now there is still warmth in the sunshine, though the air is chill in the shade beneath the tree. Her mother must away upon the morrow into the Southern Reaches upon some matter of the harvest.

"When she returns," her thoughts begin. "Not yet. When she returns."

Today, the great fish will not come to be fed however long she coaxes him. Instead she plays with the rowan berries as if she were yet a child, setting them in patterns on the stone, counting them out in games to drive from her mind the thoughts she does not wish to think, the tale she does not wish to tell.

She hears a step upon the stone and looks around. It is not her mother but the old man, the chamberlain, who has finished his day's business with the lady and walks awhile within the garden.

His eyes rake over her. She pulls her coat loosely about her, wishing there was a place to hide because he is clever and not kind. "I think you are not well," he says, holding an apple he has picked from her mother's tree. "You grow so pale and wan."

She does not want to speak of her lover, of the nights in his far away domain, the nights that by day seem as dreams. But they are not dreams and the old man is waiting for his answer.

"What is that to you?" she asks the chamberlain.

"Nothing. Everything." He looks at her sidelong. "You have heard the tale of our homeland from your mother, I think. Did she also tell you this? Your father sailed away into the west because he feared the Liùthion would come here."

She knows the look upon his face. It has accompanied a hundred homilies and lectures in the years since her father sailed away.

"I know you have never liked me. But be more than a foolish child. Even if you care only for the night, yet walk the day with open eyes. The Liùthion has never been a man. Are you quite certain he loves you?"

"He loves me," she says, sweeping rowan berries from her lap. It is not clear if it is the chamberlain or herself she is assuring of her love. "No matter what he is, I love him."

"That is good," the chamberlain says, as if she were still a child. "Where love is, there trust will be. But remember, love blinds; lovers cannot tell truth from falsehood. It is this makes it such a simple matter to deceive them."

The chamberlain goes out into the street eating his apple and she sits alone beneath the rowan tree. His question has stirred up her mind as in years past she stirred up the mud in this pool to drive the fish from their haunts beneath the lilies. Soon she must face the fear that has grown up around her love. She remembers her mother's warning and thinks of many things that fall across her heart like clouds over the face of the sun. Here in the cold daylight the night is far away.

They went on away over the heath. Liùtha pulled her hood close against the rain so its shadow hid her face. "Your words are fine and noble," she said. "I know you're a good man seeking to do what's right. But you do not know me."

"If we deal honestly with each other we can fashion our own fates," the potter answered. He was frightened of the darkness in Liùtha's eyes, of the fire she had lit within his heart.

"If you knew the truth, I do not think you'd stay with me," Liùtha said, quietly. "Kenu Vanithu told you I was hiding from you. That is true. I am afraid of what will befall you if you follow me. I am afraid of what I will become if you do not."

"Liùtha," said the potter, "I've heard enough riddles and I shall not play more games. Speak plainly if you wish to talk or else let us go on in silence."

They crossed a muddy stream that soaked its way across the heath, miring their boots. The peatbog sucked at their feet, the wind and rain blew around them. Midsummer sun seemed long ago and far away.

"In Eilanmor," Liùtha said, "it was midsummer when fires burn between the sunset and the morning and people dance beneath the trees." She paused, looking over her shoulder to be sure the piper was still behind. Quietly, so the potter alone would hear, she said, "Evening came; the dancing and the firelight. You are a man of Ittachar, Almecu mor Thorrian; you do not feel its beat within your blood but we dance that dance in Ohmorah, beyond the walls of the White City.

"Midsummer asked, and I answered. My heart cried out for what was lost, what will not live again. Once I swore I'd never again dance at midsummer. Each year in Anach I locked the door so I might not see the fires; I shuttered the window so I might not hear the music. In Eilanmor, there was no lock upon the door and my oath was as words spoken in a dream that cannot bind on waking. I told myself, *I have been seven years alone and this life is all there is.* I thought I could foreswear my past, take pleasure where I wished. That's why I made you dance with me. That's why I kissed you."

"Liùtha, you played with fire that night and burned me." He could not look at her, remembering her kiss and his desire, and what had been left behind when desire had faded. Not caring if Kenu Vanithu or any other in the world heard him, he cried out, "Is that all I am to you – a man to use and to discard? I didn't think before that night to be your lover but I thought I had become your friend."

"I was a fool that night and so were you." Fierce and quiet, Liùtha told him, "I'll not dance with you again. For your care and kindness, I thank you. For your honour, I esteem you."

Care! Kindness! These were words, and not the ones he wanted. "The fires burned, the music played, you asked – did you think I would not answer? I learnt things of myself that night I never thought to know."

She cried out in protest but he went on, "I couldn't take what you offered: it was not enough. What I want of you, Liùtha, you will not give; I saw it in your eyes at midsummer.

But, for all that, we're bound together for a little while and needs must make our way as best we can. If you cannot trust yourself, trust me."

"On midsummer's night I saw the Lord of Marac," she said. "I called to him but he wasn't there; it was only the wind and the trees casting shadows in the starlight. But Kenu Vanithu had it aright: he is waiting and I can never put aside my past." Liùtha stopped and took the potter's arm, pulling him around to face her. "Let me tell you plain, Almecu mor Thorrian: now I know he's waiting for me in Marac, it would be better for you to leave me here in the wild than love me and go with me."

He took her cold hands, shaking his head against this thought. "Liùtha, you already know my answer. I gave my word and promise: I'll go with you to Marac and face its master there."

But these were words he could have said before midsummer when no more than an oath and a promise bound him to her. They were no longer enough. There was now more he must say and she must hear.

"What I am to you," he said, "I do not know, you will not tell. But I know full well what you are to me. On midsummer's night love woke from sleeping and it's no false love, though it brings me no joy."

He spoke in anger full as much as love. She pulled her hands away from his and went on ahead, alone. The potter stood upon the muddy path and waited for the piper to catch him up. He tried to think of the garden in the White City where the blackbird had sung in the rowan tree. That memory seemed no more than a dream that slipped away as dreams do, like water through his fingers, when he sought for it. "I will have hope," he said to cheer himself. "I chose this path and I shall come to safety in the end."

But even as he spoke, he knew his words were stronger than his heart. His only hope was that to say a thing aloud would make it true. He saw now Liùtha was leading him into the dark and he would follow her, because he loved her. He loved her, and it was indeed a love that could bring no hope of happiness or harvest; in his mind's eye, he saw again the lady in her garden but now it was a garden of withered flowers killed by the frost.

He felt a touch upon his arm and saw Kenu Vanithu looking up at him with a smile in his golden eyes. "You've strength within you to see this to its end," the piper told him. "Like knows like, I've told you."

But the potter was not comforted; the rain and wind had chilled him and his love was not enough to keep him warm on the cold road.

She cannot look at him and think he does not love her. His arms are strong around her, his kiss is sweet upon her lips; they lie down together upon her bed and great joy she has of him. Her fear passes away whilst he is with her. But when she wakes in the grey daylight of an autumn morning, he is gone; her dove has flown from the silver cage; she is alone. Then she remembers that every morning since midsummer he has been gone before the dawning and, despite herself, she hears the echo of the chamberlain's voice, asking, "Are you quite certain he loves you?"

That day, the day before the equinox, such thoughts become too much to bear and she seeks out the chamberlain in his room of books and papers. From this room Ohmorah is governed, for all the detail, all the records of the White City are stored here and in his mind.

"You have lived a long time in this world," she says. "Tell me how I may know if a man loves me."

"Surely your heart can tell you that? But, if you do not trust your heart, I can give you the means to test him, so you may see clearly what he is and how much he loves you. Is that what you desire?"

She nods. He holds out his hand. On his palm lies a ring, wide enough to slide over a man's hand onto his wrist. She takes it. It is black and old, and the device stamped onto it is the sun at noontime. The ring is hard and heavy, the work of men with the weight of men upon the world.

"No greater thing than this?"

"It is its substance gives it meaning. In fire we forged iron from the bones of the earth. With iron we tamed the land. We made axes and cut down the forests. We made ploughshares and furrowed the brown earth."

She closes her fingers on the ring.

All day she wears it, high on her arm where no one will see. It is a heavy secret. It drags against her flesh but it is no more than a ring of iron. There is no power to it, no mystery. It is exactly what it seems: a little thing of no value. And as the day draws on, she grows more angry with her love because he will not stay with her past sunrise. All day this thought pulls as heavy on her mind as the ring upon her arm until, by nightfall, she is determined that she shall have the mastery.

The grey day grew darker yet. Dread sat upon the potter as they continued along the track towards the keep that seemed never to grow nearer however long they stumbled towards it. Always the wind blew, a cold wind full of sleet that cut their faces. By midmorning the track was gone, they were on the open heath and the west wind blew with never a tree to block its path, beating hard against them so they could not go straight on but turned now from one side to another, stumbling through heather clumps that caught at their ankles or into bogs that sucked at their feet. And yet sometimes, from the edges of his eyes, the potter was sure they were already there but going in circles before the walls, blown along by this wind that never dropped. Always he knew fear as he had never felt it before; as cold might numb his body so horror of that place numbed his mind until, at times, he scarcely knew where he was going or why. At last, sometime in the afternoon, they paused discouraged in the heather.

"This is hopeless," said the potter. "There's some charm to keep us back. We'll never reach Marac in this way. All we will do is wear down our strength."

"It's not the world's wind blows on us," Kenu Vanithu said, beating his hands against his sides to warm them. "I've known all the winds of all the world in the years I've walked the Later Lands and the lands beyond the Later Lands. At this wind's back is a power greater than the powers of men, older than the Tions."

"The Lord of Marac is neither a man nor a Tion," Liùtha replied. "The wind does his bidding still. This is his warning danger lies ahead."

"You know more than we do of what awaits us. Would you have us heed that warning?" Kenu Vanithu asked. "It's not too late to turn back."

Liùtha said to the potter, "I am afraid for you. The Lord of Marac cannot touch me and Kenu Vanithu is not a man." She reached out, her eyes wet with rain or tears, and pleaded, "You've come a long way, Almecu mor Thorrian. Please, turn back now and let us go on alone. I release you from the oath you gave my mother and no man shall call you coward. You've done enough, and more than enough, to bring me this far."

The potter could not see her frozen mask nor yet the false fire of midsummer's night on her face but only open concern and sympathy, as if he caught a glimpse of what she had been before her sorrow fell upon her. He rubbed her hands between his own to warm them. "More than that oath binds me to you," he said. "I'll not turn back unless you do. I am bound to Marac by your past."

She did not meet his eyes but stared at the black walls in the distance. "Now I've come so far, I shall not turn back," she whispered, but she clung to his hands and her face was set and scared.

"Then I'll go with you," said the potter, gently, and put his arm around her, feeling stronger now she was close beside him.

They walked on and again the wordless fear of Marac welled up in them but they would not turn back and struggled on, gripped by nameless terrors. Each reached out to the others by some instinct that three together might bear what one alone could not. Hands clasped tightly, they walked on through the wind and sleet towards the black walls.

The potter heard the wind was full of voices, crying out in all languages and in none, and all called out the same chorus, an echo of Assiolo's words, *You must bring death!* and of Kenu Vanithu's, *It's a dark road to Marac.* Likewise, there were shapes in the rain and figures seen from the corner of an eye that were not there when looked at straight. The potter could never remember much about the last stretch across the heath save that some small part of his mind had known he gripped Kenu Vanithu's arm and that the piper, for all he was lame and twisted, had strength within him greater than any man.

The captain wanders by night between delirium and dreaming. All the day his life has burned slowly away beneath the sun, but now his pain is far from him, as all his life is far away. For a while memory remains, but memory is fading. Soon the moment will be all that is left to him, soon the moment will pass and there will be only darkness, as there is darkness after a candle is snuffed out. The stars wheel above him and, sweet and sudden in the night, a curlew's cry floats out across the water. It cannot be: he is too far from any land for a curlew to be near; it is a bird that hugs the shore and nests upon the uplands.

The stars are very bright above the sea and very many. He closes his eyes against their light and in the quiet darkness of his mind he hears music, singing, the echo of the song he turned from long ago. It was for this he broke his oath. It was for this he came again into the west. It was for this Te-Meriku left him to drift and die upon the open sea.

The captain cries out, "If you are there, show yourself."

Within his head, the captain hears an answer. "I am here."
Behind his eyes, he sees a pale-faced man with starlight in his hair.
He is so young; he had not thought he could look so young, this
creature of the borderlands, nor wear such sorrow on his face.

"What would you say to me, man of Ohmorah, before you die?"

"You walked the earth like a man and great ill came of it," the
captain says. "Because of you, it was forgotten that death is the
price of life. Because of you, the rowan tree died. Because of you,
the eastern land was lost beneath the sea."

"Because of me, but not by my deeds alone. Tell me of Allocco."

"He lives, he breathes, and waits for you."

"How long has he been waiting?" There is no time in the
borderlands, no more than in a dream.

"Long enough," the captain answers. "The world's grown old,
and Allocco with it. He is no more the man you knew before the
flood, before the fire. When you return, when you see what he is
become, have pity on him, for what he is you made him."

"As I am what he made me. I did not come into the world to do
great deeds. I came so I might feel a summer's breeze upon my face,
the earth beneath my feet. But great deeds I was forced to, great
and terrible."

"You have the choice the rest of us do not. Why will you not
choose to be a man?"

"Because all men must die." Laughter rises out of the dark,
laughter that is very close to weeping. "Two kings by night and day
— one offers oblivion, the other death. I will not choose, and I will
keep my freedom. Tell me that, in my place, you would not do the
same."

There is no answer. There will never be an answer. The thing
aboard the ruined ship is a man no longer though the stars shine on
it and the winds blow on it and the sea bears it on its breast forever.

7: If you are there, show yourself

The fish shall fly and the seas run dry
And the rocks shall melt all in the sun
And the labouring men shall forget their labour
If ever I return again.

I Drew My Ship Across the Harbour, Traditional

The wind and the fear passed away, as the rain passed away, when they stood at last together beneath the black walls of Marac. Though the heath had been full of sleet, here the long light slanted from under storm clouds at the western edge of distance; here the sea, dark as wine, heavy as oil, restless and changeable, thrust itself against the stones of Marac. The potter saw the marks of Liùtha's fingers on his hand and bruises on the piper's wrist where he himself had gripped it on that dark path.

"Well, my friend," muttered Kenu Vanithu, "the winds blowing from Marac were strong: let's hope your heart is stronger." Aloud, he said, "Now you must do what you came here to do. Open the door, lad, your fate's within."

The potter put his hand to the great door, studded and banded in bronze, but it would not yield to him. Then Kenu Vanithu pulled the pipe from the pocket inside his coat and put it to his lips. He played, and his music rose up the walls of Marac as it had filled the gardens of the White City before he sailed away into the west. Sure and nimble danced the fingers of Kenu Vanithu across the pipe, sweet and sad as memories of long ago came forth its music, and Liùtha wept to hear it.

He kisses her gently on her brow, soft and cold as snow upon the meadows. It is all the farewell he will give her. "I renounced the storm and the fire and the knife. I will not take them up again, even for you."

The potter stood silent, forgetting where he was and why as the music flowed around him. Instead he remembered clearly all he had left behind in Ittachar: his potter's bench, his own house, the rippling waters of the burn rushing down the hillside to the sea. Too soon, the music stopped and he found himself again before the grey walls of Marac.

"Don't you listen, you fool. Open the door," Kenu Vanithu muttered. "He's locked his gate against you, lad, but you're a man and the mastery lies with you until the sunset."

Again he put his pipe to his lips to set his music free. This time, when the potter pushed at the oak, the door opened slowly.

Liùtha stepped first across the threshold, putting back her hood to look around her at the courtyard and the keep. "All is the same," she said to the potter at her heel, "though I never saw this place except by starlight."

He held out his hand and she led him across the courtyard through an open door and up the staircase beyond. As they passed through the slanting shadows he thought he glimpsed shapes and figures from the corners of his eyes but, always, when he turned to face them, no one was there.

Up the broad stairs they went, towards lamplight shining from an open doorway. They stepped into a great chamber with windows in the western wall looking out across the sea. On a table in the corner was set a lamp and a flagon of wine and four cups of silver chased with a design of waves.

Three walls of that room were hung with tapestries. There was neither glass nor shutter in the windows to act as checks upon the wind and the west wind blew into the chamber, causing the tapestries to ripple in the lamplight and sway and the figures sewn there to move in a semblance of life. One wall showed the deeps of the sea where fishes swam, and the great grey whales. Across the room, the wall was filled with the birds of the daylight skies: the gulls of the open ocean were there, and hawks hovering on the empty air; a milk-white dove fluttered towards the sun and a curlew flew low across the sea. But, on the cloth hung upon the middle wall, between the sea and the sky, men and women danced beneath a great and lovely rowan tree. Each branch was clad in leaves stitched fine in green and gold and every berry of that tree was a ruby red as a drop of blood. The rowan's roots went down deep into the earth, its branches spread wide across the land to give the dancers shade and shelter from the sun. Great-eyed owls and speckled larks perched within the tree, safe in the canopy of leaves, but a blackbird sat at the rowan's crown, its yellow beak open in song.

The piper gestured to the tree upon the wall. "A strange place you've brought us to, lass. A pretty tale to sing in the future: sunset on the stone and a memory of dancing before the world was changed."

Liùtha flushed and turned away, unwilling to meet his eyes.

The wind from the sea made the tapestries shift; shadows flickered across the walls, waxing large and dark, shrinking back. Kenu Vanithu looked steadily from the window to the point far on the horizon where the sun would dip below the level of the water. At the very moment of the sunset, he said, "If you are there, show yourself."

The lamp on the table guttered and died. The potter saw a man was there, a clot of shadow amongst the shadows in the darkest corner of the room, though he would have sworn that, but a moment before, he had been looking there and there had been no man.

In all the time since Ohmorah the potter had thought much about what manner of creature this Lord of Marac might be. He had seen despair in Assiolo's eyes when he spoke of him, and sadness in the lady's; he had seen Liùtha first frozen with grief and hatred, then burning with something much like madness. He had felt the wind blowing out of Marac and heard the warnings of his death. Now at last he saw the Lord of Marac for himself – yet all he saw at this first sight was a man, a young man and very good to look upon, though he had not a gentle face.

And then the potter looked again, and thought he might have been gentle once but, since then, he had known great suffering.

The Lord of Marac turned his dark gaze to look Liùtha straight in the eye. The hairs rose on the potter's neck as before a thunderstorm, so great was the charge passing between them.

Beyond the window, the stars are very bright and very many. The iron is heavy on her arm, surely heavier here in his domain than by daylight in her mother's house. Her lover puts back her hair from her neck and kisses her. She turns her face to his and pulls the ring from her arm, kissing him so he might not see what she is holding. She takes his left hand and pushes the ring up past his hand onto his arm.

His face writhes. He cries out in agony, a dreadful noise dragged from him by the iron. His voice is no longer that of a man: it is the scream of a seabird struck down, the hiss of the sea boiling, the cry of a falling star. He pushes her away using all his strength against her, twisting his body against the pain. Where the iron has touched him his skin is bubbling into red blisters, smoking as if she had thrust his arm into the fire.

A long while passes. She cowers in the corner of her room, her hands across her face, whimpering with shame and fear. He cannot heed her. With his right hand wrapped in his shirt he pulls at the iron ring and the flesh of his arm tears away with it. He takes the sheet from the bed, soaks it in water from the ewer upon the washstand and wraps it around his arm to soothe the burning and staunch the blood.

"Why did you do this?" His voice is broken; he breathes in great gasping gulps of air. At the agony in his face she hangs her head because, like a child caught out in wickedness, she does not want to see what she has done.

She has no answer worthy of the question. Her mind darts here and there, seeking cover for her folly but she is in a trap of her own making. "The chamberlain deceived me."

"That is a cheating answer. The iron came from Allocco; I know his work. But he could not have given it unasked. You owe me the truth, so I ask again: Why did you do this?"

"I wanted you by day as well as night. I thought it was a little thing, a charm to keep you with me past the sunrise, make you a man as other men. That was all, I swear it — I did not know. Oh my love," she cries out, "can you think I'd choose to hurt you?"

"Iron drives back the borderlands. So has it ever done; so shall it ever do," he says, implacable as sea over stone. "It matters not you did not think. It matters not you did not know. It does not even matter that you love me. The deed is done, and that is all that matters."

Beyond the window, the lights of the city burn and burn and drive away the dark. Beyond the window, the moonlight lies white on the towers of the city wall. The sea is calm and still. Iron drives back the borderlands. At last she sees clearly what he is and so she has her wish indeed. But his heart is circled with a ring of iron; at this time, in this place, she has burned away the part of him that was a man and loved her.

The white dove wakes and flies from her cage into the night.

The master of that place, he who was not a potter nor a man nor a Tion, took up the flask of wine and poured it. "Liùtha, I welcome you again to my domain."

He raised his cup to her, courteous as any great lord but there was an edge of mockery to his courtesy, and, when Liùtha stepped towards him, he moved away. And now the potter saw he was not fair in all ways. His right hand was white and elegant but his left was horribly maimed with little use to it,

three fingers twisted, two missing, and the skin up his arm into his sleeve was warped into a glove of half-healed scars.

"You raised the wind against us," Liùtha said.

"Surely. A reminder and a warning of what was before you. It did not stop you." Again, a mocking smile. "That is more like my memory of you, Liùtha. When I knew you, you were quick to act on your desires."

"I've been taught fear and sorrow and loneliness in seven years. I am no more the girl you knew."

"I remember many things about the lady of Ohmorah's daughter but not self-pity. I too have had the years alone with only my memories to sustain me. For seven years I've clutched at shadows, seeing you sometimes reflected in saltwater. As fair a sight as the sun in all its glory." Now the mocking laughter was clear in his voice, the wild note of one of must laugh or else fall to weeping. "Liùtha, let me show you yourself, as I see you. Let this man of Ittachar see what he has brought to Marac."

At his words, the potter looked towards Liùtha and saw her changed, her face and hands outlined in red and gold, like the glow from the ashes of a fire fanned by the breeze. *No*, came his second thought, *she is not changed*. He had seen her thus before, at midsummer, and thought but the fires that burned.

"This is what Allocco bought with his death: the fire to drive back the borderlands," said the Lord of Marac. "Memory of you is bittersweet, Liùtha. Perhaps, in the end, I shall teach myself the bitter outweighs the sweet."

"Seven years," she said, "I've borne the guilt I was not strong enough to love you as you are or keep alight the little flame the chamberlain snuffed out. Seven years, I was lost in shadows. I hated you, because you left me. I hated myself, because I lived on. I cursed the sunset and the morning because each marked out another night without you in your place beside me."

Again, she stepped towards him; again, the Lord of Marac stepped away. No trace now of laughter in his face, nor yet of sorrow. He raised his ruined hand and his voice bit sharp as frost upon a winter's night. "Why it was I was not there, Liùtha, you know as well as I."

Liùtha's tears were drops of sunlight shining on her cheeks but the Lord of Marac turned from her towards the piper. "Kenu Vanithu, you're a match to me, light to darkness, land to sea. Only you could have given strength to stand against the storm. But then, long ago, after the rowan died, you had strength enough to stand against the flood and flame and close the gates of morning."

The piper met his gaze with all the dignity of one great lord meeting another. "Then, as today, I did what was necessary. I wish it had not been so."

A little pause; a breath of wind; a flickering of shadows. For a moment, only for a moment, the Lord of Marac seemed insubstantial as a dream, then the wind stilled and he was again heavy in his flesh as any man, save for the touch of cold light at his brow.

"I too did only what was needed," he said. "All of us came to ruin on that longest day. Even, perhaps, Averla. For the music you bring to Marac, Kenu Vanithu, and the little space of peace it gives, I thank you. Find welcome and rest a while before your fate drives you on again. It's a weary path you tread across the lands of the world."

"Liùthion," was all the piper said in answer, but, by that greeting and by the starlight in his hair, the potter knew at last what this lord was, and knew too it was impossible. That kindred had slipped sideways into borderlands when the sun rose and the waking world began. They had no flesh that could be maimed; they had no hearts that could be broken. They were air and star; they did not love, they did not live or die.

The Lord of Marac bowed his head to him in welcome and grasped his right hand in his whole one. His touch was cold and firm. "Man of Ittachar: for your great care of Liùtha, I thank you. Eat, drink and be welcome. You will find all you need for comfort nearby. Stay this one night, but by noontime you must leave. I shall not ask your death of you, for all it would give me back my heart's desire. Allocco set too high a price, even for love."

The potter's question must have showed upon his face, for the Lord of Marac asked, "Did Liùtha not tell you what she needed, before you set your foot upon the road to Marac? *Find a man*, Allocco said to her, *who will go into the dark before his time and my fire shall die. Only that will give you your desire.*"

His black eyes wandered back to Liùtha, his face curved into a bitter smile. "I thought not," he said. "You came to Marac because you loved her. Alas, it is so very easy to deceive a lover, for there can never be love without trust."

The potter looked quickly to Liùtha. She flushed to deepest crimson and cast down her eyes. He spoke her name, wanting her to prove she was yet what he had thought her. Instead, her face blank with despair, all trace of hope gone from her voice, she said, "You came to me in Anach. A stranger who'd called a spirit out of the sea, and hope returning burned me. A dark hope, but hope where I'd had none, and so I set out with you to Marac."

He sank upon the floor, sickened she should think so little of his life. Kenu Vanithu's hand, steady and strong as on the heath, clasped his shoulder. "Her first thought, lad; hold off judgement until you know her last."

"I think we should delay further talk, lest any of us forget ourselves." The Lord of Marac spoke out of the shadow as to foolish children. "You've had a long journey, Liùtha, you and your protector, and the way has been rough. You've waited seven years to come to me, wait a little longer to refresh yourself and rest."

The wind blew into the room from the sea that lay between the evening and the borderlands; the shadows billowed and twisted round the room and, when they were still, the Lord of Marac was gone.

The piper lit the lamp and took a cup of wine; he offered another to the potter, who shook his head and would not drink. Instead, he sat with his back against the wall, his heart heavy with new knowledge.

"This is not what I expected," he said to Liùtha. "Yet now I recall quite plainly: Assiolo warned me against you, and, like a fool, I did not heed him."

Liùtha's eyes were bright with tears. The piper smiled and gently took her hand. "The Liùthion had it a-right, lass: now's not the time for talk when feet are tired and bellies empty. Best show us where we can wash and dress and find food if he'll grant it. I can wait a while longer before you tell your tale; wine and food are good and, after the wilds, to wash is best of all."

She nodded, wiped away the traces of her grief and led them though the empty halls of Marac. Empty at the first sight, and at the second, but, always, there were whispers at the edge of hearing or else a flicker, seen only from the corner of their eyes, as from the flap of someone's coat. The potter swung around, his arms outstretched, clutching at shadows. "If you are there, show yourselves."

The piper laughed. "There's nothing there, lad; 'tis but dreams and fancies taking shape within a waking mind. But it's well for us he's strength enough yet to give substance to the thought or we'd have a cold and hungry time here."

"And if I eat and if I drink?" the potter asked, old tales rising to his mind.

"You'll have a full stomach and a wet throat." The piper's hand was a warm touch on his arm, steady in the midst of strangeness. "Aye, lad, I can guess your thought, and you're not far wrong. Don't fret on it: you're bound so close already 'twill make no difference if you take the comfort offered."

Liùtha paused before a door and the potter, shrugging, opened it.

"Long ago, when even Allocco was young, I came out of borderlands to walk the waking world. The pleasure to be found in flesh is very great. In this world I can walk with flowering trees above my head, brown earth beneath my feet, with white flowers to delight my eyes; I can eat and drink, love and make love. Yet Allocco turned towards Averla and brought such ruin to your world I fled from it, thankful to be done with men and the life of men."

"You could have broken Allocco with a word, any time this sixmonth past. You should have done so."

"Now you are no more a child you must not think as a child, you must not speak as a child." His voice strengthens and she hears in his words that he knows more of the world than she does. It is too much: she wants to hear only the voice of the man who loves her.

He turns from her to look for a long, long time upon the sea and the sky beyond the city, at the first grey light leaking across the night. The day will come and who can tell what will come after, beyond the fact of sunrise. He will be gone with the dawning, perhaps forever.

"Allocco knew from the moment I stepped from my ship onto the quay I could break him with a word. It was such words led to destruction long ago. I shall not speak them because I did so once before, in another time and place, when I was another man."

He takes her chin in his hand and forces her to look at him. She sees the pain in his face, the wreck she has made of his left arm. Both these are far harder to look upon than his rage. That he has put aside; she sees he is weeping and holds up her hand to his tears.

"We were safe, you and I," he says. "As long as we kept faith with each other his hatred had no power to hurt us. I love you," he says, "but love is no longer enough. You have not yet seen me as I am. For you," he says, "I wanted only to be a man, to let my past lie with the dead in the depths of the sea. But I am not a man, and now, because of you, my past cannot lie hidden."

The wind blows across the sea, the stars fade from the sky and he is gone, leaving behind his blood upon the bedsheet and the weight of iron upon her heart.

Later, later, she looks down into the garden and sees the white dove perched amidst the apples of her mother's tree. She calls to her, holding corn out on her open hands. The dove will not come. Instead with a flutter of wings she flies from the garden up into a sky beset with storm clouds.

It was as the piper had said: the wine and the food were good but to wash was best of all. When he had washed the sea and the mire away the potter dressed in the plainest of the clothes he found within an oaken kist and went down the hallway to find Kenu Vanithu.

The dwarf sat in a shuttered chamber before a hearth made ready for a fire, a cup of wine to his hand. His blue coat was clean but seemed no less tattered than before. Kenu Vanithu nodded to the potter to sit, and himself knelt to the hearth to strike a spark and conjure it to life.

"Iron and fire keep back the borderlands, and here are both," he said with a half-smile, slipping the strike-light back into his pocket as the flames flickered and bit into dry wood. "Let's speak between ourselves first, lad, you, I and Liùtha. When you know all and can see your way, you can seek out the master of this place. It's time for you to know what you're to face, and why."

"That's the tale untold I'm waiting for," the potter said, grim and bitter now he knew Liùtha a deceiver and himself a fool. "There's danger and death all about. I've learned my lesson and, from now on, I'll be wary."

"We came into the world telling stories, we are dreams and tales as much as flesh and blood," said Kenu Vanithu. "This Lord of Marac? He's no more a man than I am. He was liùthion before the sun rose. His dancing had no weight upon the waking world and yet see what's followed in his wake."

"When I was a child, I was told stories of the borderlands. I forgot most of them once childhood passed."

"Forgot them, lad?" The Tion turned his dreadful face, his golden eyes to him. "You've not forgot the tales of Ittachar, Almecu mor Thorrian."

The potter bowed his head beneath that gaze. For it was true, as all Kenu Vanithu said was true. He had put aside the stories he had heard, not forgotten them. Now he called to mind tales told by his mother of the times when it was not wise to stray too far from the fireside. For in the long night of midwinter, a straying lass or lad might hear music and glimpse dancers in the dark, faint as the light of distant stars. Singing voices would call out of the night and then longtimes they were not seen in Ittachar or any other western land. Yet in the end, and it might be in a twelvemonth or else a hundred years, they would be found wild and wandering, crying out for the dance they danced no more. They had drunk water beneath another sky and forgotten the world. They had eaten apples beneath unknown stars and forgotten their names. No age had come upon them in their absence, although the little children they left behind might be grandams great with years when they returned. But nevermore did such things happen, except in stories told to children.

"He did not seem much like one of that kindred, if the old tales are true," the potter said at last. "Those dancers are gone from our lands if they were ever in them. Now only the wind from the sea blows in the night time."

"There's always truth in the bones of a story," said Kenu Vanithu, "even if the flesh is decked out in fancy to catch the ear. Why he is as you've seen him is the tale you'll hear this night, and what comes of it, for you and him and her, is the story not yet told. I know what this Lord of Marac was; I know what he may be, if you have the strength Allodola believed you do. Death is the price of life, Almecu mor Thorrian. So has it ever been, so will it ever be."

It is the evening of the equinox and the world is spinning to its moment of balance, the still point before everything is changed. A black-backed gull wheels above the shore while the last light, the long light, slides from under dark clouds across the land and the sea. There is a terrible brightness in that light; the western sky is gold and red and darkest blue, the sea ripples with reflected gold. On the land the shadows are hard and black and long. Behind and above the grey shore loom the walls of the city her mother has built. But now she is outside the city and the laws of the lady have no writ below the shoreline.

She watches the seagull, its white underwings burning in the sunset. It soars across the bay and settles on the tall mast of a ship. She sees the dazzling brightness of the light upon the sea as the sun touches the water and drowns. She counts one hundred heartbeats, listening to the little sounds of the water against the shingle. In the gloaming a curlew calls, once, twice, three times. Each time the same two notes, lonely, lovely, floating on the evening wind from the sea. Perfect, unexpected beauty that tears her heart and leaves it desolate. When the curlew falls silent, she shudders, a sigh escapes her. Death is close, and fear is closer.

Then, as the last sliver of the sun is devoured, the chamberlain says quietly, "If you are there, show yourself."

Her lover stands upon the shore to face the chamberlain, who has been waiting for him like a hooded crow. She sees the old man try to meet his stare but his gaze slides sideways, as repelling magnets slip past each other and never touch.

The chamberlain speaks, whispering into the wind, and the Lord of Marac must lean close to catch his words. "The iron is in your flesh, Liùthion; Lyikené is closed to you even as its apples ripen. I have written your destruction on the wind, sure as the sun rises in the eastern sky."

"You know what I am. You have seen what I have done," says the Lord of Marac. "Even now, I can call down death upon you, Allocco; even now, I can stop your heart with a word. Here, outside stone walls where the wind blows free between the sky and sea, the very elements obey me if I choose."

The chamberlain laughs into a wind that does no more than flap his black coat around him. "Then why did you not raise up a storm against me before I sent this child against you? It is true, you have that strength. But long ago I learnt to understand war. I can judge a warrior and a weapon. I know when a blow will come and when my enemy is feinting. If I could not do this, I would have died long ago."

He reaches out to the Lord of Marac and plucks the lady's silver brooch from his collar. "You will not do this again, Liùthion, you will not stand against me."

As the light softens after the setting of the sun, as the sky fades from red to mother-of-pearl, her lover looks less like a man than he had within the city. As the stars above flicker into life, his nature shines from the flesh he wears. His face is pale; his black hair blows around his face like smoke. She cannot now look into his eyes for they are darker than the night. He puts back his hair from his face and holds out his empty hands, the whole one and the broken, to the chamberlain.

"Only where there is necessity is there no choice," he says. "I will not kill again, Allocco; not even you, not even because you used my love against me."

He takes her hand. She feels the wind about her, strong as his loving arms. The last red light of sunset grows dim in her eyes and the other sea lies before her silvered by starlight. Alas, only for a heartbeat, for the chamberlain catches up the iron ring and slips it round her wrist to bind her to the earth so that the wind, however hard it blows, cannot carry her away. For a moment, the two balance her fate between them, hatred matched against love in a game neither can win. Then the Lord of Marac lets go of her hand and says to the chamberlain, "Before you make your choice, Allocco, remember mine."

He kisses her gently on her brow, soft and cold as snow upon the meadows. It is all the farewell he will give her. "I renounced the storm and the fire and the knife. I will not take them up again, even for you."

Kenu Vanithu took time to build up the fire anew, letting the potter gather his thoughts. He drank his wine and stared into the red of the fire and the black of the night until, at last, the potter asked, "Liùtha loved him? This half-man, this creature from the borderlands?"

"She loves him still. You heard the price of her desire: it is a man's life."

"Does my oath bind me to this?" the potter cried. "Is it reason to ask me to give up my life so another might have the woman I love?"

"I never yet saw that reason and love had much to do with one another," the dwarf observed. "I've heard no great tale of love that ended happily. It may be this one is no different from the rest."

"It is too much to give up the sunlight and my hope of home."

"Oh, this is a thing must be done willingly or not at all. If that's your thought, go back to your pots, lad, take up your clay and be again a potter. Forget your promise and your love and all you've seen of the world. Go home to Ittachar, a land of much peace and little greatness beside the western sea where all your joys and fears are small ones. A long life, and a quiet one, awaits you there."

The potter closed his eyes and conjured memories of Ittachar, his cottage by the cabbage field and the light upon the sea. A good place; always and always, a good place.

The two sat a while in silence, each alone in his own thoughts, until the piper stirred up the fire and poured himself another cup of wine. "I would I were a man with such a life before me," he said. "Long ago, I lost my name, my home, all I could call my own. I will not die a gentle death, nor yet find peace beneath this sky. Yet once I was the piper at the gates of morning. I sat beneath the rowan tree and made my music with Averla before ever she looked upon Allocco."

Kenu Vanithu's voice dropped to a whisper and the potter remembered the rainy night upon the heath. He had seen clearly after all.

"Such ill came of their meeting, to him, to me, to all the world," the piper told him. "And yet my greatest grief is to know I will not hear her sing again nor watch her comb out her golden hair. Instead, I must walk all the ways of the waking world where my face brings ill-fortune and people do not care to hear my songs."

When first they met the potter had seen Kenu Vanithu only as a ragged beggar-musician. That was what he was, but it was not all that he was. Even so, it was easy to forget his nature, to forget it had been he who closed the gates of morning.

"Tell me true, Kenu Vanithu, what is it you'd have me do?" he asked, quietly.

Kenu Vanithu smiled his twisted smile that was more like a grimace but for the light shining in his golden eyes. "Trust your own heart, your own strength and will; consider what it is you truly desire. Beyond that, lad, I can offer nothing. I've seen such sights and done such things your heart would break to know them."

"Your words oftentimes are bleak," the potter said, "but I have heard your music. There is no bleakness there; it is as full of life as a blackbird in the springtime. When you play, your pipe sings of the sweetness in the world, the love and the beauty, not the dark."

"Aye, I saw your face in Anach. Many listen to my music but few hear it. I'm broken in this life, a crippled, half-made thing, so foul to look upon most turn from me, but, before I was anything else, I too was a master of my craft." He took the potter's hand in a strong, warm grip. "I've said before, lad, like knows like. Allodola saw it, and so do I."

But the potter was not comforted; Liùtha's fire had burned him and his oath was a knifeblade twisting in his heart.

Though all else is lost to her she will not forget this day, the day after the equinox. Much of it she spends in her mother's garden by the fish pool, sitting there all the afternoon though it is a drear, dreich day; a few cold spots of rain fall on her now but she does not care. No day could be as bleak as her heart or cold as the iron about her arm. She longs for love, for sanctuary, but her mother is not here. She cannot speak with her of these things until after midwinter when she returns from the Southern Reaches. Whilst she is gone, the chamberlain is her regent. It is always thus.

And so, although she is within the boundary of her mother's house, although she is her mother's daughter, she does not think that she is safe.

Late in the afternoon, the chamberlain comes to her. He sits at her side beneath the rowan tree and drops her mother's silver brooch into her lap. Now she knows its meaning: liùthion dancing forever in the borderlands, those lonely, lovely lands where she cannot go. From this day she must live without him and at last the tears run hot out of her eyes.

"I have made walls to keep out the wind," the old man says. "I have lit lamps to drive back the dark."

"Why do you hate him so?" she cries out. "What harm did he do that you cannot forgive him?"

"Allodola has brought you up a fool, if you ask that," hisses the chamberlain. "We were born in the utter east, the First People when the world was young. The sunlight was warm upon us as we made the land our own. But the sun rises, the sun sets, the days are counted out, and we had such a little time before the darkness took us. It was not enough.

"Then the Liùthion came from the borderlands, free of time, free of death. And, when he would not, Averla showed me what men could be: greater than the dancers in the borderlands, more enduring than the Tions. I stopped the sun at noontime to make a day last forever, so we might also dance the dance that has no end.

"The Liùthion dared stand against me, though the lives of men are no concern of the borderlands. He called upon the wind and sea, and they rose up against us. I was torn from Averla's arms, my fire was quenched and my son drowned; now darkness creeps upon me as on lesser men."

"You made me betray him. You used my fear," she says, not loud. "You spoke truly in this garden: it is very easy to deceive a lover."

"I have lived a long time awaiting my revenge. All I loved, the Liùthion tore from me. All I desired, he denied to me. I do not forgive; I do not forget." He stands and takes her hand to lead her into her mother's house. "On the day you took him as your lover, I put from my mind you were your mother's daughter. A life he owes to me, a life I'll take from him. That will be the beginning — the ending will come after midwinter."

"Well, lad, you're here and so am I. Best you know the whole at last," said the piper, settling himself again before the fire. "I shall begin, and Liùtha shall continue in her turn..."

The potter paced the room between the windows and the door, unable to be still now he knew at last the web in which he was entangled.

"Long ago," said Kenu Vanithu, "when the world was young, the liùthion, the kindred of the borderlands, came sometimes out of the empty land, walking beneath our stars like men, like women. This tale began when one of them came to love this world as we who are born to it love it. He loved the weight of it, its substance; for him, as for us, it was real, not the echo of a dream. Alone of all his kindred, he ate and drank with the peoples of the waking world; what was ours he took for himself. No longer was he only air and starlight: he too had weight and substance, almost like a man.

"In the east the First People came to know him, Allocco and Allodola among them. But, when they knew what he was, they grew envious because they must die and he would not. Allocco stopped the sun at noontime so he and those he loved might live forever. Though by his deeds the rowan died, though with its death, we lost our protection against fear and hatred and false hope, though the light beyond the gate spilt into the waking world and set his land a-burning, Allocco cared not. In his greed for life, he broke the world and counted it well done."

This was the tale the potter had heard in the White City. He knew now it had been the Liùthion who had called a wave to quench that fire, who had made sure that light would flicker into darkness.

"And Averla?" the potter asked, knowing only broken tales of a golden witch, fire made flesh, light beyond light from borderlands east of the sunrise.

Kenu Vanithu paused and drained his cup. When he next spoke, his voice was empty as the wind upon bare stone. "Of her, I do not know and cannot tell. Maybe she is in the world, maybe she is out of it. After the fire, after the flood, all I could do was close the gate and make a new balance this side of the sunrise."

The potter stood beside the fire and held his wine forgotten in his hand. His world shrank down to four stone walls, the firelight and this voice. The blackbird and the sunlight in the garden were long ago and far away. Death was close, and fear was closer. Fear of where the deeds of others might force him.

The door opened and Liùtha came in. She had also set aside the stained clothes of travel and wore a gown of green and silver. The potter stepped back as she crossed the room so her shadow would not fall upon him.

Maybe she would have spoken, for sure the potter meant to, but Kenu Vanithu shook his head, commanding silence.

"With his flesh still on him, the Liùthion fled back to his own kindred, seeking the starlight and the stone, the wind upon the water, but no one can do such deeds and be unchanged," he said, his face made terrible by the play of fire and shadows over it. "The Liùthion fled the world, but could not escape what he'd become: less than a spirit, more than a man. He had killed, and he could not forget the faces of the dead. Because of this, because he lived, because life calls out to life, he came again from borderlands beyond the sunset and made himself the Lord of Marac."

Liùtha flinched. Kenu Vanithu saw it and said, "You need not look at my foul face. I'll turn my face from the light. Close your eyes if you want to. My voice is all I need this night."

"It is not you I turn from but this tale of yours. I've heard it before, in other times and places, and see no need for twicetold tales."

Liùtha's voice was steady but as she spoke she poured out wine and drank it fast, filling her cup a second time when she was done.

The piper said, "You've heard this tale before, you say, Liùtha? Of course, you have: it is your own story. Do not dismiss a twicetold tale." His voice rang out sharp with an authority he had not shown before. "You'll tell this man your story. The truth is what you owe him now. No more secrets, lass. Tonight he must know plain if the end he sought is the one he will find."

But Liùtha drank her wine, keeping her silence, and, after a moment, Kenu Vanithu took up the tale again. "The Liùthion came to the White City where those from the broken land had remade their lives. In Allodola, he found his friend restored. In Liùtha, he found – well, lad, that she can tell you better than I."

"But more than my mother, more even than me, he found Allocco," said Liùtha, flattening her voice to hide her feeling. "He is the matter of this tale."

"Aye, lass, he's the heart of it," Kenu Vanithu said, softly. "Alas it is, some broken things cannot be mended. Your mother trusted him and for many years he was worthy of her trust: her chamberlain, her councillor, her friend. Together they built the city; together they ruled it with justice and honour. But still the rowan tree was dead and nothing could protect Allocco from himself. He nursed his hatred and his loss across the years until not the city he had built, not Allodola his friend, not even the tree your father planted, were enough to balance them."

The chamberlain himself thrusts her into her chamber, then gives his orders. The window is nailed fast and the shutters also, so she is in darkness although without the walls it is not yet sunset.

"He will come back for me," she cries. "I'm bound to him until the ending of the world."

"Let him come. The window is barred, the door is locked. He will not get in."

They lock the door on her. The silver cage hangs yet in the blocked window. Soon she hears the flutter of wings beating against the shutter. Later, she hears a great wind, a storm, a tempest, sweep down upon her mother's house, making the walls shake. She pulls at the sealed shutters till her fingers bleed, crying "I am here, I am here!" but they will not yield and though the storm winds howl in despair she cannot let them in. Before the night is over, the gale drops and, exhausted, she sleeps and, sleeping, she dreams.

In her dream the Lord of Marac is with her. She feels no joy, only dread. His face is sad and stern, as it had been the last time they were together. One hand is whole, the other broken, and between them he holds the white dove, her wings trailing from his fingers. She cannot tell if the blood on the white feathers is hers, or his.

"The way is barred. The dove is dead."

She cries, "Not by my hand!" and reaches out to take the dove.

"That this is done is enough to give it meaning. I cannot come to you again." He turns away. "You must come to me."

She wakes screaming for him, but her room is dark and quiet.

In the morning, the chamberlain opens the door. She rushes past him down into the garden and there, beneath her window, the white dove lies dead upon the ground, half buried in the dried leaves that have drifted up against the wall. Weeping, weeping, she runs to the gate but it is barred and the guard will not let her pass.

She turns back to the chamberlain. "You killed her," she cries out. "You have no right to keep me prisoner here. But it is no use: he will come back for me."

"Listen to me," he says. "You cannot love the wind, the sea will drown you. The one you loved has left you. The guards have orders not to let you pass the gate. I shall keep you close until Allodola returns."

He leaves her, still holding the dove, still weeping.

Liùtha stretched out her hand to the fire, so close the heat must have become pain. Kenu Vanithu gently pulled back her hand from the flames. She gripped his fingers, drawing her strength from him, as on the road by day.

"Adventure you have found, Almecu mor Thorrian," Liùtha said, "but not the one you looked for."

The potter did not want to look at her, knowing she was false and wanting. He had always thought her lovely but now he saw her dressed to match her beauty and that her transformation measured out the distance between them: she was a fine lady of the White City and he but a man who had meddled with powers he did not understand. He had seen her turn towards the Lord of Marac, like a flower to the sun; he knew how she had tricked and ill-used him and, likewise, her mother, who had let him take on this quest without a word of what it was like to cost him. His heart cried out against them both who used men's lives so lightly.

So he tried to look only at the wine in his cup or the fire in the hearth, but, over and again, found he could not help but glance towards Liùtha. Each time he cursed his folly, but then he saw the fear in her face and, despite himself, she was again the girl who had sat upon the harbour wall and clung, frightened, to his hand across the heath to Marac.

"Three times," she said, "I warned you against me, Almecu mor Thorrian; three times you would not heed me. I told you the world was dangerous when first we met in Anach; I told you it was a dangerous thing to love me. Today, I told you plainly to turn aside on the road and go safely home. Each time you cast aside my warning you took a step closer to your death."

She laughed then, as she had laughed at midsummer, a heartless laughter that must end in tears. "This is where your good intentions and your kind heart have brought you, a place where all roads lead into the dark."

"That is enough!" The potter broke into her laughter, letting his anger strike at her because he loved her. "Let us speak honestly at last, Liùtha. You thought to use my love to betray me to my death, as you betrayed the Lord of Marac. Now I see the danger in oaths and in adventures. Assiolo told me I must decide a man must die. And I will not. I will not die for you: it's not by my blood you will live happy ever after."

He finds her where his father left her, in the garden of her mother's house. She sits upon the bench beneath the rowan staring with empty eyes into the water. He says her name. She raises her head to look at him, then turns back to the water and the fading lilypads, to the fish gleaming gold and red in the dark pool. He touches her face and finds it cold as the stone.

"How long have you sat here?" he asks, and wraps her in his coat.

"Since the white dove died." Her whisper is dry as the leaves about her feet. "The dove is dead and he is gone."

Three months he has longed for this; three months he has willed her lover to return to the starlight; three months he has dreamed of driving him from her but now he is gone the wreckage left behind sickens him.

He reaches out and takes the dove. He settles the stiff feathers of her wings back into their places, he strokes the downy feathers of her breast back to smoothness, but he can do no more. So he kneels beneath the apple tree and digs with his hands in the earth, then makes a nest of fallen leaves within the hole. Gently, he lays the dove upon it and scatters rowan berries over her before he presses the cold earth back. She watches and says no word, huddled in his coat beneath the tree that is only a rowan, that offers no sanctuary from fear.

He takes her cold hands in his soiled ones. "Come and get warm," he says, and leads her back into her mother's house. He calls for hot drinks and a stone to warm her feet; he makes her sit by the fireside and covers her in a shawl. Soon she starts to shiver and he kneels at her side.

"I loved him, and he left me." He has to strain his ears to hear her. "The stars shone on the sea, the wind blew across the water, he kissed me in farewell and left me."

"I am here," he says, putting his arms around her. "I shall not leave you. There is no need for fear. I shall stay with you and keep you safe."

She rests her head against his shoulder and he holds her close, his heart beating out the time until the sunset.

"Your first thought is against her," said Kenu Vanithu, steadily, quietly, a stone that would not shift however hard the stream beat against it. He had not let go of Liùtha's hand. "That's fair enough, lad. Take time to catch your breath and let your second thought be more measured."

"You do not see her treachery?"

"I see that, at sixteen, she was caught between the two who between them broke the world. What chance had she?"

To that question, the potter had no answer, but he felt the meshes of the net he was caught in tangle ever tighter. Liùtha was silent for a little time, gathering her thoughts. Then she shook her head against some memory and went on, "I've heard you repeat the tale you were told in the White City, Almecu mor Thorrian, but did you truly think to love me?"

The potter nodded.

"Then you are a fool because I have a lovely face." She near spat out her words, and he recoiled from such hatred, for all it was not meant for him. "You asked the night we met what the Lord of Marac was to me? For a while, the sun, the moon and stars were nothing next to him. Love answered love in the summertime.

"You'd have my past? It's quickly told: I loved the Lord of Marac, as ever woman loved her man. But fear came in, where love had been, and his enemy used my fear as a weapon against him. Fear calls out to mistrust, one betrayal begets another. I burned a creature of the borderlands with iron; in return, he gave me to his enemy. A life he owed to him, a life he left him free to take, and only Assiolo was left to stand between them. He loved me and he pitied me but love and pity are weak weapons against men like his father. As well try to turn back the tide with a wall of sand."

Liùtha stared into the red heart of the fire and the potter saw sparks flicker in her hair. Her voice dropped to a whisper, "Yet in the end, Allocco's hatred was so great not even a life was enough to sate it. He ran his stolen fire in me – fire drives back the borderlands surely as iron. In hatred, he lived; in hatred, he died, and used his death to set the quenching of that fire at a man's life."

Letting go of Kenu Vanithu's hands, Liùtha stood up to face the potter's anger, meeting the judgement in his eyes without this time flinching. Her wild laughter had died away; she had pulled her mask of frost across her face to cover her despair. "There's one thing more to tell. My thoughts were black and red in Anach when you found me. When we met, I thought to use you and so I did not tell all the truth. But, before even we reached Ountrie, I'd begun to doubt my purpose. As your love brought me back into my life, I knew I could not call you to your death. Some prices are too high to bear."

Letting his anger die away, thinking as he spoke, the potter answered slowly, "You spoke truly today, up on the heath, Liùtha, whatever you'd thought before. You offered me my freedom, and I chose my love. We'd not have made it through the storm had you not put such thoughts from your heart."

The piper smiled as he sipped the last of his wine, but Liùtha asked, "What can a potter of Ittachar know of these things?"

"Here, I am far from Ittachar. Here, I am not a potter: you admit as much each time you use my name. I know because I am a man. You're not the first woman I've kissed but you are the first I've loved. I'll not turn away because you are afraid. Liùtha, open your eyes! This is only the end if you hide behind your fear."

She ran from him, from the love in his eyes and the truth in his words, and her footsteps echoed down the empty halls.

He writes his letter in a common alehouse. When it is done, he sits and stares as his words writhe and twist before his eyes.

"My father has forgot his love for sake of his revenge ... banished with iron ... made prisoner in your own house...

"Madam, he has blinded men's sight and deafened men's ears... Only I can see clearly his intent...

"For your daughter's sake and mine, return."

The weight of the future presses down upon him, heavy as water. He picks up his pen and signs his name, watching the flourishes twirl across the page as if his own hand were a stranger's. Then he folds and seals the letter, leaving the smooth wax unmarked since he has not been granted his own seal and dare not use his father's.

He carries it himself down to the harbour, asking about and about until he finds a ship bound to the Southern Reaches. Its master stares and scrapes, in awe of his name and his degree, honoured to bear a letter from the chamberlain's son to the lady.

"How soon can you be away?" he asks the man, cutting through his obsequity. "This letter must reach the lady quick as can be."

"On the morning tide, if the wind does not turn from that quarter."

The wind blows cold and stiff out of the north. All across the sea, little waves are dancing and the flag at the masthead flutters briskly, a gay gold pennant crossed over and again with black.

"What chance of that?" he asks, aghast such a thing must be governed by the elements.

"No chance at all." The master laughs, certain of his craft and skill, and claps him on the shoulder. "We'll be in the southlands within a tennight, never fear, and your letter with us."

Yet, even as he walks up the road towards the gate, the wind drops away to nothing. A dead calm falls across the afternoon, no breath of wind to lift the banners at the gatehouse or play like a cat's paw across the water. He stands beneath the walls and looks back to sea a glassy mirror to an empty sky.

A curlew calls across the silence, once, twice and again, and cold sweat breaks upon his brow.

8: Love with its back broken

You crave one kiss of my cold clay lips
My breath smells earthly strong
If you've one kiss of my cold clay lips
Your time will not be long.

The Unquiet Grave, Traditional

Later, later, unable to rest within his chamber, the potter walked through the night, down the empty corridors of the domain of Marac that echoed always with the whistle of the wind and the rising of the sea. As he walked, his fear walked with him, fear of what others had done, of what he himself might do. At last he came to the room of tapestries and saw Liùtha there already, in lamplight by the window, looking out across the starless sea. He would have gone his way through the black halls but then came again the sudden breeze, the shifting shadows.

Liùtha said softly to the darkness, "If you are there, show yourself," and the Lord of Marac was there, if he had not been there before, unseen. The potter shrank back in the shadows between the tapestries, curious to see how the lovers met again.

The steward meets him at the doorway of his father's house. Taking his hat and coat, the man says, "The master's compliments, my lord, and would you wait upon him in his study."

His father sits behind his desk, his papers squared to right and left, holding a little book open at the flyleaf and his pen in his right hand. "Sit down, Assiolo." His voice is dry and cold, conjuring memories of childhood. He does not look up. The letter lies unopened, its seal unbroken, on the desk in front of him.

He takes the chair beside the desk. His father puts his pen back in its stand and lays the open book aside. The silence between them is measured out in his quick heartbeats, broken only by the sound of his blood pounding in his ears. His father turns towards some papers; he turns his eyes towards the book. A single word, a woman's name, flows across the page in his father's fine hand. The ink is wet still, glossy as a raven's wing. He reads the word upside down, over and over. It has no meaning in his mind and yet he cannot draw his eyes away. The ink dries slowly in the following silence, silky sleekness deadening to rusty black.

At last his father points one long finger towards the letter. "The man I took this from is dead."

No less than he expected but his stomach knots, remembering the man's pride in his task. After a moment, his father says, "I shall ensure his widow receives the death fee, since he died in the service of the city."

He reaches out and picks up his letter. "That price I shall pay myself, since I sent him to that death."

His father shrugs. "As you desire."

The ink is dry now, a pattern of lines and curves against the creamy whiteness of the page. He reads the name again and yet again, sounding its syllables in his mind to still his thoughts and check his rage.

"Assiolo," his father says, "do not attempt again to send that letter, or any other like it. Allodola will return after midwinter. When she returns, you may tell any tale you choose — the whole truth, if you wish it — but, until that day, remember ships can sink, the earth can shake, lightning strike without warning from a clear sky. Remember there are many ways for a man to die."

His father pauses and looks up, fixing him with his gaze. He cannot move, he cannot speak, he can scarce even breathe.

"The man who carried that letter died quickly, without pain or fear, between one heartbeat and the next. Next time," his father says, "it shall be otherwise. Next time," he says, bright eyes blazing, blue as the midsummer sky and as merciless, "it will be your part to watch and learn how much a man can bear before all that makes him a man is stripped away, leaving nothing but a lump of flesh screaming its agony to the four winds."

His breath comes quick and ragged as his father turns away, picks up his pen and dips it in the ink to write his own name below the other. This time he scatters sand across to blot it carefully. He looks up, a grey man in a grey coat; all passion gone; all fire hidden within his flesh. "You may go, Assiolo. I have said all that is needful."

He stands, as he is bid, and bows his head from courtesy and habit. Within the book, he sees the black name and the grey coupled forever on the page. His father pours away the sand, shuts up the book and lays it aside. It is a pretty thing, clad in bright silk broidered all across with summer flowers, lilies and roses, lavender and thyme.

He cannot help but ask, "Who is she?"

"A woman I knew once," his father answers, reaching for the minutes of the Assembly. "I write, sometimes. She is fond of flowers."

He pauses, wondering if there is more, but his father's eyes are fixed upon his work, his father's pen scratches across his paper. He tears his letter into two and casts the pieces on the fire. Then he goes out, closing the door behind him.

"I did you wrong," Liùtha whispered, "and sorely have I suffered for it. Surely you cannot think I meant to hurt you?"

"No," said the Lord of Marac, his bitter smile again upon his lips. "I do not think it. But still the deed was done; still Allocco had the mastery."

"When he was dead, I called to you. The wind blew, your ship dissolved to seafoam and driftwood, and I called to you out of my grief. I had not hated you until that night, when I called and you did not answer. Why did you not come back for me?"

"The way was barred. The dove was dead."

She cried, "Not by my hand!" and reached out to him.

"That it was done was enough to give it meaning. I could not come to you again: it was your part to come to me," he said, stepping away. His smile had gone; his face was set and cold.

"What hope had I to find you?"

"You had hope enough when a fool came by in search of his adventure," he answered, drily. "Have you become so much like Allocco you think my love can be bought with a man's life?"

She flushed and shook her head. "I was indeed Allocco's creature when Almecu mor Thorrian found me, full of shame and guilt. I thought to use him and found instead he was my light in darkness. He gave me his strength; his certainty cut through my doubt; his love drove back my hatred. He loves me too well to take the easy road when the storm rises against him. Today he walked towards his death rather than turn from me, although he knew I did not love him."

The potter in the shadows heard her words, and knew all of them were true.

Beyond the city, the light lingers in the west. The chamberlain's son pulls his coat tightly around him and shivers in the wind that blows cold from the sea as the light drains from the day. When at last the stars are bright above him, he stands on the tideline and says to the wind and the sea, "If you are there, show yourself."

The Lord of Marac steps out of the shadows below the city wall. He asks, "Son of my enemy, are you my enemy?"

The young man stoops to light his lantern and holds it high to let it cast its light across the shore towards the half-made man. The Lord of Marac stands at the edge of brightness, his face drawn by pain and loss, and he sees how much he has changed from the time when he walked freely down the streets of the White City.

"I have no iron and only this little flame. I came to talk with you," says the chamberlain's son. *"I know what you did not do, Liùthion, upon the equinox. Now you've had a month alone to think on it, I've come to ask if your second thought is better than your first?"*

"When she steps beyond stone walls to find me, I shall be waiting."

"You left her to my father."

"She gave herself into his hands when she put his bond upon my arm. She made her choice and, here on the seashore, I made mine."

"There will be a child."

The Lord of Marac shakes his head. "There will be no child."

"It lives! It grows!"

"There will be no child," the Lord of Marac says again. *"Have you not listened to your father's words?"*

The starlight shines upon his hair, the lamplight shines upon his face, but neither the starlight nor the lamplight reaches his eyes: no light can lift the darkness at his core. Before the Lord of Marac speaks again he sighs, a whisper of breath upon the wind. "There is always a price," he says at last, very quietly. *"This is the price we pay for broken faith, she and I."*

He bends his head and looks down at his hands, the whole one and the broken; when he looks up, he is weeping. "Allocco will take its life from me, if he chooses. There are many tales that are never told, many lives that are never lived."

"And yet you say you love her."

"What do you know of love?" Suddenly, all gentleness is gone from the Lord of Marac's face. His words fall into the silence, hard and sharp as diamonds, though tears are still shining on his face. *"You are like any young man who has not yet lived his life. Do you think love is a gentle thing, a white flower to delight you, a light in the night time to shine upon you? That is a part of love, but not the whole, not even the greater part. Love is more beautiful and terrible than you yet know: that is why it is not enough to keep us safe. Because love breeds hatred, Allocco seeks his revenge; because love breeds fear, she gave it to him; because love breeds hope, I leave him free."*

"Love is all I have to give her," he answers, hating the Lord of Marac, hating the truths he speaks.

"It was all I had too, for her and for Allocco. I cannot keep faith with all I love and so I shall be what I desire and not what they would make me."

"If you were a man, you would make a different choice."

"Allocco is a man: look to his choices. Which of us would you follow?" The Lord of Marac looks into his eyes, beyond his eyes into his mind. "You know the price of this child's life: will you pay it? Do you have the will, do you have the strength?" His words rise like a nightmare out of the dark. "How will you kill him, Assiolo? In a fight, your blood screaming in your ears? In the night time, slipping across the room on stockinged feet to stab him in his sleep? By daylight, a smile upon your face and poison in the cup you offer?"

"You'd make me do what you would not," he cries out to this creature wrought of wind and darkness. "You had him at your mercy, here on the seashore, your enemy who hated you, and you did not strike him down. Yet you'd urge me beyond the point you would not pass and make me into the thing you would not be."

The chamberlain's son swings up his lantern and sees the Lord of Marac flinch from the flame burning within it.

The Lord of Marac says no word, he makes no move, but the candle gutters suddenly within the lantern. In the darkness after the light, he steps across the space between them and his feet make no noise upon the shingle. He takes the left hand of the chamberlain's son and studies its palm in the faint starlight as his father might have done, had he been any other man. His touch is cold as stone, a cold born of the empty lands when no sun has ever shone. Very quietly, he says, "You mistake my meaning. I know all that is in your heart. I know what you desire but it cannot be. This is not your child, she is not your love, and you are not a murderer. Yours is the straight path, mine the crooked: it cannot be otherwise."

"I remember when you kissed me at midsummer," the Lord of Marac said. "You held out your hands to love and came to me, fearing neither light nor darkness. But for all your vows of love, what little faith you had in me in the end. All I could give, I gave to you; all I could give was not enough for you; all I could give you burned from me with cold iron."

His words rained down like quick, hard blows and Liùtha flinched at each as if indeed he struck her.

"I have come back," she cried. "All the rest is lost and, if you turn from me, I wish the wind would no more blow, nor fish swim in the sea, nor birds fly through the air."

Like a child afraid of the night, the potter crooked his fingers to ward off the evil that was spoken. She was far into the dark and he did not want her curse to come to pass.

"But I must turn away," said the Lord of Marac. "Allocco banished me upon the equinox but three months passed before midwinter, three months before the moment when he could turn the light against the dark and set his fire within your flesh. In all that time, you did not come out from the walls of your city to the shore where I was waiting."

"Three months! Three months from equinox to solstice he locked me in my mother's house. I was sick, the apples rotted, the harvest failed," Liùtha said, black frost upon her face, her voice cold as midwinter ice. "A life you owed to him and he collected on that debt."

"I told you plainly the first night you came to me," he said, and his face was pale and terrible, "I do not dance your dance of seedtime and harvest."

Her voice was a hoarse whisper. "Then you knew Allocco's purpose and yet did nothing. Only Assiolo tried, and Assiolo failed."

Her pain and sorrow were enough, the potter thought, to melt the hardest heart, if he had but the ears to hear, the eyes to see.

The Lord of Marac must have heard, he must have seen, but hard and cold came back his answer: "Assiolo would not become a murderer for love of you, and nor would I."

"If the tales told of you are true," Liùtha cried, "once you'd have swept that old man aside with a word. Once, you'd have conjured the wind out of the air and the wave out of the water and washed your enemy from the face of the earth."

"All those tales are true. And so too is this one true, true now as on the evening I told it on the shore before your city: I had my fill of death the day your mother fled her dying land. Some words should not be spoken, but the fate fell to me that I should speak them. Never again will I call death out of the sea with a word. I renounced the storm and the fire and the knife. I will not take them up again, even for you."

She pulled the filigree crown from the folds of her gown and flung it down upon the stone. It came to rest beside his foot, its moonstone glowing in the halflight.

"Tell me," he asked, letting it lie, "if you had seen me shatter him, if you had seen me decide a man must die, could you still have loved me?"

"Words, Liùthion, words. The child is dead."

"The child is dead, but you are not. You have blue sky above you, green trees to grow for you, a living man to love you if you let him."

She turned from him, weeping her tears of fire in the darkness of Marac, for him, for herself, for the broken life that never could come back again.

"You do not know what we suffer for your sake, Liùthion," she whispered, and, had she done no more than glance at him, the potter would have stepped from the shadow to take her in his arms.

But Liùtha did not look at him. She told her lover through her tears, "You flee away from what you do, leaving us who were born flesh behind to suffer in your place. You left Allocco when the world was young. You kissed me in farewell and left me to him, knowing what he had become, what you yourself had made him."

"Your father bade me, *Pity him*. Your mother welcomed me into her city. For your sake and for theirs, I would not be again the creature I was the day the gates of morning closed. I wanted to be only your lover, putting all the rest aside."

"You loved me by night but I had to walk the day alone because you were but a half-made man. The evening we parted you swore you loved me. Still you left me to Allocco." Her eyes were great and dark with sorrow and with memory. "That burned every bit as fierce as the iron into your arm. The hatred your enemy felt for you he used against me, he made me suffer because he could not make you suffer."

"All the power he had to hurt, you gave to him. All the rest followed from that, sure as day follows night."

"I was a fool," she answered, "but I paid a high price for my folly."

"Seven years we have suffered for it," the Lord of Marac said, desolate and empty. He sighed, his anger gone, his sadness left behind. "I do not regret my choices, Liùtha; only that it was necessary for me to choose." He made no move, he said no word, but the lamp on the table stuttered and died. "The dead are dead, and never come they back. The world is as it is. Here, in my own domain, I waited for you to come to me so we might say a last farewell before I slip forever into borderlands, free from flesh and memory."

"Is that what you desire? To slip away?"

"It is all that I can do, since Allocco sundered us."

"Yet you are here, and I am here."

He picked up the silver from the stone and held it in his right hand. For a long time, Liùtha looked about the room, at the tapestry of the rowan tree, at the darkness on the sea, anywhere but at the Lord of Marac. But all that long while, the potter saw, his own heart aching with love and pity, the Liùthion never looked except at her, a light within the darkness, and, as he gazed at her, the lines of pain etched around his dark eyes grew deeper, the trace of starlight in his black hair faded almost to nothing. The wind beyond the window died away and in the quiet dark that followed the summer rain fell down like tears upon the stone.

At last Liùtha broke the silence. "You did not slip away."

"No," he sighed, "no. Each night I told myself the time would come before the morning for me to take an apple from my king and dance again as empty as any of my kindred; each night I let the moment pass and so I am still here."

"Then you too had hope."

"As dark a hope as yours." The Lord of Marac spoke very softly, no more than a whisper of breath in the night time. "Year on year, you locked yourself away within stone walls I could not breach, not even in your dreams, not even at midsummer. And when at last you had the courage to come out, you turned your back on me to dance with other men." A pause, a breath, a billowing of shadows. "Yet the pattern changed before the dance was ended: now you are here, and I am here, and so too is that man of Ittachar. Why is this, Liùtha? What is your purpose?"

Liùtha took a step towards him and this time he did not move away. "I was a fool in Ohmorah," she said. "I was worse in Anach, thinking to use another's life to reach my end. But all is changed since midsummer and at last I know myself. I left my hatred behind me on the road between midsummer and Marac. I came today through the wind and the storm not to bring a man to his death but to ask your pardon and to give you mine."

"Ah, love, that it were enough. But still the dead are dead. Still the way is barred. It is seven years too late."

"Then there is nothing left?"

The Lord of Marac shook his head. His voice was bleak. "All the men in all the world are left to you. You are free to sow your seed and reap your harvest with any man you choose, even that man of Ittachar who kissed you at midsummer."

"All the men in all the world mean nothing next to you, not even that man of Ittachar."

The potter could not help his gasp of pain, though he had longtimes known the truth.

"I love you," Liùtha whispered. "Tell me you do not love me."

She looked up into the Lord of Marac's face, into his black eyes, and there she saw his answer. With a sobbing gasp, he reached out his hands, the whole one and the broken, and she took them between her own to lift them to her face and kiss them. He did not move towards her, he did not move away, and in a moment she let his hands fall. The marks of her lips and fingers were branded on his pale skin.

"Do not touch me again: some pains I will not bear," he said, softly, sadly. "Your touch is fire and iron, your tears burn me. The old man's curse holds fast."

The shadows shifted. The Lord of Marac was gone back into the night and, for himself, the potter was glad to see him go.

The chamberlain's son walks often at her side within the garden, through the chill of autumn into the cold of winter. She has fallen into the habit of silence and he alone can coax her from her chamber and make her go out into the air. She sits for hours beside her window, curled beneath her shawl with her arms across her belly, watching the patterns of light and wind shift across the surface of the sea. Hand in hand they walk together between the empty flowerbeds and beneath the leafless trees. Here they had played with sticks and stones and rowan berries, two children together in a garden, whilst the piper made his music on a summer's evening and the stone walls marked out a place of safety, not a prison.

She holds out her hands and he sits at her side. After a while he asks, "Do you remember when we were children?"

"You promised me when we were grown we'd make a house together and no one would come in, unless we asked them."

He nods. "I shall keep my promise."

She bends her head and says softly, "I gave mine to another."

He says, his arms around her, his face pressed against her, "No man can turn the wind from its course. He will come back to you."

"The dove is dead," she answers, "there is iron about my arm and stone walls around me. He will not come back — he cannot come back."

"Then at midwinter, you shall go to him. He will be waiting."

He feels her sigh and sees she is exhausted by sickness and by fear. He carries her to her bed and tucks her between sheets scented with lavender.

"Stay," she says, catching him by the hand as he rises to leave. "Stay with me until I sleep. I do not want to be alone."

And so he stays with her, sitting beside the bed. He holds her hand and sings to her, a song learned long ago from the crippled piper. Since those days his voice has broken, he can no longer take the tune soaring into the tall air, but still the notes are sweet and true.

> *"My love, my love, my milk-white dove*
> *That sang so sweet the whole night long*
> *Stay, stay past the dawn through the day*
> *And sing again your lovesong."*

She says, "I loved him, and I drove him from me."

He wants to speak some word of comfort, but no words will come and silence is all he has to offer her.

"Come out of the dark, Almecu mor Thorrian," Liùtha said. Now the Lord of Marac was gone the light about her had faded a little. "You have seen the worst of me."

She held out her hand to the potter. He did not take it. The strange fire was still upon her, the fire that burned those she touched, burned up the men who loved her. Now he knew what she was and what she had done. He knew, too, words and deeds could not be called back. They echoed across the world even after the speaker was silent, even when he was seven years dead and blew as dust upon the wind. This was an old, old tale he witnessed, told many times in many places. Since the world began, lovers had taken the night time for their loving, swearing great oaths of constancy and fortitude. Since the world began, their words had blown away upon the breeze, empty breath meaning nothing in the light of day.

And yet, he thought, though that was true, it was not the truth in his own heart.

"The worst of love," he said at last, "but not in you alone. You have feared and you have failed. So has your lover. But I've seen love that has been burned, love broken and betrayed, but not quite love destroyed. I do not think you are beyond hope."

He took her hand and kissed it. She was not his love but yet he loved her and would not turn aside, even if the path she led him down went so far into the dark he never came again to Ittachar. Liùtha rested a moment with her arms about him, leaning her head against his breast, and then slipped away into the dark of Marac, leaving behind the weight of her sadness and the scent of her hair.

It is not hard to find the things he needs. At the harbour, there are fishermen flattered by his interest. They show him lines fine enough for the wariest fish to miss in a cast across the water, yet strong enough to hold the kingfish after it rises to the fly. There are knifemakers aplenty in the White City, and the finest is eager to show only his best work to the chamberlain's son.

When he has a knife and a length of line, he finds yew berries and ergot; he finds foxglove, valerian and hemlock; he finds nightshade and henbane, poppy and mandrake; he finds the spotted toadstool that gives visions to a man, and the white that gives only death. All these he finds within his father's house, and, because he is his father's son, he knows all their uses for hurt and healing.

His hand is steady as he takes hemlock enough to freeze a man's blood within his veins and nightshade to open his eyes before he dies. The man he would kill has more life than most but he is still a man and so can die in all the ways a man can die, if he can find the strength and will to send him into the dark before his time.

Later, in his chamber, he looks at what lies before him on the table: three certain ways to kill a man. There is poison in the cup. There is a knife, and blood upon his finger where he has tried its edge against his skin. There is a cord fine as a cobweb that passes smooth as silk and strong as wire across his hand.

All the short winter's day, whilst the sun rides across the sky from morning into evening, he weighs one choice against the other, and sees clearly how both lead on to ruin. He is trapped in a web of others' weaving. He flinches from the horror of his seeing, but there is no escape. If he would save one life, he must take another; if he does not kill today, another will tomorrow.

He presses his hands against his eyes and screams into the silence of his skull, "If you are there, show yourself."

There is no answer. There will never be an answer whilst there are stone walls around him, a fire burning in the grate and an iron knife lying on the table.

Still the potter could not sleep nor shake off his memory of Liùtha, her fire and sadness, the touch of her hand against his face. Even so he grew weary of pacing the whispering halls of Marac and retraced his steps to knock at the piper's door. There, all whispers ceased: within were fire and iron and Kenu Vanithu himself, the monster, the musician, who bore within his twisted frame a greater strength than any man.

"Will you play for me?" the potter asked, looking down into that dreadful face, those golden eyes. "I've never heard music such as yours. Today, beneath the wall, your pipe brought hope when hope seemed lost, and tonight I am a man much in need of hope."

Kenu Vanithu held wide the door and gestured to the seat beside the fire. Then he raised his pipe and began to play, a strong, supple music very like the tunes of Ittachar the potter had known his whole life long.

The potter felt damp clay beneath his fingers and the fierce pleasure of creation, of shaping clay to reveal the form other men could not see. Colours danced before his eyes, green and gold, white and blue. He sat beside his little house in Ittachar. Before him was the sea, calm in the evening with the western light upon it. His garden was filled with spring flowers, daffodil and purple crocus, pale primroses beneath the wall, and a blackbird sang in the rowan tree beside the gate. He was no longer young but contented in his years. Behind him, the windows of his house were warm with lamplight and he could hear the voices of his children and his grandchildren. He faced the setting sun, filled with love for the world that was so bright and fair.

"A life well lived," said Kenu Vanithu, laying down his pipe. "I promise you, Almecu mor Thorrian, all that will be yours if you go home."

The potter dreamed on a while, tasting the possibility of a long life and a quiet one. At last he asked, "What of Liùtha, if I go home?"

"That, you will never know," the piper answered. "Maybe she finds another man to die for her and lives out her life with the Lord of Marac. Maybe she casts herself in despair from the tower above us and goes untimely into the dark. Maybe she returns to her mother's house and finds in time another lover."

"It cannot be." Tears ran down the potter's face, as warm as blood and salty as the sea. The piper reached out to clasp his hand, comfort for the comfortless. "I swore an oath I'd not turn aside until I had brought her to happiness. My own heart will not let me break that promise. Once, I allowed myself to be less than I should be and the clay would no longer come to life in my hands. My craft is my life; it will leave me if I am again less than I can be.

"I'm not now only a potter," he said, in answer to the question in those golden eyes. "I am Almecu mor Thorrian, the man of Ittachar who cried out for his adventure, and whose wish was granted. I cannot turn back because the way is dark. I followed my heart and found my adventure, and found love too. Now I must go on until the end is reached."

"So must we all," Kenu Vanithu told him. "You've a way to go yet, but the end will come."

"This is a drear place," said the potter, looking about into the shadows.

"It wasn't always so. There's loss here, and longing. The fear you felt today came from its master. Think what he was and what he is, thoughts and dreams shaped out of the air. He's suffered at the hands of men, has had all the force of iron and light and fire turned against him, this spirit who clad himself in flesh."

The potter shrugged, thinking much of the Lord of Marac's misfortune had come of his own deeds.

"Liùtha's suffered too," Kenu Vanithu added in a moment. "A great deal has she suffered."

"She is free to love any man she chooses," said the potter, bitterly. "She is free to love me, if she chooses."

The piper shook his head. "She's made her choice. She'll not come to love you though you give her the world and your heart and all the pleasures of the flesh besides."

"Play again," he said, wanting time to think of what he must do.

This time the music was wild and lonely, like the wind upon the sea. Again the room faded from the potter's eyes but now he saw a vision of the endless sea and land without form beneath a starlit sky that would never brighten into morning. It was the time before the waking world began, before there were trees and flowers upon the earth, before birds flew in the empty air or fishes swam in the depths of the sea. Or maybe it was the time that had not yet come, when the sea and the sky were empty once more and all joy and sorrow, hope and fear, had slipped away into the dark with all the peoples of the world and there were no more checks upon the wind.

"Such he was, such he may be," Kenu Vanithu said. "The choice is yours."

"So lovely and so lonely," the potter mused. "Yet perhaps it is not so strange to want to walk upon the earth awhile. For the trees and all that grows upon the land are fair to look upon and, of all the women in the world, Liùtha is the loveliest I have seen."

"I've one question, in exchange for all my music."

"Ask it. I shall answer if I can."

"Do you love her truly, as she is?"

"You think my love but a midsummer madness?" The potter sighed, and looked into the fire, letting the flames drive back the world and dazzle him. "Almost, I wish it were so. No, what dreams I had of her are shattered. I see her as she is, burned by fire and darkness, flawed and frightened, and yet I love her. I knew it at midsummer: I know it still."

"There's light as well as fire at midsummer," said the piper. "Sometimes light enough to make plain what was hidden."

"I wish I'd seen her smile," the potter said. "I've only seen her lonely and full of sorrow and anger. It's grief to me I cannot make her happy, full of life and love as she was meant to be."

He looked into the fire, finding shapes within like flowers and dragons and dancing trees, the wonders of the world seen and unseen by waking eyes and minds. "I think I'd like to see her happy more than any other sight in the world, even above my home again."

Then the piper played, and for a third time the potter saw the sea. There was no land but far as he could see little waves flecked with sunset dancing across the surface of the sea. A seagull flew high in the evening sky, its white feathers gilded by the light, and, following the path of the bird, was a little ship with a carved gull's head at her prow, rushing across the sea with the wind full in its white sails.

The potter flung out his hand, crying, "Enough!" and the music was shattered. "I gave my word by land and sea I'd stand by Liùtha," he said. "I swore an oath and it is as hard and true upon me as if I were a fine lord. I'll keep that oath, though it costs me my life, but I made no promise to the Lord of Marac. Let him go back into the dream he came from."

"Such straight lines, such clear boundaries to your world," said Kenu Vanithu. "A deed is done, another left undone, and so you reach your judgement. Is this truly all that matters?"

The potter laughed, short and harsh in his throat. "My death puts out Allocco's fire and gives the Lord of Marac his heart's desire again."

"Have you seen so much and still not understood? You've a way to go yet, lad. Not all ways are straight as the path of starlight across the water. Sometimes you must go crookedly to reach your end."

"It seems a short, straight path to me, and I will take it if I must to keep my promise to Liùtha." The potter reached for wine with a trembling hand. "How shall I do it? A knife? A noose? A leap into the dark?"

"Can you not see?" the piper cried. "All this has come to pass because this Lord of Marac is not a man. As he is now he'll never bring peace or happiness to Liùtha, not if you died a hundred times for her sake. He does not pay the price of life. If one will not pay, another must: Allocco knew it well, though he twisted it to his own purpose. For all his flesh, the Liùthion is air and starlight, undying in the empty land. Assiolo spoke the truth when he said you must bring death, though his meaning was not quite the one you put on it."

"Then this is a coil cannot be broken, if even my death is not enough to keep my promise and my oath. I am a potter, not a magician. Clay I can shape from one form to another but not a creature of the borderlands." He sipped his wine and tried to keep his voice quite even. "Let him be gone into those borderlands and set Liùtha free himself. That way there's no need for me to die."

"All men must die. You were born to the waking world and this life is all you have. For you, there is nothing more. No dreams beyond the darkness."

The potter said, bitterly, "I thought you were my friend, Kenu Vanithu."

"I am your friend. I brought you through the fire at midsummer. I brought you through the wind on the road to Marac."

"How do I know you are not as false as your face is foul?"

"I have no proof to offer. Only your heart can tell you that." Kenu Vanithu met the potter's gaze evenly, easily. There was no malice in those golden eyes, no deceit. "All my tales are true, Almecu mor Thorrian."

"After a fashion," the potter answered. "I think you shape them to your own ends."

The piper's twisted smile lit up his face, he threw back his head and laughed. "Even so, lad, even so."

As the first hour of the third is called the chamberlain's son hears his father's step beyond his door. He leaves his room and stands at the head of the stairs to watch him make ready for the Assembly. The chamberlain puts on his scarlet coat, he pulls his hat down firmly on his head against the wind blowing from the west, he picks up the stick he leans on now and nods to him upon the stair as he opens the door.

The old man goes out into the city. The young man returns to his room, to stare at the cup and the cord and the knife, and think of himself and of his father. By the time the sun slips into the sea, he knows he cannot do it. He has the knowledge, he has the means, but not the will, for all he is his father's son. He opens his window and pours the cup out on the ground. He slides the knife back into its sheath and lays it down upon the table. He burns the cord upon the fire, weeping all the while to find some prices are too high to bear, even for love, even for life itself.

With a heavy heart, the potter sought out the Lord of Marac in the last hours before dawn. There was much he wished to say, much he desired to know. And more than that, his anger must be told. Anger for Liùtha; anger for himself. She had suffered because of what this man, who was less than a man, had done; he was like to die because of what this man, who was more than a man, had not done.

He found him easily enough. He had only to follow the path of the breeze that ever blew through the halls of Marac. At the top of the tallest tower above the sea he found him in an unlit room where the stars could shine in by night, the sun by day. Its windows looked west across the sea, looked east across the land. An airy place enough; a cell, a cage, a trap, for one who had danced free as the wind itself upon the empty air.

This room above the land and sea was filled with papers, maps of the Later Lands and the lands beyond, charts of the sea, lists that named the many names of stars. A silver bowl stood on the table, reflecting the world in cold, clear saltwater. Images drifted over its still surface, like clouds across the sky: the towers of the White City; a house beneath a hill; a square-sailed ship; an apple tree. All the places the Lord of Marac could not reach, all the roads he could not walk, all the seas he could not sail, were spread around him. He could watch the sea and the sky from his window, follow in his mind the paths of gulls, and remember what he had been in the days before he was banished from the White City.

"I nearly killed a man because of you," the potter said. "He had forgotten it is good to be alive and thought so little of himself he was willing to take any fate a stranger offered. Now it seems I must die for you."

But why should you think to die?" asked the Lord of Marac with a twisting smile. There was darkness in his eyes, starlight about his brow. His flesh and form were real enough, but he was no mortal man. "Call up that creature and let it take you to Ittachar and your home. Or, if you do not yet wish for home, find a ship to carry you. I will send a wind from Marac to take you fast wherever you desire."

"I'll not do your bidding," the potter answered. "If you can raise a wind to blow me from this place then you can be rid of me. But for that, I'll stay with Liùtha until she needs me no more."

"You need not stay for long. You know my flesh is real? As it is real so must it die. Liùtha's touch drags me down into the dark as Allocco intended. My death will follow from her kiss before midwinter: thus ends our tale."

"I'd expected much from the Lord of Marac, but not self-pity," the potter said with scorn. "You will not die, as she will die, or I. Your flesh must wither and decay, that's all. You danced before her world began. You'll dance when it is ended and she and I blow as dust upon the wind. What you did long ago, I do not know. But for what you did seven years ago I shall judge you; aye, and condemn you too."

"She turned first from me and let him guide her into folly."

"You made her what she is, you as much as that old man who hated you but had only her to play with, tormenting her as a cat does a mouse because you slipped like starlight through his fingers. Was that well done, Liùthion?"

"You did not kill a man who came at you with a knife. Why should I do differently?"

"My life's my own: had he held that same knife against my lover's throat I'd not have held back my hand. But then, I am a man."

"Allocco died, alone and wretched. You've heard of him only as an old man, twisted with his failure and his loss. He was not always so. I did great harm."

"He is dead, and gone into the dark, and none need mourn him. Liùtha is alive and loves you. She faced her fears to find you. But what is she to you?" asked the potter. "A pretty toy to take up when she pleases, to cast aside when she does not? The usual tale of man and maid?"

"I loved her more than the starlight on the sea, she was more dear to me than the wind upon the water, my hope when hope had gone," the Lord of Marac answered, fixing the potter with his dark gaze. "But, even if I desired it, I could not dance her dance. I am no man, nor can I walk beneath the sun."

No man could meet those eyes for long. Within the flesh and blood and bone of the Lord of Marac was something older than the waking world that would outlast its little shell of skull and skin.

Rage rose like a fire within the potter's heart. He loved Liùtha, and did not want her to suffer further. He loved his life, and did not want to die before his time. And so he let himself be angry, as a man faced with a force of land or sea will rage against the elements that can destroy him without care or knowledge.

"You were enough of a man to take her from her mother's house," he cried. "Man enough to lie with her. Man enough to kindle a child on her."

There is no advantage born of such anger; no man's rage can change the path of the wave nor halt the blowing of the wind.

"There is no child," said the Lord of Marac. He held his maimed hand in his whole one; his face was marked by the pain of iron and fire.

"There is no child. How does that weigh against your hand?" asked the potter, careful now to pick his way through his anger, to use it not be used by it. "A life you owed the chamberlain, a life he took from you, and so there is no child. Did you know? Did you care?"

Beyond the window a pair of herring gulls drifted across the sky in the time before the morning, their curved wings slicing through the wind, no weight upon the world.

The Lord of Marac fixed his eyes upon the gulls. "Yours is a world of light and iron and fire. Mine is everlasting starlight, the wind upon bare stone. Iron she put on me, iron burned me, iron drove me away. That is its nature. That is my nature."

And to that, since it was true, the potter had no answer.

When the gulls had gone away into the distance, the Lord of Marac said, "When I am gone and the midsummer fires burn, Liùtha may turn to you. It would be easy for a woman to love you, a man with the strength and beauty of the Sea People mellowed with the clay of Ittachar. Is that not what you desire, Almecu mor Thorrian? Why, then, would you give up your life for me?"

"Because I love her as she is," the potter replied, trying to call back the rage that was falling from him, leaving sorrow in its wake. "She is not a dream, she is not a vision."

He wanted Liùtha for himself, wanted her smiling in his arms, warm within his bed. She had kissed him at midsummer but only to drive away the memory of love burned and betrayed. Perhaps she would come to him again, but it would be love with its back broken, haunted by the ghost of what was lost. It would not be enough.

"Liùtha does not love me," he said, forcing himself to meet those black eyes. "She will never love me as I would wish. I would learn her dance if she would have me, but she loves you and so this is all I can do for her. *No price at all, if you love her,* said Kenu Vanithu."

"Perhaps you love her better than I did." The Lord of Marac's voice was cold and empty as stone or star. "You are, after all, what I am not."

"How can I know that?" the potter cried out with all the passion of his heart. "All I can know is her love for you is real. I saw it when she kissed me at midsummer. I would it were not so! But for that I'd gladly peg you out beneath the sun myself and watch you burn for what you did. You've suffered? So too have all men suffered. Learn mercy from it."

The months that began with the equinox have dwindled away into a night. That night, the chamberlain's son stands before her door and says to his father, "You have done enough, and more than enough. The Liùthion has fled back into the dark he came from. All of Ohmorah knows you are the stronger."

"A life he owes to me, a life I'll take this night," the chamberlain retorts, "and if the Lord of Marac could not gainsay me, Assiolo, I do not think you will."

The house is filled with people but the old man has set a wall of silence around himself, has walked through the lady's house carrying a silver cup in his right hand whilst its people stand aside to let him pass without ever seeing clearly he is there at all. Only he stands before the locked door and dares defy him. He holds the key in his left hand and meets his father's eyes.

"You have done enough," he says again. "You must not pass this door tonight."

"There is no man within this world, Assiolo, who may say must to me." His father's voice is scarce more than a whisper; he has never been quick to anger. He is a man who thinks before he speaks, thinks twice before he acts, and his will always overcomes that of lesser men. "If you set yourself against me, I shall prevail."

He sets his back against the oak. "I gave my promise and I shall keep it. With all my strength and will, I stand by her and so I set myself against you."

His father says no word. He makes no move but, between one heartbeat and the next, he is outlined by fire, by the brightness of the rising sun. Light surrounds him, driving back the darkness, and he is dazzled, blinded by the old man's brilliance.

His father speaks out of his borrowed light. "You are a fool, Assiolo; you have always been a fool. You are no more than a moth dancing round the moon. You have no will, you have no strength, else you'd have slipped that knife between my ribs or offered me that cup you poured instead upon the ground. The only end is death, for me as for any other man who lives and breathes and walks upon the earth."

The old man holds out his burning hand. The iron key glows white hot as within the heart of a fire. He gasps in pain and drops the key, his hand burned and blistered by the iron. He bends for it but his father is there before him.

"Very good," said a voice behind him. "You're a wise man, Almecu mor Thorrian."

Kenu Vanithu, the monster, the musician, who had walked all the lands of the waking world, stood in the open doorway. He could walk quietly enough when he chose to, for all his twisted leg, and, if the Lord of Marac had noted him, the potter had not, being too filled with love and anger to mark his footsteps as he climbed the stair.

"For a potter?"

"For a man who loves and does not see his love returned. You start to see the patterns in the world," replied the piper.

"Your friend condemns me as less than a man. How do you judge me, Kenu Vanithu?" the Lord of Marac asked.

The piper gave him answer, speaking not as judge but as witness of deeds done long ago. "I saw the rowan die. I saw the sun stand still at noontime, a red moon rising and fiery dancers setting the very wind to flame. There were few choices left on that day; all you did, all I did, was as necessary as it was dreadful." The piper was never good to look upon but now all the pain and hatred he had seen sat heavy on his face, and the sight was horrible and pitiful. "The world we made is not the world that was lost. After the fires burned out and the waters fell back there was a new balance this side of the sunrise."

He looked up, golden eyes staring hard into black, and, just as night is driven back by day, the Lord of Marac turned down his gaze before him. Kenu Vanithu was little, he was twisted, but suddenly he was terrible.

"You chose to walk again beneath this sky, Liùthion. You came in flesh out of the borderlands, sought love in the waking world. Allocco chose his path in the streets and gardens of the White City, you chose yours, and Liùtha was broken between you."

The Lord of Marac reached out his hands, the whole one and the broken, pleading for understanding, or for judgement, or, perhaps, for absolution.

"I did not know what she was due from me," he whispered, "and thought love itself enough. Allocco understood me well for all his hatred; he knew what I was, what I was not, and measured out each blow he struck at me."

"There are choices," said the piper, "and there is what follows from those choices. There is no judgement, Liùthion, save in your own heart. You have your freedom, Allocco had his: all that might have been, had you chosen differently, will never be. There is a price for all things, and that is the price of freedom."

The words fell into the silence in that room hard and heavy as a stone falling to the sea. The Lord of Marac wept, but now his tears were for Allocco and Liùtha, for the child that died before its birth, for all that might have been.

The door is locked and all his strength is not enough to shatter it. He screams his failure to the night but his scream is muffled as a cry in a nightmare, not even so loud as the squeal of a mouse beneath an owl's talons.

A very little time passes – time for a hundred sobbing breaths to rise and fall within his breast – and the door is opened. Out walks his father and both his hands are empty.

"It is done," the old man says. "I offered her the cup and she drained it dry. Thus I take from him what once he took from me."

"Let us talk no more of the past but decide the present," Kenu Vanithu said. "You know what this man has done, Liùthion; you have heard all he has said. By his words and deeds you know him, as I do. He is the one who will bring this to its right ending."

Both looked to the potter, and he saw his death reflected from their faces. He saw the path laid out before him, the path he had chosen when he called forth a creature from the air and sea, and found it must do his bidding. Yet who had been called that day, and who had answered?

In a voice he had not used before, the Lord of Marac said, "Almecu mor Thorrian, you spoke to me of mercy: seven years since, I held back my hand, though I knew Allocco was my enemy, hoping it would be enough for him to stay his. Alas for all of us that it was not."

Then, as at his first sight, the potter could see only that he was one who had suffered. He looked away, desiring only to hate him, not to pity him: pity would demand compassion.

Through the open window the first shimmer of light could be seen above the land of Marac. Kenu Vanithu said, softly, "There is one choice more you must make, Liùthion, if you truly love her."

The Lord of Marac bowed his head, acknowledging the truths in Kenu Vanithu's words. He paused a moment, then knelt before the potter and placed his head between his hands.

"I cannot walk beneath the sun, nor cross the sea into Lyikené, so I must ask a boon of you, before you die." In the last of the night his face was very sad, yet the potter saw hope there, where there had not been hope before. "Will you bring me an apple from the firstborn tree so I may eat and be no more liùthion?"

"I can and I shall, but not for your sake," the potter told him. He took the cold hands in his own to raise him to his feet. "If I am to let Allocco's hand fall upon me, then I must know death will be your ending, as for any other man. Only then can I trust you will love Liùtha as she deserves."

All is as silent as the night is dark, the only sound the drumbeat of his heart, counting out the rhythm of his life. His hand is branded by iron and his heart by knowledge. For all the time until the morning, he sits hunched against the wall, knowing all the promises he made have been broken tonight, that love is not enough.

At dawn, the door yields to his hand and he slowly opens it. The fire burns bright within the grate and he retches at the smell of spilled blood and spilled wine.

She lies before the fire in a tumble of stained linen, the silver cup lying near her outstretched hand. He screams, a raw howl made up of equal parts of agony and failure. This time his scream smashes through the silence and, out of every door and chamber, come pounding feet and clamouring voices as the house wakes around him.

Soon the room is full of strangers. He sees the midwife there, and the doctor. He sees her lifted to her bed, and ice and hot water brought to her. She is the still centre of the chaos of that night. No one looks to him or to the little thing of blood and bone within his hands. He slips out of the room, out of the house in uproar, into the quiet of the wet garden, and stands again beneath the apple tree.

When he had been a child, he had heard how it been brought as a slip from a tree at the world's end, a symbol of hope when hope was gone. Now he is a man, hope has proved as hollow as the rotten apples it bears on its bare branches.

With one hand, he scrabbles in the soft earth beside the hollow bones whilst with his left hand, burned by fire and iron, he holds his dead hope against his breast. Its father has abandoned it, his has destroyed it, and no hope, no love, no tree, is enough to bring it back. He lays down his burden gently as a father lays his child within its cradle, singing it to sleep as he tucks the earth softly round it while the night thins into a grey morning.

Then, with blood and soil upon his hands, he goes back into the house to sit a last watch beside her so when she wakes he will be there as witness.

9: Open your eyes and look at me

I have climbed into a tree that is too high for me
Seeking fruit where there wasn't any growing
I've drawn warm water from beneath the cold, cold clay
And against the stream I was rowing.

False, False, Traditional

The potter found Liùtha in the room of tapestries in the bright morning. The window was wide open to let the wind blow in from the sea and the golden summer sunlight flood across the room to drive back all the shadows. Liùtha crouched on the floor beneath the rowan, her arms locked around her knees. It was but an image of a tree and gave no protection from the guilt and grief gnawing at her heart. She had wept last night but now she was done with weeping and her face was bleak and lovely.

He knelt down and wrapped his arms around her, offering comfort to the comfortless.

He sits beside her bed holding her hand until she should wake from her drugged sleep. He sings to her, one verse of a song he remembers from their childhood:

"The year dies slowly, bare is the tree
And the blackbird turns dead leaves in the frost.
No more, no more will my love come to me:
My heart is sore dark, all my hope is lost."

When at last she wakes she does not speak of herself or of her child or of its father but stares into the dark in some wretchedness beyond pain or sorrow that is reflected in his eyes. Neither can weep, neither can speak, so, silently, he withdraws his hand and, silently, he leaves her. Both know he will not come to her again.

"Hatred drives love out," Liùtha said. "I loved the Lord of Marac, yet I drove him from me; I love him now, and his flesh is dying at my hand. I lost him when the white dove died," she whispered, pointing to the milk-white dove flying across the tapestry of sky and birds. "Now he is lost to me again."

"You live and love," the potter said, "and so does he." And he would give much, he thought, for it to be otherwise. Were it otherwise, he could have hope that he would see his home again and feel cold clay beneath his hands.

"Love was not enough in Ohmorah. It is not enough now."

"That is not true," he told her gently, remembering her mother in her garden, bright and lovely because she had learnt her way through the world. *Lead her into the dark places where she is afraid to go.* So would he do.

"Last night," he said, "I saw the light beyond the fire, the root beneath the frost. You spoke last night of love, not hatred. What you are is not the chamberlain's choice, unless you make it so."

"You do not know. You were not there. I sought death at midwinter but Assiolo dragged me back into a life I did not want." She raised her head and looked him in the eye. "The only end is death. Allocco made that certain when he set his price at a man's life."

"You sought death but did not die," said Kenu Vanithu from the doorway, "and any time these seven years your lover could have slipped from flesh back into borderlands. But you came out from your stone walls and he waited in his flesh. Now he's set his face towards the waking world: would you turn from him again?"

"He's like a star that seems close but is far, far away. False hope is all I can find in Marac."

"Your mother thought otherwise," said Kenu Vanithu, "and so do I, though I've seen much evil in my time."

Sitting himself down beside them, he set his back against the wall and played his wooden pipe, weaving a tune from dreams and sunlight.

The potter saw the fear seep from Liùtha's face as she listened to the music, but not the sorrow. When his tune was done, the piper said, "Liùtha, lass, your mother set her borrowed fire aside and made a new beginning before ever you were born, and yet she sent this man on his adventure, thinking he could find a way to undo what Allocco did."

"Assiolo tried." She hid her face within her hands and cried out of her torment, "Assiolo failed! He did not have the strength to stand against his father. There is no man beneath this sky has strength enough for that."

"Are you so sure?" asked Kenu Vanithu, quietly, steadily. "You are here, and so is Almecu mor Thorrian, a man who called driftwood into life with dreaming. How is this so? Surely it is not by chance?"

With those golden eyes upon him, a new pattern came swirling into the potter's mind out of the sights he had seen in the White City, the stories he had heard. He remembered the vision shown in light and running water, and Assiolo's bitter smile as they parted on the shore. Then he had wondered why a man who could conjure such images should have done no more and been content to be a tool for others' using. Now he remembered his creature's tale of its creation from dreams and from despair, and was ashamed to think he had offered Assiolo nothing, not even understanding.

"Assiolo is Allocco's son, and learned much from his father. I am not a man and leave it to men to judge men," the piper said, a half-smile on his lips as if he read the potter's thought. "But this I know: Assiolo made a beginning, seven years since, and now the end is up to you. And the beginning of that end lies in an apple from the firstborn tree."

"That tree is a song, a story told to children."

"That's so. It is also real and grows in the west at the edge of the world. Two kings guard it, lad, beneath two skies, and each offers what the other cannot. But, from whichever hand you take it, to eat of that tree is to accept all that is offered." Kenu Vanithu bowed his head, stretching his face into a hollow smile. "I found it was a bitter fruit but I've heard others call it sweet. You'll find one end or another in its apples: it is the end of all things."

The potter sighed. "You know your way across the world as I do not. Why can't you go, when you have so much more understanding?"

The piper looked up; his face was sadder than the potter had seen it yet and his voice full of regret. "It's as I said: I am a half-made man. So now is the Liùthion. You are whole and we are not."

"For all your music and his dreaming? For all the life you have?"

"Music and dreams are not a life. We are strangers in this land for all the years we spend in it. I am a stone upon the earth. He is the wind that blows. You are a man."

"I envy you your life. I do not want to die."

"I shall die, Almecu mor Thorrian," Kenu Vanithu reminded him, "and a far harder death than yours."

In the silence afterwards, the potter asked the piper, "What must I do to reach that tree?"

"From Marac the way lies across the sea. You must take a boat and sail west from this coast as the day dawns," answered Kenu Vanithu. "Keep a straight course all the day with the wind at your back and, in the evening, you will find what there is to find."

He was a man of Ittachar: he knew whose eyes watched all the ways into the west; he knew of bronze swords and square sails and death striking out of the sunlight. He asked, "And what of the Sea People who guard the open sea? Will they let me pass?"

"If they see you, they will hunt you. If they hunt you, they will catch you. Then you will know the value put upon your life." The piper smiled his twisted smile. "They are all you think they are, the Sea People. Ruthless and terrible, jealous of their freedom and of the open sea, but Imacah mor Tamarhak their king kept the balance of light and darkness on the day all the rest forgot it, though he did so with a sword. They live closer to the borderlands than any in the Later Lands can do, and many times their strength has been all that stood between folly and destruction."

"Then I'll do what I can," the potter said, though his heart was heavy with the weight of the future he had chosen. To strengthen himself against that knowledge he held Liùtha close and whispered, "I'll keep my promises for your sake. I am no less a man than any in Lyikené."

"I cannot bear the price," she said, her hands clutching at his.

Much as he loved his life, he loved her more, and so he said, "I shall bring an apple from the firstborn tree and leave you with a man to love you."

Liùtha squeezed his hands to silence him. "If you die, I'll not outlive you," she said, fiercely. "I cannot be bought by your life: some prices are too high, even for love."

Her hands in his were hot and dry. He looked into her eyes but she could not face his love more than a moment and looked away.

"Many lives have been lived in this world since your people first danced beneath the flowering trees," he told her softly. "It's not always a gentle place. Hatred and cruelty rise up out of the minds of men and sometimes they are not checked. But hatred and cruelty do not fill all men's hearts."

He held her close, feeling her tremble like a hare within the heather. Quietly, he said, "I love you, Liùtha. Trust me, and have hope. I'll not abandon you to fear and hatred but shall give you back your life to live as you wish, not as Allocco or the Lord of Marac desire. Now I will fetch an apple from the west. After he has eaten, we can decide what is necessary."

She hid her face against him, finding some comfort in his arms, but the sunlight glowed on her skin, the light danced across her hair, and the brighter she burned, the fainter his memories of his home became, fading like the stars at sunrise. He did not want to die, but death was the only way to keep his promises.

It is as the chamberlain promised. He keeps her close within the house, like a dove in a silver cage, but for her there is no open door. From her window she can watch the wind dance across the sea but at night, though her window is wide open, her curtain never stirs. The iron band is very heavy on her arm and she knows her love will not now come back to her. For hours or days she cannot remember him, not even his face or the touch of his skin against her own.

As the day dawned, the potter walked with Liùtha and the piper down the halls of Marac and out of the gate to where a little boat was waiting, moored to a rock at the water's edge.

Kenu Vanithu looked up at the potter, a strange, sad look in his golden eyes. "The Lord of Marac must learn to draw his hope from life. There is none elsewhere. You must remember this."

Surprised, he answered, "You told me I must die."

"Should you find the gates of evening, you must remember it. There is neither life nor death, neither fear nor hope, beyond those gates. The apples of the borderlands are not the apples of Lyikené, though they grow on the same tree."

"I thought all ways into the borderlands were lost?" Liùtha stared at the piper. "My mother said so, and the Lord of Marac, in Ohmorah."

The piper shook his head. "From Ohmorah, for certain; from Ittachar, perhaps; from Lyikené, never."

She asked, "How can we know you speak the truth?"

"I know all the paths of all the world, even those I cannot walk again," Kenu Vanithu answered, and neither thought to doubt him. "And this is neither Ohmorah nor Ittachar. This is Marac. You've been here before, Liùtha, seven years past. Were the lights down this coast all you saw then from its windows?"

She bit her lip upon her answer, and flung her arms around the potter. "Thank you," she whispered, "for all that you are, all that you offer." Her lips were soft against his cheek and warm as the sun upon a rose.

He held her close, loath to leave her, burying his face in the darkness of her hair, wishing himself into another life. But leave he must and so he gently freed himself. He stepped into the boat and let the piper cast it off. He raised the sail and set off into the west.

The only sounds he heard that day were the slap of the waves against the boat and the grey gulls screaming as they followed him across the sea. He looked often towards the horizon, hoping to see another, greater gull shape, fearing to see the square sails of Lyikené. Each time he saw nothing between the sky and the sea. All the long summer's day he was alone upon the sea and the silence grew about him until he no longer knew if he was awake or dreaming. He tried to sing to break the silence, but his voice cracked and broke, and the tune halted out across the water:

> "The blackbird sings in the apple tree
> And the blackbird's song is of need not art,
> But come to me, oh my love come to me,
> Is the song in every beating heart."

Then he wept, for his love would not come to him and he was going to his death. The piper had said, *Where there is necessity there is no choice.* Perhaps Kenu Vanithu had wisdom enough to see the patterns in the world, to know necessity, but he himself was only a man and had not grown weary of his life.

As the sour dusk falls upon the city streets the chamberlain raps his stick against her mother's gate, and the guard steps back to let him pass. The old man has set aside his scarlet coat of office and wears instead plain grey; he has grown thin in the days since the equinox. She cannot deny him entry to the house. She has not the strength, for she has grown dull in her grief and fearful in her captivity.

"One thing more I must do," he tells her, "then in the morning you shall go free. You have been too long alone. Allodola will return within a sennight; let the new year be your new beginning."

Vaguely, she thinks of answers, but she is too tired to speak. It does not seem to matter. Hope died the night all promises were broken.

"I am an old man," says the chamberlain. "I have overtaxed my strength and I am dying. It is midwinter's night and I must

speak to you, so when my son finds me dead in the morning you understand what I have done and why."

Still she does not answer. It is easier not to think, to let him talk if he wishes, and not to listen. He lights a lamp, a little lamp filled with scented oil, and sets it on the table. The small flame burns up bravely and drives back something of the darkness. The smell of the warming oil is fragrant, like rosemary in summertime within her mother's garden.

He takes her hand and removes the bond about her arm. "This has served its purpose. I want you awake, to listen to me and remember."

As the fog within her head grows thin, first memory returns, and then a hatred stronger even than her grief. "You slew my babe before its beginning."

"The Liùthion killed my child, as bonny a boy as ever saw the sunrise. Why should I not kill his?"

"Did you kill him too? Is that why he has not come back?"

He shakes his head and laughs. "He is no man to die at a man's hand."

Now she is awake, one thought shines like a white light through her grief. She says, "All else you can kill but not my love. He is mine and I am his. Forever."

"You were born beneath this sky. You do not have forever. When your lover's flesh decays he will be what he has been since the world began: wind upon the water, starlight on the sea. It is not so for you and me. We dance the midsummer dance because this life is all we have. I'll leave you free to dance beneath the trees at midsummer with any man of this world."

"I will not dance that dance again. The man I love does not dance beneath the flowering trees and nor shall I."

"He is no man. I saw clearly what he was on the evening he came into the city. He was yet a half-made man; he did not walk beneath the sun." The old man's voice is low and quick. Suddenly, he can no more keep silent than a lid can be kept upon a boiling pan and all his secrets and his hatred come spilling out into her chamber. "Had he become a man, had death been his end, then his life would have paid for the life he took from me. But he chose to remain liùthion, to take his pleasure and to keep his freedom. And so a life was not enough to pay his debt. All he desires I will deny to him. Only then will he suffer as I have suffered."

"You cannot keep me from him when you are dead," she says, remembering all her promises of love. "Dead men have no weight upon the world."

Since he took it from her arm, the chamberlain has held the iron ring in his hand. Now he holds it out and, quick as thought, it glows white hot as on the day the smith forged it in his fire. The ends of her hair singe and curl as she flinches from the heat. The ring burns and burns upon his open palm and his flesh is not consumed.

"My death is the price of my vengeance and I pay it willingly. All that was hers, Averla gave to me. Once, the fire of the sun ran through my veins. There is fire enough left in me for my purpose. You gave yourself into my hands when you took this iron from me."

She unfastens her mother's brooch from her dress and drives the pin into the ball of her thumb. The blood springs out in a great red bead. As with the iron, it is the nature of these things which bears their power. But now it is too late. She stares at the chamberlain, hating him, seeing in her mind's eye the cat she had found with her white dove: it too had enjoyed its power of pain.

The iron dulls black and cold again as the old man tosses the ring aside into the empty grate. With his handkerchief he wipes the blood from her thumb. He turns her hand gently within his so he can study the palm of it, as her father might have done had he come back to the White City.

"The fire within my flesh has been long years damped. I let it smoulder out of sight and mind until it should be needed. Tonight," he says, *"all that is mine, I give to you. You will carry my hatred in your flesh. Go to him, and you will serve my vengeance. Yours shall be the burning hand that pulls him back into the empty land he came from."*

"He is greater than you are. He will undo your work."

"Only a man can undo what a man does." The chamberlain shakes his head and laughs. "Find a man who will give up the sunlight and the starlight, find a man who will go into the dark before his time. Only then shall my fire die and the Liùthion come to your bed again, if you can make your peace with him."

The boat came softly to the shore, grounding itself upon the shingle. There was no line of weed and driftwood to mark the boundary between sea and land, no rocks upon the empty shore. Almecu mor Thorrian pulled it a little up the beach, though no tide would rise upon this shore to float it free. This sea was empty. No fish swam in these waters; there were no shells amidst the shingle. This sky was empty. No birds flew across this shore. The only sounds in all the land were the small shifts of stones beneath his feet and the rattle of shingle as he dragged the boat up the pebbled beach. The stars were very bright, closer and greater than stars seen in the waking world, and there were more of them: all the stars from the night skies above his home were there, and many others whose names he did not know. He looked towards the land that stretched endlessly away, rising from the seashore in gentle hills, all alike covered in the same grasses. He wrapped himself in his coat against the wind. His hands were cold on this shore that the sun had never warmed.

He stepped above the shore and walked into the borderlands. The wind rippled across the hill, bending the grass into soft waves, but he could not feel it on his face. When he looked back towards the sea he saw he had left no trail behind him; his feet had not bent one blade of the grass growing upon the empty land: he had no weight to mark the borderlands. With each step he took away from the shore he left behind more of the memory of his life, his home, his skill as a potter. Before he left Liùtha in Marac, she had kissed him in farewell and all the way across the sea he had felt the soft touch of her lips burning on his skin. But that too was lost when he left the shore and the sea behind. Here, in the borderlands, he was only a man, and to be a man was to be nothing.

He could not tell how long he walked. He tried to count his heartbeats or his breaths but always the numbers slid out of his mind. He did not tire; he did not hunger or thirst. All the land was alike beneath the stars, each step like all the others he had taken before, all the ones he would take after. There was no time in these borderlands. He closed his eyes and looked into the dark.

At first he heard nothing except the blood pounding from his heart. Then music. Music like none he had ever heard in the sunlit lands: wild music, high and sweet, that made him want to laugh for joy and cry for sorrow, to dance until he dropped or else to sleep and dream, never to wake from dreaming.

He opened his eyes and now he saw an apple tree standing black against the starlit sky atop a little hill. Beyond it the land stretched towards another shore and a little spring rose at its foot whose waters ran clear and cold down to the sea. In that empty land, he should have seen that tree from far away, but he had not. Yet, when he came to it, he knew it had always been there at the gates of evening, for this was the firstborn tree that marked the western edge of the waking world. It grew beneath one sky by day, beneath another sky by night. It had grown on the day the sun first rose out of the sea; when it died, the sun would set for the last time and the waking world would pass away as if it had never been.

Outside the garden walls, the watch are the only men abroad in the city streets. They walk midwinter's night because they must; all who have a choice are safe behind locked doors with their lamps lit against the dark. It is very cold within the garden but she cannot bear to spend another night within the house that was three months her prison.

The apples rotted this year on her mother's tree. No one thought to pick them with the lady from the city and she herself had other cares than apples on her mind that autumn. Now the shrivelled fruit are black clumps on the bare branches or rotten clots beneath the tree, a mocking memory of sweetness. The fruit is withered dry, so has her heart decayed.

The hour is called. Another hour, and the year will change.

She feels her skin flush. With fear that knowledge does not lessen, she sees her hands shining bright in the night time. She cries out in pain, burning with the fire running through her blood. She had not thought she could know so much pain and live. She puts her hand on the frozen pool and the midwinter ice melts at her touch. For a moment she is outlined in light, bright as the rising sun, and sparks leap and crackle in her hair to make a fiery crown. She burns and burns within the darkness but is not consumed. In a heartbeat the pain and light fade back into nothing and she is herself again, or as near as she will ever be. The fire is hidden within her flesh, not gone from it.

She covers her face with her hands and weeps within the garden at what she has become.

The firstborn tree stretched out its branches beneath the starlit sky, its growth bent low by the wind from the western sea. Its little apples were pale and round in the starlight. Almecu mor Thorrian felt the music of the borderlands throbbing through his soul, a wild song sung by the wind and stars, and heard the voices whispering his name among the leaves of the apple tree.

"If you are here, show yourselves," he cried, his shout a little noise within the vastness. The wind carried his words away across the empty land. Again he shouted, "Show yourselves!" for he knew they were here, dancing on the land and in the empty air.

They showed themselves. All around him, light as leaves blowing on the wind, soft as snow falling on a winter's night, whirled a pale-faced multitude with darkness in their eyes and starlight in their hair. They were not men, they were not women. They were the kindred of the borderlands, the dancers in the empty land. They were older than he was, older than the land he came from. He remembered what Kenu Vanithu had told him, *Once all the world was theirs. One day, it will be theirs again.* Very lovely they were to look upon, full of a grace not seen in the waking world where love and death have their dominion.

There was one among them greater than the rest. His eyes were blacker than the darkest night. His cloak was tattered and his feet were bare but he was crowned with stars. He stood beside the firstborn tree and it was to him less than a mayfly is to a man.

The king of the borderlands held up his hand and the music died away to a memory of sweetness and loss; the dancers slipped away into a dream; all that remained was the king, and the wind shaking the leaves of the apple tree.

"You are welcome, Almecu mor Thorrian. Only here, in borderlands between your lands and mine, can we meet."

He knelt before the king of the empty land. "How do you know me?"

"I know all the names of all the men who have ever walked beneath the sun." The king's voice was not the voice of a man. It was the rise and fall of the sea upon the shore; it was the wind blowing across the empty land. "I know all the places you have been, little potter, all you have seen, all that you seek."

He looked up into the king's eyes and saw they were empty of love, of hatred, of fear and hope. There was nothing beyond the starlight and the borderlands but the black eyes of the king. He closed his eyes but he could still see the king looking back at him, the stars tangled in his hair, his cloak like nightfall, his eyes dark as the deep places in the belly of the earth. Then he was certain he had seen the king's face before, had heard the king's voice of star and stone. He had known him in a dream that fades fast in the morning or else in the time before he was born. Yet if he had seen this face, if he had heard this voice, how could it be he had forgotten?

"Then you know why I have crossed the water into these borderlands," Almecu mor Thorrian said, his heart beating out the fast rhythm of his life.

"There is only one reason why those born beneath your sky come into these borderlands."

"Will you help me?"

"The lives and deaths of men within the waking world are no concern of mine. I cannot be bound with oaths and with adventures. I make no promises, I offer no hope, I grant no boons and I make no bargains. I do not judge. I do not pity. I dance the dance of sea and star and stone, and those who will dance with me."

The sea and the stars are beyond the law of any land, the wind blows where it will and no beating heart can turn it from its course. Yet still he pleaded, holding out his empty hands to the king. "The Lord of Marac is of this company. He came out of these borderlands."

"Think you he wishes to return and dance again upon the wind?" The king's voice was the clash of stone on stone, cold as a mountain of ice floating across the northern seas.

He looked up and saw branches stark and black against the sky. The firstborn tree was here but the apples of the borderlands were not the apples of Lyikené. There was an end beneath these stars, but not the one he had promised to Liùtha. That lay the other side of the sunset and the way was guarded by bronze swords and hard hearts and the dead men of Ittachar. Looking into the king's face, he saw he might with as much reason look for mercy from the sea or seek pity from the stars as from the king of the empty land.

"Then I must die," said Almecu mor Thorrian, in despair at last.

"All men must die." The king's speaking was the raging of the storm across the sea. "Death is the price of life. You have taken the day and night for your own. You dance between the sunset and the morning. You have blue sky above you, brown earth beneath you, white flowers to grow for you all the days of your life in the waking world. Do you think, as did the Lord of Marac, all these could be had for nothing?"

He did not answer. Any answer he gave would be mere words, empty breath upon the air. He could not remember the sunset and the morning. He could not imagine a sky not filled with stars. All he could remember of the waking world was how all its ways led into the fire of Allocco's hatred.

"I can set you free," said the king in answer to the thought unspoken. "Here you can slip sideways into a dream and nevermore know joy or woe." In his left hand he held a silver cup, in his right he held an apple. "Eat, drink and be welcome."

Almecu mor Thorrian bowed his head to the ground so he could not see the king's face. He did not take the apple;

he did not take the cup. He stooped to pick a single blade of grass and held it up to the starlight. It was as any other of the millions growing across the borderlands. They put out no stems of feathery flowers, they bore no seed. It was no more a blade of grass than the king of the empty land was a man.

"Why do you not eat?" the king asked. "Why do you not drink? There is no need for fear: here in these borderlands everything is as it seems."

"I have heard," he said to the blade of grass, to the shadow of the tree, to the king in the borderlands, "that those who eat and drink beneath this sky forget the world and dance forever between a dream and waking."

"You do not have forever. You cannot escape your fate. But you may stay to dance here, if you choose, and forget your loves and sorrows in your dancing. Many men and women have chosen to dance in these borderlands since the waking world began."

He knelt in silence. The king's eyes were upon him, the kindred of the borderlands stood about him, the firstborn tree stretched over him.

"There can be no love, no death or hope within these borderlands." The king's voice was the soft cold of snow upon the meadows. "They followed when men and women woke in the sunlight of the waking world. What I offer is releasement from the knowledge of such things so you may dance empty as the wind itself upon the empty air."

"Then there is nothing else?"

"Not here. But this is not your place. In the waking world there are many choices but here there is only one. All who come into these borderlands must make it." The king's voice was the rustle of the wind through the leaves of the apple tree. "Stand up, Almecu mor Thorrian, come out from behind your fear, open your eyes and look at me. Put your hand upon the tree and consider what it is that you desire. Is it to be the potter of Ittachar or to lose yourself upon the wind?"

He laid his hands upon the trunk of the firstborn tree. The bark was rough beneath his touch; he saw the scars where branches had broken away in winter storms, the darker patches on its leaves where the salt spray had burnt them and the spurs of this year's growth that next year would bear fruit. The land and sea and empty air were filled again with music and shadows as the liùthion swirled round and around, reaching out their hands, calling him into their dance. Almecu mor Thorrian paused for an hour, a day, a fragment of a life, and watched the dancers trace their patterns on the empty land, beyond dreams, beyond time.

He looked up and saw the king of the borderlands. The king's face was bone white in the halflight. The wind blew from the sea but it no longer stirred the folds of his ragged cloak. His hair fell down about his face and he stood proud, crowned with stars. Around him, the sky was jewelled with starlight. Thus he had been before the beginning. Thus he would be after the end.

Yet, as Almecu mor Thorrian stood with his hand upon the firstborn tree, one living thing reaching out to another within the empty land, life called out to life. All the beauty he had known in the waking world came back to him. There, nothing was constant; everywhere and always there was change. The sun rose and the sun set, counting out the days between the beginning and the end. And, in that time, the flower set its seed; the wheat grew gold and was cut down; little children grew into women and men who lived and loved and went into the dark. It was enough and more than enough for any man.

He took his hand from the apple tree. Reaching out across the space between them, he took the apple from the king. He took the cup in his right hand and raised it to the stars as if to drink a health. Yet now the ground was firm beneath his feet and the wind blew cold into his face. He remembered his home and his craft, the feel of cold clay, the joy of creation. He was only a man but that was to be part of the pattern of the world, the weft within the warp, and so, though he stood in the borderlands, he knew all he could do before the darkness claimed him.

Almecu mor Thorrian shook his head and the liùthion drew back. He had made his choice and the distance between them could never now be bridged. He did not eat. He did not drink. Slowly, carefully, knowing well what he did, he poured the cup out onto the empty land, telling the king, "This is not my place; I cannot drink from this cup."

He opened his hand and let the apple drop. "I cannot eat," he said, "this fruit is not for me. I will take apples from this tree beneath the sun or not at all. The price of life is death, but the blue sky and the brown earth and the white flowers are mine before I die. I have my life, I have my love – these are not little things and they are worth the price I pay for them."

"Do you know me now, Almecu mor Thorrian?" The king's voice was the joyful rush and tumble of the stream.

"Yes," he answered, smiling, "yes, I know you. And so I know myself, and think I am no less than you, for all your starlit dancing."

"It is not a little thing to be a man." The king's smile was the starlight rippling across the sea, his laughter the dance of the wind across the water. "What is yours to take is not mine to give. Another hand must give you what you need beneath another sky."

The king drew the man close and kissed his brow with his cold lips. "Farewell, little potter, we will not meet again. Go carefully, all your days within the waking world."

The king was not gone but he no longer wore the likeness of a man. He was the stone beneath the land; he was the silence before a word is spoken; he was the darkness after the light.

Almecu mor Thorrian could still hear the music, the wind still blew through the branches of the apple tree, but he turned his back upon the music and the dancers to return across the empty land. He had heard the song he could not sing, he had seen the dance he could not join; now it was time for him to go back into the sunlight and find the firstborn tree again beneath the other sky. He pushed the boat down the shore into the sea and set a way towards Lyikené.

He has bound himself to her in love, but this does not make him a man. He walks by night beneath the trees, but this does not make him a man. He can suffer all the pains that flesh and blood can suffer, but this does not make him a man. His flesh must die, but even this does not make him a man. For then? Then he will be free. Free of flesh; free of time; free of love and death. Death is the price of life, but not for him. This is why he is not a man.

But she is a woman, and this life is all she has.

The potter slept upon the open sea for a night and half a day, easy as a child upon its mother's breast. The borderlands were unreal as a dream on waking but his shirt was torn, his feet were bare, and he had lost his coat. Beneath the noontime sun, he saw the sight to drive all memories of dreaming from his mind, the sight he had been taught to dread, the sight not seen by any man of Ittachar for near two hundred years: the square sail of Lyikené. There was no escape upon the open sea. This was the domain of the Sea People: here, what they hunted they caught.

The ship waited for him. It kept its place upon the sea as a hawk hangs in the air, dreadful and lovely, with its simplicity of purpose written into every line and curve. There was an eagle's head at its prow, its hooked beak open in an eternal scream. There were three blood-red eagles on its white sail, their talons outstretched to rend the world asunder. A harsh burst of laughter rang across the water, a snatch of song, the clash of bronze on bronze.

The helmsman led him between the ranks of oarsmen down the length of the ship to where their king waited. He was as fair a sight upon the world as the noonday sun, and full as merciless. The wind lifted the folds of his cloak that was near as red as his hair.

The king watched in silence as the little boat was scuttled. Only when it had sunk beneath the surface of the sea did he say, "Years since, I hunted these seas. I caught then what I hunted: the oathbreaker of Ohmorah. I gave him the death I promised. I keep all the oaths I swear." The king's eyes were bright and fierce, used to looking into the distance beyond the sight of other men. "I have sworn no man from the Later Lands shall take an apple from the firstborn tree whilst I am king of the Sea People."

But, with no little pride, the potter answered, raising his voice so all there might hear, "I will take an apple from that tree though it cost me my life. No man can turn me aside, not even the king of the Sea People. I also keep the oaths I swear."

The king smiled to see the potter's pride that was no match for his own. "So it was for fight you sailed into the west? I am ready, if that is your desire. Do you think you can take me? I with my bronze sword and armed men at my command, and you without even a knife to your hand?"

"I think I must try," he answered, "for I must have an apple from that tree. And if you are an honest man then you will put aside your sword or give me one to match it."

"The sword I can give, if you are certain, but not the skill to wield it." The king's voice rang out like a great bronze bell. "If you set yourself against me, you will die."

"All men must die," said the potter, quiet and desperate. He saw the folly of it, and the necessity. He realised he was shaking and had pride enough left to hope the king should think it was only because the wind blew cold across the sea. Then all the rest drew back, making a little space around him and the king. The king cast aside his cloak and nodded to the helmsman. He stepped forward and held out a sword to the potter. He took it in both hands. He had not thought it could be so heavy, the work of men with the weight of men upon the world.

The king of the Sea People did not move towards him; he did not move away. He waited that the potter might have time to learn the balance of the sword. There was no way of knowing whether this was courtesy or the waiting of a cat that wishes to play a little with the mouse beneath its paw before it crushes it.

"All the advantage is mine," said the king, when the potter looked towards him. "You may strike the first blow. Kill me if you can."

The potter took a step towards the king. He raised the sword but did not strike. Instead he looked all around him at the Sea People of Lyikené, at the sunlight on their bronze spears. In the ship were young men, strong and beautiful as the heroes of old stories, men who would fight for a song and a day of glory and go laughing into death. Such men cast long shadows across the world like to the dark of the moon: burning houses, scorched fields and the harvests ungathered; hollow faces doomed to live on when all wish for further life is gone; women weeping for their children.

With these thoughts in his mind, he laid down the sword and stood with empty hands to face the king of the Sea People.

"It is easy to kill," the potter said, "if you do not pause to understand death, if you are swept along on the world's wind like a hawk rising to the sun." He had knelt to the lady of Ohmorah, potter before a queen; he had knelt before the king of the borderlands, man before eternity, but he did not think to kneel again. "I do not have the wisdom to know when or why a man should die. It seems that others do."

He had never noticed before how bright and clear were the colours of the world nor heard so intensely all the little sounds: the small shifts of men's feet against the deck, the slap of the waves against the hull, seagulls mewing on the wind. He saw the light upon the water and the white wings of the gulls shining against a blue brilliance of sky, and his eyes pricked with tears of wonder at such beauty.

The king stepped forwards. Pale-faced, dry-mouthed, the potter waited for his death to come, at the stroke of a bronze sword, on the point of a bronze spear, a death like the deaths of the men of Ittachar on that midsummer morning, long ago. The sword in the king's hand caught the sunlight with its blade and dazzled him, bronze no longer but a flame. He closed his eyes against the sight and his mind against the thought. His life shrank down into a moment and the sound of his own heart beating drowned out all the rest.

There was no pain. There was no darkness. The moment passed into sunlight shining red through his eyelids and, above the thunder of his heart, he heard the king calling him back into the day: "Death will come to you, but not at my hand. Open your eyes and look at me."

The potter opened his eyes to see the king had laid down his sword beside the other. For a long, long time he looked at him and, despite all, he was worth the looking, clad in the colours of his life: red and gold, bronze and blood and fire. And he saw at last that this king's face was the mirror of another face seen beneath another sky, save for the eyes. Those eyes were all his own. They were not grey nor green nor blue but each and none in turn as one moment passed into another, like the surface of the sea itself as the patterns of light and shadow shifted across the day. Not long ago the potter would have turned from those eyes, flinching away as from the sun. No longer. Now he would look any man of the waking world full in the face, even the king of the Sea People. So he looked, and saw, and understood what this king was, his weight upon the world, the glory and the terror of his purpose.

"It was not to kill you that I met you upon the open sea," said the king. "I too have walked in borderlands beneath another sky. I too know all that happened on the day the gates of morning closed. I know what you would have of me. But until you ask, I cannot answer."

The king held out his hands to the potter in friendship and in welcome. "We are on the same path, you and I: we do not seek to change the world, only to make safe what we love."

"Though you do it with a sword," said the potter of Ittachar, remembering midsummer shadows. Knowing why his fore-fathers had died did not make it easier to bear the knowledge of their deaths. Knowing why he was going to die did not make death more welcome. "Is this balance worth the lives of all those you have sent into the dark before their time had come?"

"Even so. It is not a game we play with life and death across the morning," the king answered, as certain of himself as of the sunrise. "I keep the covenant but I cannot mend the world. Not even the kings of the Sea People can put together what is broken. One tree is dead already and I am all that stands between the hearts of men and the world's ending. It is no longer the right of all and any to stand in sunlight beside the firstborn tree. There is a price on its fruit that was not there when the world was young."

"So said Kenu Vanithu."

"All the tales he tells are true."

"And what am I?" asked Almecu mor Thorrian.

"You are a man," the king told him, and smiled, simple and powerful in his life as the sea eagle itself.

"There are many men beneath this sky."

"Many men, but few like you, who walk quietly and see clearly and keep each promise made. It falls to you to show the Lord of Marac the way into the dark: do you have the strength? Do you have the will?"

In his question, the potter heard the echo of Assiolo upon the shore before the White City but now he knew many things he had not known on that day, and knowledge had brought understanding. Quietly, he said to the king, "All my will and all my strength are not enough unless you help me. Will you give me what I need?"

The king pulled a little bundle of scarlet silk from the pocket of his jerkin. He unwound the cloth and offered the potter a little apple, ripe and golden, glowing in the sunlight. "I picked this yesternoon from off the firstborn tree. Take it, if it is what you desire."

The potter closed his hand upon the apple. He held his future in the palm of his hand and shivered in the sunlight.

"Allocco was a man. Even this apple is not enough to undo what he did and make an ending."

"The only end is death. You know this as well as I," said the king. The shred of silk fluttered from his fingers, red as rowan berries, red as the flames at the heart of a fire, red as blood. He opened his hand and let it blow away upon the wind. When it was gone out of sight, the king took the potter's hand and pressed a second apple into it. He held him close a minute, whispering so he alone might hear. "My gift to you. Eat it, and I promise you will no longer fear the dark."

Then, on the king's word, the ship of the sea eagle was turned towards the east and the drum beat out the rhythm for eighty oars to cut the water and carry Almecu mor Thorrian back to Marac. And on that ship, he stood beside the king of Lyikené beneath the sail that was as white as snow, as red as blood, and ate the apple from the firstborn tree. It was sharp and sweet and very good to eat.

> Then death sailed from the western land,
> Death sailed across the sea,
> Death held an apple in his hand
> Grown on the firstborn tree.

10: Falling ... but knowing why I fall

A man may drink, and no be drunk;
A man may fight, and no be slain;
A man may kiss a bonie lass,
And ay be welcome back again!

Duncan Davison, Robert Burns

As the sun sank towards the sea the potter climbed the path up from the shore to stand again beneath the walls of Marac. This time the door yielded at his first touch. He had not expected otherwise. No shadows stirred the edges of his vision as he walked through empty halls of stone towards the room above the sea, only whispers fainter than he could remember, a susurration on the edge of hearing. For a moment, all seemed as it had been but, at his second glance, he saw the tapestries were threadbare, their colours dimmed, their rubies dropping like berries to the floor. He held out his hand to touch the tattered web, his mind filled with its meaning. But such thoughts were forgotten at the sound of footsteps behind him. A pause, a soft cry of joy, and again the sound of footsteps on the stone, pattering more swiftly now. He span around as Liùtha ran towards him and caught her up into his arms.

"You are changed," she told him, after that first moment had passed, all too quickly, by. "I can see the western light shining in your eyes."

"Smile, love," he told her, holding her hands. "I have the means to bring the ending you desire."

"I do not think I shall smile again," Liùtha said, shaking her head, pulling away to point at the fading tree. "In the time you've been gone the Lord of Marac has suffered all the pains Allocco meant for him. Kenu Vanithu keeps the watch on him I cannot; night by night, he's sat at his side and seen him fade from the world. Soon, not even his music will be enough to bind him to his flesh."

He shook his head and gave her the yellow apple of Lyikené. She drew in her breath with wonder: such a little thing; an apple; an end and a beginning.

"This is the gift of the king of all that lies this side of the sunset," he told her, smiling. "He offers it to the Liùthion and, with it, all the joys and sorrows of the waking world. It's time for him to make his choice: the starlight or the sunlight, the straight path or the crooked. Let him eat and be a man, or slip forever into the borderlands.

The apple was a slight weight upon her hand but in its substance was its meaning, as much as iron or fire. The rowan tree was long years dead and there was no protection left against fear or hate or vain hope. But in Lyikené, at the edge of the world, the firstborn tree lived yet, with the promise of life rising in its sap, of love in its fruit and of death in its falling leaves that blew away upon the wind. She cupped the apple in her palm and looked up into the potter's face, but, in a moment, bent her head to hide her tears.

He held her loosely in the circle of his arms, knowing some choices still remained and it fell to her to make the first one.

"I love you," he said. "I've loved you since I first saw you beneath the birken tree in Anach. You were so lovely and so sad. Since then I've wanted nothing so much as to take away your grief so I would see you smile."

His heart beat fast and strong. There was one more question he must ask; one answer would decide whether his path led him back to Ittachar, to be the potter on the shore and live a long life, and a quiet one, safe beside the sea, or if he took the shortest path up the twisting staircase of the black tower of Marac, to leap into the dark with the wind in his hair and the song of the borderlands in his heart. "Liùtha, will you be his love again or mine?"

Liùtha did not pause to think but raised her face and gave her answer sure and clear, for all her tears still glistened on her cheek. "That I am his," she said, "and he is mine is as certain as the sunrise and the nightfall. The world is as it is."

He had hoped, of course, as any man would hope, she would give another answer. But, as she spoke, he knew she would never answer differently, though he wait for her a hundred years and ask of her a hundred times, and so his path was marked out by the certainty of his love, by the choice she made.

"Then I swear to you, Liùtha, you shall have a lifetime dancing with your love, a woman and a man, equal beneath the flowering trees."

Looking at her, he did not mind the price; there were greater things in the world to fear than darkness and silence.

"What I am, I am, Liùtha. And I promise I can heal your love and bring you to your freedom. I know now what must be done." He took her hand and the fire within her flesh no longer burned him. "I've stood at the gates of evening and heard the music of the borderlands. I've eaten the fruit of the firstborn tree. I no longer fear the end."

She pointed to the hangings on the wall, the faded rowan and the ragged dancers. "Here is the other tree that stood at the gates of morning: they counted its death a price worth paying, my mother and her kind. Its death paid for their lives. Her life gave me life. Even before Allocco died, I was born of fire and death."

He shook his head against such thoughts. He had seen the love the lady of the White City had for her daughter; he had heard from Kenu Vanithu the love Liùthai bore for both of them. This world had beauty and happiness enough to fill her heart, if she would but hold out her hands to grasp them, if she had the strength to trust love over death.

"You are your father's daughter too, born of his life and of his love. Your mother put aside her desire for fire before ever you were begun. Your father knew it when he planted an apple tree from the world's end within her garden. The whole of the waking world is yours. You can make a balance in your heart, Liùtha, between light and darkness, between your joys and woes, and so go safely through the world."

Her hand clutched tight. "But what of your own dancing? All flesh must die, all love must end. Far better I am alone forever than have your death upon my love."

Still she burned with the light of the chamberlain's hatred but he could undo that curse and it no longer had the power to make him fear or doubt. He had come to know himself, to feel his weight upon the world and so the meaning of each choice, the price of action, the cost of inaction. He must think carefully so as to say what was needed, to make her understand what he did was necessary. She had been too much alone, too long afraid. He did not want to add to her fear: she could never be free whilst her fear was upon her.

"You've made your choice, love," he said. "This one is mine. It is not your freedom only. It is mine, and his, and even Allocco's. I cannot have you for my own but I can free you to live out your days in love, as you were meant to do." He smiled, though tears clouded his eyes. "Here and now, Liùtha, love is enough."

In return, Liùtha took her silver brooch and pinned it on his shirt. He had seen the dance captured there in silver, it had been his for dancing but he had chosen to return because he loved her. She had no words just then to say what was in her heart and so she held him close and said nothing.

The wind hurls the night against the window but these stone walls have stood for many years and are proof against the wind. Within the chamber, out of the wind, a dozen lamps are lit against the night. They burn and burn and consume the midwinter darkness. Their light shines upon the young man who sits weeping by the bedside and the old man who lies dying in the bed.

"If I had offered you the cup, would you have drunk?" Grief hangs heavy on him, as the years hang heavy on his father.

"Drunk a health to life to come?" The old man's breath catches in his throat as his son waits for an answer. "You turned aside, your moment passed, it will not come again. You shall never know what might have been, had your resolve matched your longing."

The young man flinches and the old man smiles, a bitter smile that curls his lip and does not reach his eyes. So has he smiled a thousand times upon his son, measuring out the distance between them. Now he tells him, "I did not turn aside — I took all I wanted, and I did not mark the price. So came I to my desire and you to desolation. Mark me well, Assiolo; it is the last lesson you shall have of me."

"I shall learn nothing from you. The piper taught me better long ago, the Liùthion showed me another path, though neither was a man."

The old man turns his face slowly and his son bows his head. He dares not look his father in the eyes from fear he will see himself reflected there. He stares instead into the lamp and lets the flame dazzle him. From behind the light, he hears his father say, "Fine words — fine words that have no meaning to them. The piper is gone into the west, the Liùthion is banished, my fire is set and your hope lies cold beneath the apple tree."

All this is true, and so the tears run down his face. Blood and earth were washed from his hands by running water, the wind blew the last leaves from the apple tree, but no wind can blow his memories away nor water wash them from his mind. His dreams have faded, his love is gone, the dead are dead and never can come back again.

"Tonight my will is done," his father says. "Tonight my end is come and with it all I desire."

This too is true. But out of the silence left by the death of love, out of the grave where hope lies buried, out of the darkness of his grief, another memory rises through his mind, a memory of green leaves and golden eyes and a blackbird singing in the springtime.

And this is also true, and, at last, he has the strength he needs to stand against his father.

He says aloud, "I knew well what I did when I poured that cup away. I shall not live as you have lived."

Then the chamberlain's son puts out his hand and snuffs out the lamp beside the bed. Slowly, he walks around the room and puts out every light. In darkness he tells his father, "She lives and breathes and walks upon the earth, and so do I. I shall make a beginning out of your ending."

He closes the door behind him and leaves his father alone in the dark.

Kenu Vanithu had kept his promise and his watch. The potter heard singing as he walked through the shadowy halls of Marac, the piper's voice clear and high as sunlight in the noontime sky:

> "The apples have ripened on the tree,
>   And the blackbird's song awhile does cease.
>   Oh come, my love, oh my love, come to me,
>   My poor heart is sore and cries out for peace."

Then he saw the shapes of the shadows had changed upon the walls and floors. The light left after sunset was lower, longer. Summer was gone and the world span again towards its moment of balance.

When he came to the room high above the sea, he found the Lord of Marac lying there, still and silent as a figure carved in stone, very lovely in the halflight but very little like a man. Perhaps he slept, perhaps he woke, certaintimes he dreamed, at once in the world and out of it. The wind from the west blew freely through the open window and, all around, voices whispered on the edge of hearing; all around, the shadows danced, figures swirling on the edge of vision. The borderlands were very close and his kindred were here to call him home.

"I saw a square sail in the distance and looked for your return, Almecu mor Thorrian," said Kenu Vanithu. "It is the evening of the equinox. Tonight all is in balance and there is but a step between the waking world and borderlands."

"I have seen two lands and met two kings and I have made my choices. I know now what is guarded in Lyikené and it is a great deal more than whale ivory and amber. The old songs are all true."

He looked at the piper, seeing him clearly and with pity. Time out of mind Kenu Vanithu had lived on, past the deaths of friends and enemies, and seen the world remake itself anew, a kaleidoscope of ever-changing patterns. He was not, and never could be, the stone he longed to be. He must live on knowing that, for him, all hope was false; foul without and flawed within, for all his music; his only certainties an empty life and an ugly death to follow it, aching always for the love he would not find.

"You knew what I would find beyond my dreams," the potter said. "How did you know I would not eat and drink and lose myself upon the wind?"

"Nay, lad, I never doubted you. You are all I am not, all I would wish to be," said Kenu Vanithu. "Once I stood where you stood, where Liùthai stood before you, and made the choice you men did not. I drained the cup to its dregs, hoping I would forget the world. I ate the apple to its pips, hoping I would forget my name. Alas, that I am not a man. For me, there is no oblivion, no refuge, in those borderlands and but one path before me, a long road beneath the sun.

"For me, all hope died beneath those stars. In this waking world I know all the ways of cruelty, all the faces of hatred and fear. Children throw stones at me; women laugh at me; men curse me. I'd fled this broken world into the borderlands because I wanted to forget I lived and breathed and must walk my days beneath the sun. So too did the Liùthion, the day the world was changed."

"He has the choice you do not. He need not be what he is now," said the potter, wincing at the piper's words because he could not lift this fate from his friend even if he died a hundred times. "Let him wake and find the strength he needs."

He filled a silver cup with water and held it to the sleeper's mouth to wet his lips. The Lord of Marac opened his eyes and asked, "What did you learn in the borderlands?"

The potter refilled the cup and held it close so he could drink deep. "The truth behind what we say so easily. Death is the price of life, because death gives life its meaning."

The Lord of Marac nodded, understanding. Then with his right hand he touched the silver brooch upon the potter's shirt, turning it about to study the device. "It is not a little thing to be a man. To fall from the light into everlasting darkness, nevermore to dance in borderlands between a dream and waking."

The potter said, gently, "Liùtha cannot dance your dance. But you can choose to follow the steps of her dance instead. There is great beauty in the waking world at midsummer. To dance with the one you love beneath the flowering trees, knowing the harvest shall follow."

"Falling in the end into the dark, but knowing why I fall," the Lord of Marac mused, and the potter saw him balanced between the light and darkness, between what he had been and what he could be. "What of Allocco's price?"

"No price at all, if we love her."

"Then both of us must die."

"All men must die. It is what we do before we die gives us our weight upon the world."

"You are a rare man, Almecu mor Thorrian."

"You know your part and I know mine. Rest awhile; Liùtha shall come to you before the morning."

A curlew calls out of the dark, two sweet notes that blow away upon the wind. When there is nothing left, the chamberlain's son holds out his hand. "Come home," he says, "come home."

She screams to him and to the wind, "All you promised me is gone. All he promised is gone. Only Allocco kept his promises."

Her face is pale, its beauty marred by rage and grief. He sees the hatred in her dark eyes. It is for her lover, because he has abandoned her. It is for him, because he has broken all his promises. He tells her, "It is midwinter. You are free of him."

She shrieks out her answer, and he hears she has passed beyond grief and hatred into something close to madness. "Only death can set me free."

She puts her hand on his and her touch burns against his fingers. He backs away, his heart beating out the fast rhythm of his fear as he reads the truth written on her skin and hair. The guards see nothing, no more than they hear the music in the wind, but he is his father's son and has spent half his life learning to see the things other men cannot. He closes his eyes against her. She is bright in his darkness as the rising sun, and as hard to look upon.

She turns away to stand upon the harbour wall, her arms open to embrace the wind. "You loved me – will you die for me?"

It is too late. If it could free her he would give her his death gladly but he could die a hundred times and it would not be enough. His love is gone, buried with his hope beneath the apple tree; all that is left is sorrow, a grief as great as hers.

He hears her cry, "Since only death can make an ending, let it be mine!"

Too late, he reaches out to her. She slips through his curving fingers to cast herself into the water. The wind blows high, and the wind blows low, but the wind cannot blow her away. He hears wings beating against the storm. The curlew passes from one darkness to another, so close beside him its feathers brush against his cheek.

Between its first note and its second lies clarity beyond despair. In that moment, he comes into his inheritance. Once, his father stopped the sun at noontime. His father has gone into the dark: all that was his now falls to him to use in any manner that he chooses. He holds out his empty hands and determines this moment shall not be her last. Standing alone between the sea and sky, he twists a future out of broken dreams, out of salt foam and driftwood tossing on the water, out of the memory of love, out of rage and grief and shame. So it is the waves do not crush her, the waters do not close upon her. Instead, a creature of storm and strangeness snatches her from the foam and carries her to a place where she must live on past the death of hope, foresworn and desolate. But, as he turns back into the city, he knows this much is true: she lives, and so it is not ended, for the only end is death.

But, in the end, it was the Lord of Marac who came to her. Liùtha sat beneath the silken rowan with fallen rubies all around her, listening to the potter tell his tale of ships and kings and golden apples. The Lord of Marac came into the room like a shadow in that room of shadows.

He was changed, as unlike his past self as morning is from evening, for all starlight clung yet to his hair. Smiling, he met the potter's eyes.

"For me, you went into the borderlands and stood at the gates of evening," he said, "where I shall not dance again. I shall be no more liùthion but a man of Marac who will dance all the dances of the waking world."

The potter gripped his hand tightly. "It is well said," he told him, "but in the time to come, when you are a man, when you lie awake at night and fear the dark, remember it."

Kenu Vanithu slipped away into the shadows. He had been burned by the fire, he had been tumbled in the flood, and he had lived to see the world remade. Now he had played his part and must leave it to a man to undo what a man had done.

The Lord of Marac had no more eyes for any but his love. He turned to Liùtha, to seek her love, to offer himself to her again. Liùtha looked at him fearfully but he smiled and his face was very gentle.

Liùtha's face was soft and lovely, freed from frost and fire. The Lord of Marac held out the moonstone crown, saying, "The world is a strange place. Forgive me, love; a poor lover I proved to be. I left you once – I would not leave you now. I am sorry it has taken me so long to learn the lesson you have taught me. Only half a life may be spent beneath the stars."

She gave a cry of wordless love and grief.

"Come back to me, my love, for whatever time is left to us," he said. "Let me eat the apple of Lyikené and know I share your fate."

Liùtha ran across the little space between them. "Hush, love," she whispered. "We are together tonight. Forget the past and the future, and let this moment be enough. I cannot touch you, may not love you as I desire, but at last I have you as my own again. I shall love you until my heart is still, until the wind blows no more upon me."

The anger between them had passed, as, in the morning, a storm passes into sunshine; they were lovers again, each forgiving the treachery done by the other. What had been broken was now mended. He offered her the moonstone crown and she placed it on her hair.

The Lord of Marac said, "Let your fate be mine," and Liùtha dropped the golden apple into his hand. He ate, and his eyes fixed upon her face held love and longing enough to melt the hardest heart.

"We shall watch the sun rise together in the morning," he told her, "whatever follows after."

The potter watched with love and silent understanding, knowing Liùtha would not come to his arms again.

"One thing more I must do," he said, "then in the morning you shall go free. You have been too long alone."

He left them to tell the truth in their hearts, though his own was heavy for his end was very near. Only a living man's love was enough to balance a dead man's hatred. He had given his word and he would keep it, and, besides, his wish was granted: he had seen Liùtha smile.

As he walked the empty halls of Marac all the remainder of the night, he heard Liùtha singing. Her voice was sweet and true and her song a lovesong old as love itself:

"The blackbird sings in the flowering tree
 And the year has turned again into spring.
 At last, at last, has my love come to me,
 And my heart the blackbird's song doth sing."

Such beauty was enough to tear his heart from his breast, for
he knew full well the cost of it, and that the price was not yet
paid.

Is this a true dream?
   *In his dream he is dancing in borderlands between sleep and
waking, beyond joy and sorrow, outside of time and memory. He
is what he has always been: starlight on the sea, the wind blowing
across the empty lands. But somewhere a man is crying the hopeless,
wordless sobs of a child afraid of the dark. And it is very strange,
both that there should be weeping here, and that he has the ears to
hear it.*
   *He turns his back upon the music and the dancers. It is the
hardest thing he will ever do. He is heavy in his flesh as he walks
towards a light that shines out brighter than the dark light of the
stars in this land where no sun will ever rise. Because of this light
there is darkness in the borderlands, and this too is strange.*
   *The sobbing ceases as he walks out of the dark. A man raises his
face from his hands and his tears fall like sunlight from his eyes.*
   He kneels beside him. "Is it you?"
   *In the borderlands there is no fear, but this man has brought fear
with him. In the borderlands there is no hatred, but this man has
brought hatred with him. In the borderlands there is no shame nor
guilt nor penitence but all these this man has brought with him. The
man cowers from him, hiding his shining face in his bright hands.*
   *In the borderlands there is no mercy, but he has walked as flesh
beyond the borderlands and there he has learnt mercy. In his right
hand is a silver cup, in his left an apple.*
   "Drink and eat with me in friendship."
   "Am I your friend?"
   "Before you were anything else, you were my friend."
   "Then I shall eat and drink with you."
   *He holds out his broken hand to the light. The man takes the
apple and they embrace beneath the stars, as they had in the days
when they were young. He gives the cup to his friend and, in turn,
they drink from it. They drain it dry between them; together they
eat the apple and then, for them both, there is nothing more. No
dreams beyond the darknes, only the endless silence as before either
man began.*
   *He wakes from dreaming in a room flooded with the morning.
His left arm is withered but his pain is long years gone. His love
lies sleeping at his side. He looks from his window and sees the
sunlight dancing on the waves. The colours of the land and sea and
sky have never been so clear and pure as they are this morning. A*

herring gull soars in the high air, white wings carrying it effortlessly across the periwinkle blue vault of the sky. It sweeps across the land and sea and cries aloud for its lost soul.

He asks himself, "Was it a true dream?"

The herring gull screams back the answer, and he smiles.

And so it was, in the time before the morning, the man of Ittachar stood on the high tower of Marac and the wind from the sea blew upon his face. There were stars in the sky, pinpricks in the night above him, and his heart sang the song of the borderlands. It was still too dark to see his hand before his face but in the east the blackness shivered into grey. Soon a new day would begin.

He felt across the width of the little wall. Three feet high it stood, one foot across, and beyond it the unseen drop to the black rocks and the swirling sea. In the east, the grey light thickened, taking on a faint touch of pink, pale as the inside of a shell. Now he could see his hands on the black stone. Night grew thinner; day was coming and with it the leap into the unknown. As the night faded from the face of the sea, so did the strength of his will fade a little from his mind and his fear rose from his stomach, like an animal's fear, for the call of life for life was very strong. His mind showed him the vision of his little house in Ittachar, the goatpen and the cabbage field, snug and tight between the shingle and the hillside. "No turning back now," he told himself, but knew, though he did not fear death, he feared the dying; perhaps he did not have the strength to do this, to leap and fall, to be smashed upon the rocks or rolled forever in the margins of the sea.

"I do not want to die," he said to Kenu Vanithu, who said nothing but waited at his side to bear witness to his death because it was all that was left he could do. "I want to go home and live out my days in Ittachar, growing old watching the sunset on the western sea."

He had been too long away and wanted to use his skill to bring the clay to life between his hands again; to have no thought beyond today and tomorrow; to be only a potter.

"I shall wait for the sunrise," he said, thinking of the choice he had made in the empty land beneath the brilliant stars. "I shall leap into the dark but I need not leap into the night. I shall go with the sun on my face: there is darkness enough ahead of me."

The wind blew high and the wind blew low around the tower of Marac, and another stood beside him. In the darkness of night's ending, there was still a touch of starlight at his brow, but his choice was made and, when the sun rose to shine upon him in the morning, the Lord of Marac would be a man at last. Life he had taken for himself; love Liùtha gave him; death would come to him as to every other man who kissed his love beneath the trees at midsummer. Never again would he dance hand in hand with his kindred in the empty land.

There came the rustle of beating wings in the darkness below and then a curlew's cry, two sweet, sad notes, clear as Kenu Vanithu's pipe. The potter clutched at the cold stone. Around him there were shapes in the darkness, the other witnesses to his fall from life into the dark, no brighter than the light of distant stars seen from the edges of his eyes, their song the echo of the song within his heart. Very soon the sun would rise above the land to shine upon the sea; they would be gone with the dawn and his death.

He heard Liùtha's quick footsteps behind him. She put her bright hands over his fingers that gripped the stone.

"I do not want to be free if this is the price of it. You have already given me so much."

He did not look at her but to the east above the land of Marac. The sky was taking on more colours, shading from night into indigo, then to palest blue, pink and pale yellow. His heart ached for what he would lose because of her but, now she was beside him, his last doubts were gone. He remembered the king of the Sea People, who bore more than any other man the weight of what had been lost. He remembered the king of the borderlands, who was not a man, who had not offered hope or fear or life or death but who had showed him what he was. Though here upon the tower of Marac, the borderlands were but the shadow of a dream, he knew he had seen clearly. His life was too full of beauty to be cast away upon a whim. Nor would he become one like Allocco, who clung so close to life he destroyed all it offered.

"I want nothing more than to live for you, Liùtha. I cannot do that. The world is as it is: this was begun long before I met you."

He let himself look down at her and saw her face glowing in the thin light before dawn. "Do not let your life go by in regrets or remorse. We were all led here by the choices we have made, by the words we have spoken and the deeds we have done. Now for all three of us there is no other way this can end. It is the last of Allocco: you will go free today and all your choices be your own again."

He pulled Liùtha's hood from her hair and tilted her face gently towards him, kissing her forehead in farewell. Then, despite himself, he pulled her close as he had longed to do, pressing the warmth of her body against his. For the space of one hundred heartbeats he held her, his face buried in the darkness of her hair. He raised his head and, though his eyes were closed, he knew the night had ended. He kissed her and his tears fell down upon her face, then he put her from him and she did not resist. Her lips formed out the words she did not speak aloud.

The sun was a ball of fire above the horizon. The sky was red and gold and a path was marked out in dazzling brightness where the light fell across the water. Like a man in a dream, he fixed his eyes upon the sun so the world was hidden behind the light and leapt lightly upon the wall, paused there for a single beat of time before pitching himself forwards into the empty air, his eyes blinded by the sunrise and his face still wet with tears.

He seemed to fall forever. Time enough to wonder if he would be broken upon the rocks or swallowed by the sea. He spent a lifetime falling. He had no memory of why he fell but his mind screamed out his name, a seagull's cry upon the wind. Then there was nothing left to fall: no man, no memory, no name. Not even the dark.

But, impossibly, something came out of nothing. A man saw the sun and the sea below him and felt the cold pricks of starlight as the stars wheeled around him. The man found his name again, his memories. He was no longer falling but flying. No, he was not flying and the sea was below and the sun far, far above. He was safe in the soft feathers of his creature of dreams and driftwood that had snatched him out of his death as a sea eagle seizes its fish from the water.

"You chose your moment well," it said, and its laughter was older than the laughter of men. "The third time was indeed the most important. You have done well in your adventure. Did not I and others say you were a man of skill and strength? Which other man could give himself to death to undo the evil a man's heart let loose upon the world, yet come safe back into his life?"

Down below he saw the black tower of Marac rising from the sea. He saw Kenu Vanithu fling up his hand in salutation. He saw Liùtha locked tight in her lover's arms, their happiness blazing from them like the light upon the sea. He saw what he had done and knew himself for what he was. Then exultation filled him, as the sunlight filled the empty air.

"Shall I take you to them?" the creature asked, in its hissing voice of sea and air.

He saw the light flash on the silver brooch he wore, upon the dancer on the empty waves beneath the stars of another sky. The Lord of Marac, Allodola, Allocco, Liùtha, all had held this a little time whilst the wind blew across the land and sea. Now it had come to him. He unpinned the brooch, weighed it a moment in his hands, then tossed it up into the sunlight and watched it drop, shining like a falling star, towards the waves before the sea swallowed it forever.

"No," said Almecu mor Thorrian. "Take me home. It is time for me to be a potter."

That is the end. Of the potter, and Liùtha, and the Lord of Marac, there is nothing left to tell. There are other stories, of course, other beads upon this chain, and some of them concern Kenu Vanithu, the monster, the musician, as he wandered long and lonely across the Later Lands and all the lands beyond them, but those are other tales, to be told another time.

Acknowledgements

This is a book long in the making. I would like to thank: firstly, all who read the early drafts, especially Anna and Jane; secondly, Louisa, who read *every* draft; thirdly, Douglas, who drew the map and set the text; fourthly, Yana and Molly, who created the artwork and designed the cover; and, finally, Terri, the very best of editors.

About the Author

Harriet Goodchild was born in Glasgow and lives in Edinburgh. This is her second novel.

Also by Harriet Goodchild, published by Hadley Rille Books

After the Ruin
An End and a Beginning (short stories)
Tales from the Later Lands (short stories)

Lightning Source UK Ltd.
Milton Keynes UK
UKOW02f0611100716

277996UK00001B/22/P